D1760791

NOVEMBER NIGHT TALES

NOVEMBER NIGHT TALES

HENRY CHAPMAN MERCER

with a new introduction by
CORY M. AMSLER

VALANCOURT BOOKS

INTRODUCTION

There are very few creative endeavors to which Henry Chapman Mercer (1856-1930) was a stranger. Mercer, a collector, archaeologist, historian and tile-maker, may be best known for the museum of pre-industrial American hand tools he established in his hometown of Doylestown, Pennsylvania. Or, for the extensive array of Arts & Crafts-era architectural tiles he designed and produced at his nearby Moravian Pottery and Tile Works. Mercer's castle-like home, Fonthill, also remains as an enduring monument to its builder's architectural creativity and romantic vision. All three buildings, imaginatively constructed of reinforced concrete in the early part of the twentieth century, were designed and built by Mercer within the span of about eight years—a one-man building boom.

Mercer took time out from his scholarly, historical and architectural pursuits—and the pressures of operating his tile business—to engage in a variety of other artistic ventures. Often these were pleasant diversions—rest and relaxation for the mind. He played the fiddle, composed poetry, sketched and painted, produced etchings, and listened to and fancied himself a connoisseur of Irish dance music. Leaving nothing undone, or unexplored, he also tried his hand at writing short stories—as this volume attests.

Originally published in 1928, near the end of his life, *November Night Tales* drew together a collection of stories that Mercer had written and reworked over several years. Another tale, "The Well of Monte Corbo," though not included in the original volume, was discovered among his papers and published posthumously. All the stories are set in a world of the fantastic, the mysterious, the horrific, and the magical. In his writing, Mercer found inspiration in the romantic, gothic fiction of the nineteenth century. Authors like Poe, Shelley, Stoker and Conan Doyle were his muses. Along with many other aspects of an emergent modernism, it was the writers of the early 1900s that Mercer disdained. Hemingway, for example, was a particular target of Mercer's scorn.

The publication of *November Night Tales* seems to have been an important item on Mercer's "bucket list," something he wished to accomplish that would enable him to feel complete at the close of his life, his personal ambitions fulfilled. After so many years, it would certainly please him to find his collection of stories reprinted here.

As a young man, Mercer traveled widely in Europe, in Mesoamerica, and around the United States. His curious and inquisitive mind seems to have been on "record" for much of his early travels. Later in life, he would switch to "playback," in which remembered places and scenes found expression in his architecture, tiles, and artwork. Even Mercer's efforts at writing fiction convey the distinct impression that he is resurrecting memories, and that the pictures he paints with his prose are drawn from settings and characters he had encountered years earlier.

Some of the stories in *November Night Tales* do indeed appear to be autobiographical. Most obvious is "Castle Valley," in which the village of Doylestown is thinly disguised as "Highborough," and the central character and narrator, Charles Meredith, is a stand-in for Mercer himself. Like Mercer, who eschewed a career in law to pursue a more creative path, Meredith decides to set aside political ambitions—and his family's expectations—in order to explore his true passion and calling as an architect. But even in Mercer's other stories, especially those narrated in the first person, the reader has a keen sense that it is the author himself who is wending his way through the tale.

Though not an especially religious man, Mercer nonetheless had a spiritual side and possessed a strong affinity for the metaphysical. As his thumbnail biographer, Joseph Sandford, once noted, Mercer was not one to dismiss flippantly either "coincidence" or "trifles." Even in the smallest of details or most trivial of circumstances, he imagined some higher or transcendent power at work in the world. Though chance plays a role in his stories, Mercer might rather attribute such coincidences to forces beyond mortal comprehension, not to seemingly random fortune.

Throughout his life, Mercer's thoughts often turned to castles, and all the romance, intrigue and mystery they represented. Captivated as a boy by the engravings he discovered in his grandfather's print collection, he later visited some of those ancient edifices firsthand during his travels in Europe. Even in Doylestown, Mercer's eye was drawn to the Romanesque turrets and central spire of the 1878 courthouse building—his hometown's very own castle, set on a hill in the center of the village. It was a theme to which he would return frequently. Mercer injected the castle motif into his art, his pottery, and of course his own architecture. It is small wonder that the image of the castle appears also in his fiction.

Whether it is the folly begun by a local madman on a hilltop in "Castle Valley," the ruins of the fortress of Golubacz on the Danube in "The Wolf Book," or an evocative sketch of a citadel beneath the clouds that launches "The Well of Monte Corbo," the image of the castle imaginatively complements the tale. Indeed, to Mercer the very presence of a castle suggested an almost infinite number of narrative possibilities. "Castles, Castles, Castles—Where do their stories begin or end?" he queried rhetorically in a 1921 correspondence.

As much as his extraordinary buildings, extensive collections or inventive tiles, this collection of stories offers insight into Mercer's original and creative mind. In his life, Mercer adopted the phrase *Plus Ultra*—"more beyond"—as his personal motto. It thrilled him that there might always be more to discover, to learn, and to do. There is certainly more to Mercer than is revealed in these tales, but they offer a fine beginning to anyone encountering the author for the first time. In exploring the stories, I hope the reader takes Mercer's personal motto to heart, and makes this volume only an initial foray into the mind of an extraordinary individual.

Cory M. Amsler
Vice-President, Mercer Museum
2015

The Publisher gratefully acknowledges the assistance of the staff of the Mercer Museum and Library, Doylestown, Pennsylvania

CONTENTS

CASTLE VALLEY

A FEW MILES west of the town of Highborough, a well known stream bends sharply to the southward, around a hill, at a place called Castle Valley. There is a mill-dam there, and a covered wooden bridge, built upon stone piers. But the hill is not conspicuous, unless seen at a distance, when its conical top rises smooth above the treetops, commanding the whole landscape.

You see it best, and the park-like meadows beneath it, from the bend of a road that follows the high north side of the valley; and there, one fine summer day, many years ago, when coming home from a walk, I found my friend Pryor, then a young unfamed painter, whom I had not met since he gained his first honors at one of the winter exhibitions.

Decidedly talented and, in spite of a lack of earnestness that might well have handicapped his later success, he was, nevertheless, such a rare compound of eccentricity and convention that the sight of his well-dressed, slender, slightly stooping figure, ruddy cheeks, and carefully-parted "back hair," gave me a thrill of pleasure.

He was standing under a very large oak tree, by the road side, packing up his box of colors. His umbrella and folded-up camp stool lay on the grass beside him. After our greeting, he said that he had just come to spend the summer in the neighborhood, with his mother, had established himself in a farmhouse nearby, and was out that day on his first painting exhibition.

"That tree," he exclaimed enthusiastically, pointing to the trunk whose mighty arms overhung us, "must be three hundred years old at least. The boughs frame the picture. Look under them. They give distance to the meadows, the bridge, and the hill yonder. The scene has a curious effect upon me. I hardly know how to describe it."

"No one goes into raptures over it here," said I.

"Probably not. Not everybody would feel it. But there is something not quite real about it,—a sort of illusion. So much so that I must come again, for I have hardly had time to grasp it."

"Yet, you have painted it." I pointed to his covered canvas. "May I look?"

"You won't like it," he answered, laughing, as if at something that he didn't intend to explain. "I haven't put down what I saw, but what I thought I saw. I am not a realist, you know."

"Yet," I observed, "judging from some of your work, you compromise at times with the new idea."

"I suppose I do," said he. "But we must make our way. Fashion is fashion. Not this time, though," he added, as he unstrapped the cover and held out the canvas.

At a first glance, I saw that I was expected to look at the performance, from some point of view that might escape me. It was evidently a fantasy, in which he had caught the spirit of the scene, but had chosen to widen the stream, exaggerate the size of the hill, and set a purely imaginary castle on its top.

"Very delightful," I said; "but I don't quite understand. You have idealized things, not too much, perhaps; but why the castle on the hill? Isn't that going a little too far?"

"I expected you to say that," he returned laughing.

"The legend," I continued, "is somewhat vague, and hardly justifies you in deliberately putting it on canvas."

"What legend?" he asked. "I know of no legend."

"Do you mean to say," I returned, "that you have painted a castle on that hill, without knowing that there was a castle there at one time, or the beginning of one, at least?"

"Never heard a word of it," said he, in astonishment.

"Why, the place is called Castle Valley," I exclaimed, "from that fact, and I ought to know something of it, as the builder is supposed to have been one of my ancestors. But it's all gone long ago, the stones were used to build the bridge yonder."

Pryor listened in surprise as I went on to explain that my ancestor in question, according to a family tradition, had been in some way thwarted in a singular project of building a castle on the hill before us. Whether because of the hostility of his father and friends, or his own mental derangement, his architectural dream had never been realized. The walls had hardly risen above their foundation, when the poor fellow died.

"I always felt very sorry for him," I added. "But it is one of those unfortunate memories that lose their tragedy and blend into folklore as time goes on. What strikes me as very remarkable, though, is the fact that you should be ignorant of the castle story and yet paint the castle one hundred and fifty years later."

Pryor seemed to be as much surprised at the coincidence as I was. But he denied that he was composing a drop-curtain for a theatre, in the Italian style, which would have required a castle, or something of that sort; and as he was much interested in the name of the place, the folklore and the family tradition, in justification of his artistic fancy, I entertained him with further details of the legend, to which I had never given much attention, until we parted at a lane, where the gray roofs and chimneys of his summer quarters showed through the trees.

II

A few days after this, as I happened to be crossing Castle Valley Bridge, and saw Pryor on the bank below, I got over the fence beyond the parapet and joined him. He said he had been examining the stones in the massive piers, as relics of my ancestor's demolished castle, trying to estimate its size from the amount of material visible; and as he supposed that some traces of the ancient foundation must remain on the neighboring summit and suggested an examination of the place, we climbed the hill together.

A careful search of the skyline at length revealed the ground plan, as we thought, of the old building,—all that was left of it, a bramble covered hollow, with faint traces of protruding walls.

"Nothing here now but a woodchuck," I remarked, pointing to a hole of one of the recluse animals on the east slope of the depression.

"You forget the view!" exclaimed Pryor. "Look! Miles and miles of park. And the grass so old and close! Don't they plough the meadows below there?"

"No, nor cut the trees, on account of freshets. The cows keep down the grass."

"No wonder your unfortunate ancestor wanted to build a castle here," said Pryor. "But think of a dreamer of that sort, all alone, so long ago! What possible sympathy could the men of his day have had with an artist,—probably a great architect, born before his time? You say his mind was deranged. I doubt it. Judging from what you tell me, he probably died of disappointment. Call it a broken heart."

"You may imagine anything you please," said I. "It was a long time ago, and the tradition becomes more and more vague. There were other particulars that I scarcely remember, about his losing a treasure, or burying a treasure, or something of that sort. But I never heard him called a great architect; and do you know, I have never been to this place before in my life?"

"I am surprised at that," said Pryor. "It seems to me that if I were studying architecture, as you say you are, I would buy back the land and build the castle."

"I believed in such things once," said I, "but I have changed my point of view. I have discovered that life is practical, and propose to stick to common sense. By the way, I think I shall drop architecture for politics."

We had walked some distance down the slope, had stopped, and were taking a last look at the hilltop, now brightening in the glow of sunset.

"What's that?" said Pryor, pointing to a sparkle of light in the brambles.

I saw nothing until I stepped behind him and, looking over his shoulder, caught, at his angle of vision, a small point of flashing light, through the bushes on the grassy slope of the old excavation.

"It's a piece of broken bottle or chinaware, reflecting the sun," said I.

But on going back to the place, we lost sight of it; and, failing to find it again after a careful search, gave it up, and descended the hill.

III

Who ever knew Highborough in the 'eighties would remember Lane's Tavern, standing at the crossroads, overlooking, then as now, the south sloping streets of the hill town. One hundred years had brought many enlargements, renovations, and so-called improvements to the hospitable, well-equipped, many-roomed building, but none less objectionable to the man of taste, in those days, than the high double-storied porch that followed its south front. A few discerning guests had long known the place as a sort of observatory, within easy reach of refreshments, whence they might look down upon the street drama of the little town, as from the gallery of a theatre. And, as an outlook of this sort could not long have escaped the observant Pryor, I was not surprised to hear his cheerful voice call me from above, one afternoon, as I walked by.

"Hello, Meredith!" he shouted. "You are the very man I wanted to see! Come up here! I have something to show you!"

He was seated in a comfortable armchair, near the shady corner of the porch, by a table supplied with bottles, sandwiches, and a siphon.

"Delightful place, this," he remarked, as I joined him. "Better than a play. The slope of the streets makes an ideal stage-setting, and the actors seem so absurdly unconscious. I was looking over their heads into the sky, building castles in the air. But sit down, and prepare to open your eyes."

He pushed his glass of whiskey and soda to one side, laid down his cigar, pulled with difficulty out of his pocket a large, heavy bundle, wrapped in a handkerchief, and laid it on the table.

"You remember that glitter that we saw, or thought we saw, the other day on Castle Valley Hill, as you call it?"

"You mean the piece of broken bottle that we tried to find in the grass?"

"No bottle about it," said he. "Here it is." He unwrapped the handkerchief and displayed what appeared to be a very large and beautiful piece of transparent quartz or rock crystal. It had a high polish in some places, but rather as if water-rolled than ground by a lapidary. He held it up to the light and turned it about until it flashed.

"Where do you suppose I found it?" he said, looking at me intently, as if waiting for me to speak. As I said nothing, he continued: "You remember there was a woodchuck burrow on the hilltop that we never thought of looking into. When I went back there the other day and saw the glitter again, I kept my angle better, and managed to trace it. This thing was just inside the hole. The woodchuck had barely missed pushing it out. What do you think of it?"

IV

"I am not much of a mineralogist," said I, "but it looks like a very fine specimen. Far handsomer than if ground or faceted. I suppose you will give it to some museum."

"Nothing of the sort," he replied. "I had brought it up to give it to you, but I have changed my mind,—for the present, at least."

"Very kind, indeed, my boy. But you must keep it yourself. I never took the least interest in minerals. Why should I have it?"

"Because it belongs to you,—or to your family. What is more, I believe it to be the treasure that you were talking about. Examine it."

I picked it up as it caught the afternoon light, and looking from various angles into its lucent depths, turned it slowly over, until I noticed a flat interval between two of the projections. Then, as I followed the line of polished surface, my eye caught the words of an inscription, in large deep cut letters:

PER VARIOS CASUS

"Why, how in the world did that get there?" I exclaimed. "It's our family motto."

"I thought it was something of that sort," said he; "but if so, all the more remarkable. I remember the words in Virgil, don't you? The shipwreck episode; Æneas preaching to his followers about misfortunes,—*varios casus*,—a sermon on disaster. But my idea is that your ancestor must have had it in his possession when building the castle, and if, as you say, he lost, or buried, a treasure, here it is."

"He may have lost it," said I; "but why call it a treasure? Excepting as a family relic, it would have no particular value."

"On the contrary," Pryor objected, "if I am not mistaken, it is one of the scrying stones, used by the old crystal gazers in their second sight, prophecies, and warnings. Your people probably brought it with them from Wales."

"All very well to say so," I contended; "but how are you going to prove it?"

"I have proved it. I have looked into the stone and seen enough to convince me that the thing has what is now generally recognized as hypnotic influence."

"What do you mean?" I asked.

"I mean that I have seen a vision,—a castle,— three times at least. So beautiful that if your ancestor saw it, as I am convinced he did, no wonder it inspired him as an architect."

"No one has ever called him an architect but you," said I.

"Yet he was one, and so, you tell me, you are, or will be if you follow your bent. Besides that, you are his kinsman and ought to see more in the stone than I do."

I told him I didn't mind trying, and, incited by his words, helped him move the table into the sunlight, where I sat down and, fixing my eyes steadily upon the brightest point of the relic, stared at it for a long time, in vain. I took off my coat and threw it over my head, shifted the table, tried new angles; but without success. Pryor himself tried it; but failed.

"It won't do here," said he, much disappointed. "You must look by candlelight, with a piece of black cloth. Till now it has generally worked well for me,—too well, in fact, considering the headaches it brings with it; which, by the way, I find hard to get rid of."

He wrapped up the stone again and put it in his pocket.

"My mother has taken a dislike to it," he continued, "and wants me to destroy it. Now that I have told her your story, she insists on my giving it back to you, as your property. The fact is, I came up today for that purpose; but, on second thoughts if you will allow me, I will keep it for a few more experiments."

"Keep it as long as you please," I consented, as we parted. "But, considering your mother and your headaches, I should say the sooner you hand it over to me the better."

v

In order to make clear the following narrative, a serious difficulty, which confronted me at this time, should be well explained. It was a moral dilemma evolved from unexpected circumstances, which, rapidly growing into a crisis, had stirred me to the depths.

At the political convention, then sitting at Eastport, the party leaders, owing to a series of embarrassing rivalries not understood till later, had suddenly offered to nominate me as Congressional candidate for the Eastern District of D——, and since the chance, in no way sought for, thus thrust upon me seemed too good to lose, I had almost decided to seize it. If I did, my reasonably certain election promised a short cut to rapid official preferment,—at the expense of nothing more serious than the abandonment of my chosen profession as architect; the loss (if it were a loss) of the few years already spent in preliminary study.

As the smiling goddess beckoned, I saw no difficulty in locking up my draftsman's tools and throwing my blue prints into the wastepaper-basket. But before I got through with the matter, I realized that there were obstacles on the political highroad that I had not bargained for. At college, as an outspoken idealist, I had not confined myself to literature and art, but had carried my doctrines into politics, as a preacher of reform, an opponent of race hatred, labor unions, socialism, corrupt journalism, political humbug, and so forth. But before I had been long graduated, some of my enthusiasms had been talked out of me by my friends as being impractical and Quixotic, and when, on getting my instructions from the "powers that be" at the Convention, I had found that the time had come to stop preaching what I had never had a chance to practice, I concluded to make the usual bargain in the usual way.

The job was not altogether easy; for I found, on summing up the sacrifice, that some of my old college war-cries were nearer my heart than I had supposed. But at last I got rid of them, and when the Convention broke up, I thought I had my political ship well insured for a prosperous voyage.

Nevertheless, I came home out of spirits, disgusted with myself. It was one thing to pretend to give up my career as an architect and laugh at my old ideals, political and artistic, in conversation with the great men, but another deliberately to sell my soul in writing. Hence the moral dilemma, which, in spite of what I called reason and common sense, oppressed and disturbed me on my return. As I had a week left in which to conclude the bargain, I put off my requisite letter of acceptance to the last moment, and took counsel with several of my acquaintances on the subject. These oracles condemned what they called my ill-timed scruples, but failed to relieve my mind; and I had got through with them all, when I thought of my artistic friend Pryor. Since my return from Eastport, I had seen or heard nothing of him. Yet, as I well knew that I could depend on his sympathy, if not his judgment, I chose one fine autumn afternoon in which to pay him a visit.

VI

Why I had never visited the house once belonging to my father's family, in which the artist was spending the summer, I scarcely know. It stood in a hollow, between two close-set hills, a damp-looking stone building, so gloomy that I remember fancying, as I reached it, that if my castle-building ancestor had ever lived there, he might well have been repelled by the contrast of the place with the hilltop he loved. There were several outbuildings, and at some time in the day the sun's rays, if they ever penetrated the trees, must have fallen upon a grape-arbor, at the lower end of the kitchen garden. There, as I came in from the rear and turned the corner of the barn, I noticed the tall, bent figure of old Michael Shronk, well known in the then superstitious neighborhood as "the powwow doctor," at work pruning the grapevines. He was on a ladder set against the arbor and had blocked the path with a wheelbarrow. As I stepped aside to avoid the obstruction and waved my hand in greeting, I stumbled over a projecting stone and fell headlong upon the grass. When I rose to my feet, the old man, whom I had known since boyhood, had turned upon the ladder, and without the slightest attempt at a smile, had fixed his large, sombre eyes upon me.

"He calls you," said he in his sepulchral voice.

"Calls me!" I exclaimed. "Who calls me? I heard no one."

"It is from the dead."

"What do you mean?" I asked. "Who is dead?"

"A young man, like yourself. He died more than a hundred years ago. But his grave is under your foot."

I felt the subtle power of the man's domineering manner, with the touch of threat in his voice that had always frightened me, as I looked down at the flat piece of native red slate over which I had fallen. It was evidently a gravestone, and protruded about a foot from the ground, with another smaller piece close to the barn wall beyond it. Upon the larger stone, I saw the faint outline of the initials H.M., cut on the weathered surface.

"M for Meredith," I remarked. "My father's people lived here, I know. But I never heard of a graveyard."

"Here is no graveyard." Again that touch of threat in old Shronk's voice. "There are no friends for him. He lies all alone." He paused, still keeping his extraordinary eyes upon me. "Are you alone?" he added.

"Why, no!" I answered. "But yes," thought I, as I walked away. "Today I seem to be alone. I feel as if I hadn't a friend in the world."

VII

At the house door, I learned that my friend Pryor was upstairs in his room and was asking for further particulars, from the little girl who let me in, when his mother, a tall, well-dressed, grey-haired old lady, whose careworn face and appealing eyes betrayed her anxiety, came downstairs. She led me into the rural dungeon, smelling of musty carpet, called the parlor, and when she had illumined the place by forcing open two pairs of shutters, we sat down.

"Will has been talking about you, Mr. Meredith," said she, "and I want to speak with you. He has never been very strong, you know, and now he is not well,—not at all well. Our visit here this summer has been a failure, and the sooner we get back to town, the better."

I was surprised and somewhat startled at the news, and still more so when she declared its cause. It was the stone, she said, which her son and I had found earlier in the summer. He had been crystal-gazing,—staring into it, at a vision that he saw, or thought he saw, "the Castle," as he called it,—until his health had given way. The dangerous trances that followed his experiments resembled boyish attacks that she thought he had outgrown. Sometimes they lasted nearly all day, sometimes all night, and were getting worse. The doctor called it catalepsy, but could do nothing,—could not even arouse him. Neither could any one else, until, on the advice of one of the neighbors, she had sent for an old man, now at work in the garden.

"Old Shronk," said I; "a friend of mine. You know, they call him a 'powwow doctor,' if you believe in such things."

"I don't care what they call him. He is my only hope, and this is the second time, thank God, he has wakened Will."

She had lost her influence over her boy, she said, and had begged him, in vain, to destroy the stone, which she didn't dare do herself. On learning that it was an heirloom of my family, she had made him promise to give it to me.

"It's ruining his health, Mr. Meredith," she exclaimed, weeping. "He talks of what he calls his ideal,—says he is going to paint a great picture; but he never does. In fact, he has given up his painting, and his walks do him no good. Won't you get this dreadful stone away from him, before it is too late?"

She stopped suddenly at a sound of footsteps in the hall, when the door opened, and the subject of our conversation entered the room.

He had lost his high color, and in spite of the fashionable cut of his clothes, the brilliant opal-pinned scarf, and freshly brushed hair, he looked feeble and haggard.

"You feel better, don't you, Will?" asked his mother anxiously as he stepped slowly across the room, with a forced swell of the chest.

"Not very much," he replied, greeting me and grasping my hand. "I must get rid of this headache first. But it's all rather ridiculous, don't you think so, Meredith?"

"Too serious for that," was my answer; "but I hardly know what to think, except that——"

"That I am a first class hypnotic subject, no doubt," said he gloomily.

"So it seems." Then I added: "But if you had given me back the stone the other day, your mother says nothing would have happened."

"But, then, I should have learned nothing. I should never have been quite sure that the vision I see in the stone is something that has appeared before,—appeared to your ancestor. Call it the inspiration for his castle,—his ideal. Call it my ideal. But then——"

He stopped and looked intently at me: "Why not yours? You are his descendant, and a would-be architect, at that. Why shouldn't you see it better than I?" He pulled the stone out of his pocket and handed it to me. "Mother says I must stop crystal-gazing," he added; "and as I have promised her to give you your property, here it is. You can lock it up in a safe; but mother would say 'don't look into it.' Wouldn't you, mother?"

"I'd say, 'throw it into the lime-kiln down yonder, when it is on fire,'" said the old lady.

Her earnest face beamed with delight as I took the relic from her boy, wrapped it up, and squeezed it into my pocket.

Under the circumstances, I realized that events had defeated the purpose of my visit. Another glance at my friend convinced me that it was no time to add my burden to his troubles, and after a short talk on other subjects, in which I found him almost too weak to listen to me, I took my leave.

In crossing the garden, impelled by curiosity, I took the crystal out of my pocket and held it up to the light. Then, near the corner of the barn, I stopped and laid it down on the top of a barrel that stood there. Could it be possible that it had had such an effect on Pryor? After examining the inscription and turning the stone over several times, I had fixed my eyes on one of the bright spots and was staring at it, when I heard the deep voice of Shronk behind me.

"Why will you look today, my friend, when you see nothing?"

As I turned upon the tall, thin figure, I noticed a slightly contemptuous smile on the rigid fleshless face.

"You are right," I agreed; "I see nothing today, or any other day, and I have looked into it several times. Mr. Pryor, in the house there, believes in it. I don't think I do."

"When you are blind, you cannot read. Allow me," said he, grasping my pulse as he placed his hand on my shoulder. Then, pushing back my hat and resting his long, bony fingers upon my brow, he fixed his sullen black eyes upon me.

"Yes, you are far away today," he muttered, "but he can bring you back. There," he continued, pointing to the marked tablet that I had fallen over, "there is his grave. There we will place your wonder stone."

"Not now," said I, repelled at the singular proposal. "I must go home." I walked along the wall, paused at the corner, and looked back.

"But I may bring it to you some day, and you can show me the trick."

"Trick, my friend! When you bring me your wonder stone, you learn your tricks,—not from me!"

VIII

My grandfather was living in Highborough at the time, and though in general he understood my political situation, I had not yet asked his advice upon the moral crisis that clouded it. He was a small, delicately-built man, of noble appearance, popular in spite of his austere manners, admired, if not imitated, for his principles,—an idealist, whose inflexible hostility to slavery years before had lost him his political career through an anti-party vote. Hence I hesitated to risk opposition by consulting him in a case so similar to his own. But, as the time for my decision approached, and as the chances of help from my other friends, including Pryor, had failed, I determined to put my relative's opinions to the test.

On leaving my room for the purpose, late one rainy afternoon, while putting on my overcoat, I happened to see Pryor's crystal in the corner of an open drawer. I picked it up and put it into my pocket.

It had grown chilly when, about dusk, I reached the large white house on the north hillside, at the corner on Wood Street, where I found my grandfather in his study. He was busily arranging some legal documents piled upon the table and protruding from the pigeonholes of an open cupboard, near which he stood. A fire was flickering under the black marble mantelpiece. He pointed to a chair beside it. "Sit down there, Charlie," said he. "It's cold tonight."

Several moments passed while I waited for him to leave the cupboard. I looked about the room. Why it happened, I hardly know; yet, as my eyes wandered, in the deepening shadows, from the mantelpiece to the chandelier, and from one well-remembered engraving to another, my decision to consult him on my political crisis suddenly left me. I got up, took my crystal out of my pocket and, finding a place for it among the law books, laid it down on the table. After locking the cupboard, my grandfather, who had heard nothing of the relic as yet, lit the lamp, and then, leaning over the table, picked up the stone and examined it under the light, while I surprised him with its story. We discussed the possibilities of the case, the fate of our castle-building ancestor, the lost treasure, and details of the family tradition that I had never heard before. But above all things, the inscription interested him. The Virgilian motto, which I had often noticed on my late father's bookplates, had never been explained to me. It hinted, said my grandfather, at calamities, hostile to human effort at all times, typified in this case by a shipwreck.

Holding the singular relic in his hand, he sat down, and for some time looked in silence at the fire. . . .

"Shipwrecks . . . misfortunes." He spoke in the slow, impressive voice that had thrilled many a jury. "What have they meant to those who have come and gone before us? What do they mean to us? . . . What teaches us to reconcile them with Divine justice on this earth?"

"Certainly not this motto of ours," said I. "It dwells on the difficulty, but suggests no remedy. We are left in the dark."

"In the dark?" he repeated. "Never,—if you take it with Virgil's full text: *Tendimus in Latium.* Don't forget that. Those men were pressing on to found Rome. Shipwrecked in body, not in mind. They never abandoned their purpose."

"I have been wondering," said I, inspired by his disclosure of a meaning that I had not before heard of, "whether our ancestor's project was a mere freak of fancy, or, as Pryor contends, the dream of a great architect, and what induced him to give it up. This crystal, which he must have owned, and mislaid or buried, seems to confirm the tradition of some misfortune or illness,—perhaps a quarrel with his father. Pryor would say: 'a lost ideal?'"

"Why lost?" asked my grandfather. "We lose our ideals only when we sell them, betray them for money or for fame or power. Otherwise, they are always ours." He paused, and for a while we watched the flickering fire in silence, while boyish memories echoed in the once-familiar ring of raindrops on a tin spout just outside the window. The time to unburden my heart to my grandfather had come. But I let it pass. At length, he handed me the stone.

"What do you propose to do with it?" he enquired.

I had intended making a few more experiments in crystal-gazing, and told him so; but he objected.

"We have learned too much of crystal-gazing and hypnotism in late years," he declared. "With Pryor's experience as a warning, I should advise locking it up in my safe."

To this, I made no objection. Nevertheless, the project failed, for when, on lighting a candle, he took me to the large bolt-studded safe in his outer office, the key could not be found. Whereupon, after a long and fruitless search, we gave up the plan, and I returned home, carrying the family treasure with me.

IX

I had hardly reached my room when I realized that, instead of quieting my mental turmoil, my interview with my grandfather had made matters worse. I went to bed late, but could not sleep. As I tried in the wakeful hours to weigh popularity, renown, power, in my moral scales, his broken career rose before me, now as the Quixotic failure of an impractical theorist, now as the lonely triumph of a knight errant, whose polished armor reflected star-gleams in a dark night. The restless day that followed was the last possible interval for my indecision. As its hours passed and evening approached, I sought in vain to reason away what seemed to be my over-estimate of ideal things, to consider as settled the question that I had feared to put to my grandfather. Again and again I got up from my writing-desk, pen in hand, with my unwritten letter before me. The crystal was lying on the table, where, several times, I had noticed it during the day, while its strange association with the questions uppermost in my mind came and went on my thoughts, without relieving them. Now, as my eyes fell upon it, I suddenly remembered my conversation with old Shronk, and with a breath of relief at the thought of a long walk and possible distraction in an interview with the remarkable man, I put on my overcoat and, finding an umbrella, hurried out of the house, with the stone in my pocket.

The wind had risen. The cloudy darkness was broken by glimpses of moonlight and distant flashes of sheet-lightning, as I walked rapidly over the nine miles of rough and winding road, until where the highway entered the river hills, a deserted lane led down a ravine to the old man's cabin. There I stopped, to hold my own against the wind, which, whirling in sudden gusts, nearly blew me off my feet. The light, seen as I approached the little house below me, shone from under a rotting porch, where, after stumbling through a bed of periwinkle that obstructed the path and pulling forward a rickety gate, I reached the door. When it opened in answer to my knock, the cadaverous stooping figure of old Shronk stood before me.

x

No doubt the old man was accustomed to night calls. At any rate, he showed no surprise at mine. On the contrary, he pretended that he had expected me.

"Um-um-um," he chuckled, nodding his emaciated head for a while without speaking, as if something, denied by somebody, had been proved to his satisfaction.

"When I wish you, then you come," he at length said. I felt my boyish fear of the deep-set eyes, turned upon me with their peculiar, sullen glitter.

"What?" I asked. "Do you mean that you knew I was coming?"

"More, my friend: I know you bring me your wonder stone."

With the usual fortune-teller's knack, he must have read my face, I thought, as, entering the little room, I pulled the relic out of my pocket.

"Here it is," said I. "You told me you would show me the wonders. But when I look in it, I see no wonders. Nothing at all."

He took it from me and closed the door against the boisterous wind. Then, carrying it to a kerosene lamp that stood on a table in the corner, he raised, lowered, and turned it in the light.

"Are you well tonight?" he asked, looking back upon me,

while the deep shadows from the lamplight upon his vellum skin seemed to transform his head into a skull.

"Well enough," I answered. "But I feel nervous,—I'm worried. Though it has nothing to do with the stone."

"You are wrong, my friend. It is all in the stone. There you will see what you hunt for tonight."

He opened an inner door. Then, going to the mantel, pulled a long paper-twist out of a glass, and holding it to the lamp until it blazed, lit a candle.

"Wait here," he ordered, as, picking up the crystal, he went with the candle into the dark inner room and closed the door.

XI

The wind was making a loud noise in the trees outside, and I felt the little house shake. But, in spite of the sounds and rumblings of thunder, I could hear him moving about behind the thin board partition. At last the door opened.

"Come here," said Shronk, beckoning me from the threshold with several long-circling sweeps of a black cane held in his left hand. Then, as he turned back, I followed him. The whitewashed inner room, with its log walls and low rough-hewn ceiling, was lit by four candles, set upon a table, in bottles, between which, on a piece of fur, lay the crystal. Reflecting the light in all directions, it seemed to glow more brightly than ever before.

Deliberately placing his cane upon the table, where I noticed that it was twisted or carved into the form of a snake, the old man turned, and, looking fixedly at me, stepped forward. At his request, I held out my wrist. He seized it with one of his gnarled hands and, pressing the other upon my forehead, slowly brought his palm downward toward my eyes. Just as I closed them, the little room, through its two small windows, was illumined by a flash of lightning. The following clap of thunder seemed delayed for a long time, during which I felt a twitching sensation, as the old man's knotted fingers bore upon my closed eyelids. When I opened my eyes again, the black cane was standing upright in a hole in the table-top. Shronk was pointing at the stone.

"Now look, my friend," he said, as his forefinger approached the brightest part of the crystal, touched it, and drew back. Just then another still more brilliant flash was followed by a tremendous report that shook the whole house. I felt a quick-passing dizziness, followed by a shortness of breath, and drew back in alarm.

"Hadn't we better wait," I asked, "until this is over?"

"Look now," came the answer in a loud threatening voice, "or you see nothing. It is all for you."

I leaned forward and stared intently upon the gleaming stone. For a moment its glitter seemed to contract into a scintillating focus, then to increase and quiver in the outlines of a Gothic castle. Slowly the picture grew, until the candles, the stone, the snake-cane, the room, expanded into a transcendent radiance of innumerable gables, turrets, and pinnacles. I saw a swirl of clouds and a waving of banners. But the blast of trumpets I heard was a terrible crash of thunder, annihilating consciousness, as the vision vanished in darkness.

XII

When I awoke I found myself lying upon a pile of straw on the floor of a barn, through the open door of which I saw a red glow, with clouds of smoke, and moving figures of men. Slowly recovering my senses, I got up with difficulty and, in spite of my dizziness, staggered out, to a freshly-fallen tree and looked about me in the rain-cooled air. At length, from one of the farmers, I learned that the red illumination, a cellar full of live embers, was all that remained of Shronk's cabin. He told me that I had had a very narrow escape from the burning house, which had been struck by lightning, had caught fire, and from which Shronk had dragged me at the last moment. The old man had lost everything, and as he had burned himself badly, had been taken to a neighboring house and put to bed.

Postponing my plans for his help and comfort, that night I

accepted the farmer's offer to take me home, and without again seeing the singular character who had saved my life, climbed into the wagon, and we drove off.

Not until we reached the top of the hill, did I remember with dismay the stone that had brought me there. Could Shronk have rescued it from the fire? No. It was gone, buried under the embers, melted, shattered, lost. But as I looked down on the scene of desolation and thought of its motto, it seemed that, after all, evil had triumphed. Fatal facts contradicted my grandfather's fine theory. Had I dabbled in sorcery? If so, what but misfortune had clung like a curse to the relic,—and even now rose from the smoke and fire below me? For a time I gazed upon the red glare, and never lost it until, turning the corner of the hill, I closed my eyes and sank back upon the seat. Then slowly, unexpectedly, and without effort of will, the dazzling vision seen in the cabin, again rose upon my inner sense.

In wonder, growing into ecstacy, I watched it, as several times it dimmed, to brighten again before it slowly faded away.

While we jolted onward upon the stony road, a joyful elation, as of final relief from a crushing burden, replaced my gloomy doubts. Shut off from the reality of the sights and sounds about me, I scarcely heard the driver's voice as he talked on, of the fire; until, after trying in vain to listen to him, I fell asleep.

At last, we reached home. The morning was half gone, and, after a bath and change of clothes, I had just finished my breakfast when, following a ring of the door-bell, my friend Pryor appeared. To my pleased surprise, he seemed to have recovered his health and spirits, as, with his old smile, he grasped my hand and held it for some time.

"We have decided to prolong our visit," said he, "and, thank Heaven! I am all right again. But how are you?" he asked after a pause, as he looked anxiously at me. "It is a curious thing, that ever since I reached Highborough this morning I have had a fancy that something has gone wrong with you."

"So it did, or rather it didn't," I returned contradicting myself, as I hurriedly related my narrow escape.

"You ought to be in bed," said he.

"On the contrary, I believe I feel better. I have had an infernal incubus on my mind for the last week, and this thing has lifted it. That letter on the table there that I have been trying to write was too much for me. Could I, or couldn't I, sell my soul to the Devil,—or the politicians, whichever you choose to call it? The question was driving me mad; but I have seen your castle, and it has settled the matter. I wouldn't have missed it for anything."

"Yet, you might have missed it. It seemed hopelessly hidden from you at first."

"So it did," I admitted. "It may be hypnotism. But it is none the less curious that you, of yourself, and I, thanks to old Shronk, should have seen the same thing. Both times a castle."

"And both times with a dose of misfortune thrown in," said Pryor. "My trances and your thunderstorm. It's that unfortunate motto of yours."

"No! We're wrong there. According to my grandfather, we misread the motto and lost the point."

"How so?" asked Pryor.

"We must go back to Virgil. The real meaning of the poet is in words the motto leaves out,—the idea of final victory. Read out the text: *Tendimus in Latium.*"

"You mean that they went on to Latium, in spite of the shipwreck and the misfortune."

"Yes,—they founded Rome."

"Splendid!" exclaimed Pryor. "I lost that in Virgil. But it reconciles the motto to the vision."

"Exactly," I agreed. "The castle becomes an ideal. That we hold on to, in spite of the Devil and all his angels."

"Just as I thought it was from the first, without knowing why," said Pryor.

"Now that the stone is gone, it is fortunate that I have seen your castle, thunderstorm included," I continued, "or I should never have known what you were talking about. So much for hypnotism. But how wonderful, how astonishing it is, merely as a picture! Don't you think so? Those unearthly pinnacles that pierce the clouds! If I were a painter, as you are, and saw a thing like that, I would feel that I had got hold of my ladder of fortune and only needed to climb up—up—up."

"But the ladder is yours as well as mine."

"Why? I am not a painter, and never could be."

"What are you?"

I got up, seized his hand, and looked deep into his glowing eyes.

"I didn't know, till just now," said I. "I thought I was a politician. But I have decided that I am an architect!"

THE NORTH FERRY BRIDGE

I

When, about forty years ago, as a young doctor, I came to Bridgenorth to begin practice, I was unmarried, and my means, though sufficient to provide me with comfortable quarters, did not warrant me, as I thought, at the start in keeping a horse and carriage. Hence, I walked to my patients. This did very well for a time. But Bridgenorth in those days, before the hand of modern improvement had touched it, with its sagged and winding streets, interrupted by two ill-directed streams, with its weary detours and dead intervals, was a very exacting place for a pedestrian doctor. Bad enough in the day time, but worse at night; and, as my practice grew, my exhausting beats, among poorer patients, drawing me farther and farther into the widespread suburbs, and often protracted until the early hours of the morning, began to tell seriously upon my strength and sleep.

It was during these late and fatiguing walks, when unfamiliar shadows creep over the sleeping city and things half seen mask in exaggerated shapes before the tired mind, that I came by a series of impressions, vague, elusive, yet strangely disagreeable, from passing glimpses of a man often met upon the deserted streets. Judging from his looks and the large glazed shoulder pack, he might have been one of the then not uncommon itinerant pedlars. Always hurrying and always alone, he never appeared before midnight, and generally much later. I saw him in widely distinct parts of the city, vanishing across commons, or at street corners, sometimes entering, sometimes leaving private enclosures. But at first nothing seemed more remarkable about him than the late hours he kept, and I paid no particular attention to him, until one windy night, at the house of a patient, when I had gone down stairs to get some hot water and was about to light a candle in the kitchen, I happened to see him through one of the shutterless windows. He was standing in the bright moonlight against a background of swaying trees near the corner of a wall and had set his pack upon the ground, when, as I watched him, he partly removed the glazed cover, opened a lid, turned the bundle upside down, and jostled it against a pile of rubbish close by. After the process had continued for some time, although I saw nothing fall out, he stood up the pack and closed it. As he shouldered it, by means of its arm-straps, and walked out of range of the windows, I noticed, under the broad hat brim, his very pale aquiline features, protruding teeth, and a peculiar unpleasant glitter in his prominent eyes.

The incident impressed and puzzled me; but, on going upstairs, where I found the wife of my sailor patient devotedly nursing her sick husband, I concluded that the woman was too much worried at the time to be needlessly disturbed by my experience, so finished my work and went home without mentioning it.

II

At that time my distinguished uncle, who for years had been living alone at Bridgenorth and had been instrumental in my coming there, was my only friend. He was a very handsome man, past middle age, who since his retirement from the Bench, on the death of his wife and only son, had turned his back upon public life, and in spite of his success as a legal essayist and his rare social talents, had made few friends.

But beyond all ties of blood, the sparkling wit that graced his gifted mind, the eager yet kindly manners, had won me from the first; and as he seemed to enjoy my company when he honored me with his, we often exchanged visits.

One evening, I well remember my satisfaction at the sudden advent of a thunderstorm that had detained him with me after supper, when, as we sat at the table, watching the flashes that broke the premature twilight, the subject of our talk turned, from the house in which I lodged, to the notorious Dr. Gooch, its former tenant. In his vivid and graphic style, my uncle described the singular personal appearance of the great chemist, the later events of his career, and, finally, the dramatic criminal trial that had ended in his downfall.

At this trial, presided over by my uncle as Judge, which had closely followed the great cholera epidemic at Bridgenorth, the evidence, charging the doctor with the atrocious murder of one of his assistants, had been altogether circumstantial. The murderer when seen had worn a mask, and the identification, always short of certainty, rested on inferences, comparisons, dates, and so forth. Considering the brilliant and plausible efforts of the doctor's lawyers, the quick verdict surprised everybody; but the sensational feature of the case was a savage speech made by the condemned man, cursing my uncle upon the bench, and threatening impossible vengeance on the inhabitants of Bridgenorth in general.

"What could have been his grudge against a whole city?" I inquired.

"There were facts preceding the trial that must have embittered him," said my uncle, "ghastly rumors about a cholera serum, tested upon his patients, resulting in the loss of his practice, and finally, a disgraceful flogging by a mob. Owing to the state of popular feeling at the time, when his life was in danger, the reports no doubt influenced the jury. I disbelieved them, and therefore suppressed them from the evidence. Nevertheless, he denounced me."

"Was his mind deranged?" I asked. "How could he have failed to know that you were only the abstract mouthpiece of the law?"

"There may have been some jealousy," said my relative. "I had criticised his theories. He was a man of ungovernable temper, and very vindictive. Long before the trial, I had an interview with his supposed victim, and hence could have been associated in his mind with the rumors."

As my uncle talked on, the storm that howled outside, and shook the room in which we sat, seemed a fit accompaniment for his description of the blasted career of the great man and the furious outburst of diseased eloquence that ended the trial.

In his chivalric way, he touched little upon the personal side of the affair, dwelling rather upon the great talents and well-known discoveries of the fallen man, whose creative genius, wrecked through moral depravity, might have been of high service to mankind.

By the time evening had turned to night, and as the storm died down to distant rumblings, the talk ended in a sketch of the fatal inroads of the scourge of ten years before, from which the city had not yet recovered. Whole streets depopulated, a scattered black list of *To Rent* placards had given the place the sombre and deserted look which still clung to it.

The dilapidated house in which we then were, said my uncle, as I followed him downstairs, had been since used for storage by its owners. The evil fame of the doctor, more injurious than the aftermath of cholera, having kept off tenants during the whole interval.

"No idea of ghosts, I hope," said I, as we stepped out upon the wet grass and looked up at a few stars in the still threatening sky.

"I never heard of that. The murder was not committed here, and the doctor has not yet gone to ghostland. He got off with life imprisonment."

"Where is he?" I asked.

"Serving his sentence in Fetterfield Jail."

"Is there any chance of pardon?"

"No," replied my uncle as I left him,—"nor of escape either; the prisoners are well guarded there."

III

Several weeks had passed, and I was slowly becoming familiar with my new difficulties, when an incident happened, which, though scarcely noticed at the time, deserves mention as strangely relevant to the events that follow.

It was on a breezy summer afternoon. After mounting the hillside along the shady end of M—— Street, I had stopped to visit my sailor patient above mentioned. His wife, as usual, answered my ring at the door-bell. We had passed through the little stuffy hall, and I was about to turn upstairs, when, glancing through the open kitchen door, I noticed a little white animal dart across the floor, almost too quickly to be seen, and disappear down the cellar stairs.

"What's that?" I asked.

"It's one of our rats," replied the woman, stepping into the kitchen, to close the cellar door.

"But it seems to be white," I remarked.

"Yes, sir. They are all white."

"White rats!" I exclaimed. "Are you keeping them as pets?"

"No indeed. No such pets for me, if I have my way. There's bad stories about those rats, sir."

"What stories?" I asked.

"Charlie won't believe them, sir; but it's about the cholera, years back. They say that the white rats brought it here."

"What!" said I. "I never heard of such a thing."

"Yes, sir. It may be all nonsense, I know; but yet, there is something wrong with them. Both our cats were afraid of them, and both died after they came. They say that white rats have pink eyes. These don't. Not a single one of them."

I told her that a little rat poison would soon settle the matter, and offered to send her some.

"I wish you would," said she; "but Charlie wouldn't hear of it. He says there's a mint of money in white rats, and he is going to trap and sell them as soon as he gets well."

IV

About a week after this I met my uncle on one of his evening strolls, and as I walked home with him by way of a dismal suburb near the river, which had been notably depopulated by cholera, I inquired as to the origin of the great epidemic, for which, he said, no reasonable theory had been advanced. There had been East Indian ships in port, but they had been well quarantined.

"Did you ever hear that the infection had been brought in by white rats?" I asked.

He had been looking out across the harbour, and turned to inquire, with surprise: "Who told you that?"

"One of my patients seems to have heard a report to that effect. She tells me that her cellar is full of the animals."

As we walked onward in the deepening twilight, I related my experience, at which my uncle seemed very much impressed.

"That white rat story," said he, "was at the bottom of the rumors that ruined doctor Gooch. One of those wild fancies that get possession of the popular imagination in moments of fear and lead to outrageous injustice. As I told you, I got the details of it from the murdered man before the trial, but suppressed them from the evidence. He declared that the doctor, during the panic, had discovered a method of sprinkling rats with a serum containing cholera germs, whereupon their fur turned white, and they became wholesale absorbents of the contagion."

"One way of exhausting its virulence," I remarked.

"Possibly, provided he had no other motive, but though otherwise non-infectious, his rats could still contaminate human food. Therefore the discovery would have been a highly dangerous secret, a *carte blanche* for universal murder, with perfect safety to the murderer.

"The man's charge to me was that the doctor had not only boasted of his serum, but had proved it, by foul play upon several of his patients. In other words, he had introduced his white rats into the houses of his victims, in order to infect their food."

"Frightful idea," said I, "but almost too atrocious to believe."

"So it struck me at the time. Considering that the informer had had a quarrel with the doctor, I was not disposed to put too much faith in the story. It was late one night when I heard it, and, as some of the details seemed insufficient, I postponed the interview. The result was that I never saw the man again. He was found dead in his bed about a week later. When the post mortem disclosed poison, suspicion fell upon the doctor; hence the accusation and trial."

I suggested that if white,—or whitened,—rats had existed at the time, those seen by my patient might be survivors of the old breed.

"Hardly," said my uncle. "The town was overrun with rats, but the general opinion, as I heard it later, is that the white ones died out long ago. Still," he added as I left him at his door step, "rats are very curious creatures, particularly the breed of so-called albinos. Suppose we go down and investigate the cellar you speak of."

Whereupon, after arranging an appointment with me for a rat hunt several days later, we parted.

v

My house, a rambling building on high ground, rather too much shaded by trees, was far too large for my needs. With its musty outer office and laboratory, ending in a ruined green-house, it had taken a long time to clean, but at length the work was done. I had congratulated myself upon the final junk-heap and the final bonfire on the lawn, when, one afternoon, on my return from a long tramp, my housekeeper, a thin, neatly-dressed woman, with tightly plaited hair and gold earrings, met me in the office.

"I hope it won't offend you, sir," said she in a hesitating voice as I took off my coat and threw it on a chair; "but I am afraid I can't stay here."

"Why not?" I asked, somewhat hurt at the sudden news, for I thought I had done my best to treat her well and make her comfortable.

"It's nothing against you, sir,—not at all; and I did like the house well enough, though I must say it's damp. But I'm fright-ened here; so I am, sir; and I can't help it."

"Frightened!" I repeated. "What do you mean? Who fright-ens you?"

"There is somebody prowling about the house at night,

when you are away and I am all alone, and I don't think I can stand it sir."

"Haven't you made a mistake?" I asked. "It sounds impossible. Nothing has been stolen. Who would want to come here at night?"

"It's a man," said she, after looking uneasily out of the windows into the trees. "I've heard him several times; and I believe he gets into the cellar."

"Have you seen him?"

"Never but once. He was coming out of the greenhouse, carrying something on his back; but it was too dark, and I couldn't make out what it was."

I tried to reassure the woman, told her I would inform the police, and finally satisfied her by promising to employ her niece to sleep in the house with her until we could get the thing looked into.

The information worried me for a while, but I heard nothing further from the woman, and by the time the little girl had been with her several days, I had dismissed the subject from my mind.

VI

As autumn approached, the increasing range of my nocturnal practice often led me past my uncle's house, and one night on my way home from a tiresome round of late visits, when the usual gleam from his study windows beaconed through the trees, I stopped and crossed the street.

Unlike some students, whose talents quicken in the flush of morning and who tax the patience of servants and housekeepers with breakfast-calls at peep-of-day, my uncle worked at night. For him memories, waking with the silent hours, brought an inspiration, which kept his light aglow long beyond the bedtime of common men. That night, as on many a night before, the mellow ray, with its sure promise of welcome, cheered me, and I stepped across the little lawn and rang his doorbell. The housekeeper had long since gone to bed, and he let me in himself.

"Come upstairs, Ned. I have something to tell you," said he.

His brilliantly-lit study, lined with bookcases, was on the second floor, and there, at one end of a large table, piled with law reports and manuscripts, a punch bowl, with some lemons and a glass stood on an outspread napkin.

He went to the cupboard for another glass, ladelled it full of punch, and pointed to a sofa against the outer wall.

"My boy, you look tired," he said. "Lie down there."

A refreshing sea-breeze, blowing in the open window, was lifting the chintz curtains and rattling the manuscripts on the table as I drank his health and sank back upon the comfortable couch.

"I have just had a curious bit of news," said he presently, after sitting down at the table and helping himself. "Speak of the Devil, and he is sure to appear. It seems that Dr. Gooch has broken out of Fetterfield Jail."

"What!" I exclaimed. "Didn't you tell me that Fetterfield was supposed to be proof against escapes?"

"Yes," he replied; "but it seems it's not. The thing happened nearly a year ago," he continued, as he filled my empty glass; "but it has been kept out of the newspapers by the police. I only heard of it in tonight's mail."

"He has left the country, of course," I remarked.

"I doubt it," said my uncle. "Men of that type rarely do. There is a sort of moth-and-candle infatuation that seems to lure them back to their old haunts. I shouldn't be surprised if he were in Bridgenorth now."

"If he is," said I, laughing, "I hope he won't pay his old house a visit. I can't say that I want to meet him."

"Don't concern yourself," said my uncle; "my house rather than yours would be his first objective point. Read that."

He picked up a letter lying on the table and handed it to me. Written on a small blue-lined half-sheet of paper, in a disguised hand, in imitation of printed letters, I read the following words:

If you think you are safe, you will know better when you read this. Dr. Gooch is out of Fetterfield Jail. You know him, and he knows you. BEWARE.

The last word was written in double-sized letters in red ink.

"What an infernal thing an anonymous letter is," I exclaimed, after looking at the unsigned paper on both sides. "The more you read it, the worse it gets. Why don't you destroy it? Though perhaps you had better show it to the police first. In any case, I hope you won't worry about it."

"Not a bit of it," said my host; "I have encountered too much of that sort of thing in my time; but I wanted you to see it as a curious sequence to our conversation about the doctor the other night."

"The doctor would hardly have written it himself," said I.

"No; it is someone who knows his history. Some fellow-criminal, perhaps, whose motive may not be altogether unfriendly."

Declaring that he would make an effort to learn the particulars of the doctor's escape, he enlarged, as he had done before, upon the brilliant attainments, prostitution of talents, and so on, of the great chemist, and finally the danger to society involved in the freedom of a genius, unrestricted by any inborn principle.

But I was almost too tired to listen; and, after nearly falling asleep twice as my uncle talked on, got up, at last, and bade him good-night.

VII

My first summer at Bridgenorth was ending in a growing practice, with bright hopes for the future, when the city, which had not yet lived down its past, was startled by the reported appearance of several cases of Asiatic cholera. The sudden threatenings, breaking out in widely diverging districts and at first doubtful, soon showed their well-known symptoms; and when more than one death had turned suspicion into certainty, the whole city was in a panic. Wealthy persons left town, houses were quarantined, and elaborate precautions taken. Meanwhile, a rush of fresh work had soon monopolized my time and interrupted my visits to my uncle. For at least a week I had seen nothing of him, when, late one afternoon, I called at his house.

The old housekeeper let me in, and as she fixed her red and swollen eyes upon me, I saw that she had been crying.

"Oh, Mr. Edward, I hope you have brought good news!"

"What's the matter?" I asked,—"what news? I don't know what you mean."

"It's your Uncle James," she said, in a frightened, trembling voice. He went out after supper day before yesterday, and he never came back. It's that dreadful cholera, Mr. Edward,—I know it is. Oh, what shall I do?"

No ordinary devotion spoke in the appealing look of the aged and wrinkled face; and the eyes, swimming with tears, told of half a lifetime warmed in a genial flame of kindness and sympathy.

I tried to cheer her as she wept. Probably he had gone to the country with some of his friends. We would look for a letter at any moment. I would tell the police. The cholera was well in hand,—so I said.

But, utterly unprepared for the news, and knowing the range of my uncle's walks, I found it hard to sham a confidence I did not feel; and, dreading the worst, hastened home, only to hear of a sudden accident to one of my patients in Rockhaven, which hurried me supperless over the river, into the sister city.

VIII

It took me a long time to finish with my Rockhaven patient. There were instruments needed, which I had forgotten to bring with me and had to borrow from a neighboring surgeon, so that it was past midnight when, after a hasty sandwich at a tavern, I had gone down Tower Street to cross the North Ferry Bridge.

The wind was blowing almost a gale, with a wild whirling of moonlit clouds, and, in the chasm below me, out of which towered the great wooden bridge and pile-built warehouses on the Bridgenorth side, I saw that the tide was running out fast. I was walking rapidly; but before I got half way across I heard the click of machinery, the rattling of chains, and then the ringing of a ship's bell, which I knew preceded the opening of the draw.

Whoever remembers the place may know that the draw-bridge, turning horizontally, opens on the river, where the channel runs close upon the south waterfront. I saw the circling of lanterns as the great turnstile swung out from the roadway, but my yearning thoughts were with my uncle,—the time lost, the things left undone for his help. I remembered the long delays that often occurred at such moments; and, without waiting to calculate my chances, sprang forward, and, leaping across the widening gap, ran along the draw. But though just in time at one end, I was too late at the other. The moving streetway had cleared the opening, and I stopped at the corner and looked out along the railing at the oncoming mass of spars and rigging. I heard the whistle of the tug boat, the hoarse orders of the captain, and, blending with the noise of the wind, a loud scraping, as of a projecting spar along the bridge-rail. Then suddenly came an irresistible thrust that swept me out into the darkness. With a rush of air, I felt a pounding plunge, a wild mental turmoil, and the stifling instinctive submarine struggle, with gulps of water, that at last brought me swimming to the surface. I saw a ship's hull glide past; but, being at home in the water, kept my distance in the light of the bridge lamps, and, as the tide swept me towards the forest of piles ahead, I swam with it until I reached one of the barnacle-covered posts. For a moment I clung to it; then, letting go, floated on into the darkness. Clutching or grazing the prickly pillars, I followed the current, and after several kicks in deep water, my feet touched bottom. I felt a steeply-sloping bank of mud, and waded slowly through it, upward, until at length I stood waist-deep and looked around me. Save for the water-gleams and dim-lit patches of river seen beyond the posts, the place was pitch dark. I felt a dry slope of earth above me, but in vain looked along it and up at the blackness overhead, for an opening. For a while I wallowed and clambered onward through wedged masses of slimy flotsam and ramparts of mud and pebbles. Then I got up on the bank. The roof of the place,—in other words, the floor of the warehouses under which I had been swept,—was still high above me, and

I stopped continually, to feel my way across deep hollows and over blocks of stone. At length, passing round a muddy cape, I halted at sight of a gleam of light ahead,—a faint ray of lamp-light, which, as I got nearer, showed the rungs of a ladder reaching downward through a bright opening in the planks above. I approached it cautiously. The ladder rested on the bank, a few feet above the water, and the trap-door through which it penetrated showed a very large, dimly-lit room, with blackened beams and roof-lines lost in shadow. I looked and listened for some time, but heard no noise.

"Hello, up there!" I called out.

There was no answer. I shook the ladder, called again, and waited a little longer. Then I slowly climbed up through the opening.

IX

The place I got into showed a vast roof space, with overhanging floors and galleries, extending back into the darkness, and looked as if it might be one of the wings of a deserted foundry.

By the light of a hanging lamp I saw piles of lumber, rusty machinery, and casters' flasks. Another lamp, with a half-barrel and some bottles and dishes, stood on a workbench behind me. Across the floor, near a pile of boxes stuffed with straw and close to a cupboard, I saw a long wire cage, built against the wall.

As I looked from a distance, a moving white mass, seen inside the close-woven meshes, seemed to expand and contract, like a shifting cloud of vapor, until I stepped across the room; when, leaning close against the wire, I saw to my astonishment, that the cage was swarming with rats. White rats!—hundreds of them,—darting in all directions, or crouched in groups upon a long pile of mould or grass heaped against the inner wall. The cage was wet inside, from a dark liquid that had formed pools upon its metal bottom, and was oozing out upon the floor of the room. It took me some time to see that the moisture was dripping from a long tin trough in the cage; and I had just made out a barrel fixed upon a framework above it, when I heard a noise as of the splash of oars and presently, voices. I stepped back and looked across the room.

The sounds came up through the trap-door from below, indistinct at first, then clearer, until I heard words, plainly spoken in an urgent, rasping tone:

"Doctor, I don't like this. He never did me any harm." And then, after a pause: "Let's throw him overboard and be done with it?"

A harsh laugh and some talk that I could not make out followed. I saw the ladder move, and with a quick premonition of danger, stepped into the high empty cupboard and closed the door.

As I did so my legs grazed some bars of iron, and instinctively I stooped down and seized what I found to be a pair of blacksmith's tongs. A few moments of silence were followed by a noise of heavy breathing, a grating of footsteps, and a dull, scraping sound. I pushed the door slightly open and, holding it by a nail just within the crack, looked out. A bleached-looking, thin-bearded, long-haired man, without a hat, in a dingy cutaway coat, was leaning over the ladder, pulling at a rope. The high-cheeked white face, under a commanding forehead, was turned downward; but there was something about the protruding close-set eyes and overshow of teeth that seemed familiar, until, as the man's muscular body strained at the rope, a peculiar flare of the ears and fall of the hair convinced me that he was the pedlar of my night walks.

I had hardly made him out, when the hole was filled with a sight that overwhelmed me with amazement and horror. The gray hair, flushed face, then the shoulders of my uncle, slowly rose into the room. The lower features were concealed by a wad of white rags, stuffed into his mouth; and as the arms, tightly bound under the rope that lifted him, and then the body emerged, I saw a pair of dirty hands push him up from below. I was trembling, and as my hand bore upon the closet door, I heard it creak, closed it, and drew back. For a few seconds I waited in the darkness, listening to the shuffling of feet, followed by a dull bumping sound. When I pushed the door out again, and looked through the crack, my uncle was lying upon the floor, and another man, with close-cropped hair, and staring eyes, was standing near him. The formidable man I had recognized bent down, and I watched him loose and pull out the rope noosed under my uncle's arms, deliberately coil it up, and throw it across the floor. Then, stooping the two men seized the tightly-bound prostrate figure, lifted it, and carrying it across the room, placed it on the floor close to the cage.

The pedlar walked back to the work-bench, and pouring some liquid from a bottle and a pitcher into a basin, picked up a large brush, and, returning to the cage, sprinkled my uncle with the mixture. While he did so, I thought I recognized the pungent aromatic smell of oil of rhodium. And as it filled the room, I heard a loud noise of scampering and squealing inside the cage. The younger man, who had been peering through the wire meshes, gave a low whistle.

I saw the pedlar look down at my uncle and push him with his foot.

"Do you hear that?" said he.

There was a door about two feet square in the front of the cage. The pedlar pulled out an iron pin in its staple, opened it, and stooped down.

"Now, in with him," he ordered savagely; and the two men, seizing the tightly-bound body of their prisoner, pushed it head foremost through the hole. As the door closed, the younger man stared at his assistant with a look of fear. He seemed to he trembling.

"Good God!" he cried. "This is too much for me."

He stepped across the floor to the ladder, started to climb down, then stopped, calling back:

"Come along, doctor. I wouldn't look at it, if I were you."

A contemptuous smirk played over the grim face of his companion. I saw the white of teeth and a diabolical glitter in the eyes. Then, as the head and shoulders of the speaker disappeared down the ladder, the man or monster whose terrible purpose I at last understood, gave a low chuckle, walked back to the cage, and placing a stool near it, sat down, and leaned over towards the grating.

X

For a few moments, while an irresistible impulse to rush upon him sent the blood tingling through my veins, I waited and listened, until the noises from the boat below died away. But I had no thought of parley, or of juggling with the chances of my uncle's fate, when at length I pushed the door slowly open. Safe, then, from interruption, and clutching the iron weapon in my right hand, I stepped out upon the floor, noiselessly approached the ferocious villain, and struck him a tremendous blow with the tongs. Without a groan, he fell heavily upon the planks; but I hardly saw him, when I rushed at the cage door, pulled out the staple pin, and swung it open. I heard the rats scamper and squeal, as I squeezed in across my uncle's body, stooped over him, and looked close. Thank God, I saw no wound! The voracious vermin had not yet tasted his blood. He was breathing in deep gasps. His flushed face was streaming with perspiration. His swollen and inflamed eyes were winking, as if he hardly saw me. I threw down the tongs, seized his legs, and dragged him through the door. Pulling the rags out of his mouth, I cut the ropes from his arms and legs with my pocket knife, and, finding my flask, held it to his lips. But I had to wait several moments, as I chafed his stiffened arms and turned and shifted him, before he managed to get on his feet, stagger forward, and clutch the side of the cage. At length, the strong spirits had their effect and he found strength to lean upon me and stumble across the floor to the ladder. I got my feet upon it, and with a last look at the villain, who lay perceptibly breathing near the open door of the cage, I held fast to the dazed and trembling man until, slowly descending through the trap-door, he had followed me to the bottom.

The stony bank under foot was reasonably level, and while we groped forward, his trembling sentences became coherent enough to make clear the full meaning of his ghastly experience. Several times we halted in the darkness, while the broken details of his capture and imprisonment verified my suspicion that the stunned man left behind us,—the pedlar, the monster, who would have watched the rats devour his victim alive,—was the terrible Dr. Gooch.

With arms extended to meet the continued obstacle of the thick-clustered posts, we struggled on in the watery cellar of the great buildings above us until finally a platform leading backwards brought us to a rotting staircase choked with rubbish, and thence upward into a long, narrow yard between high walls. Passing piles of waste iron and then a labyrinth of ruinous sheds faintly lit by the moon, we reached a gate at the end of a paved alley and pulled back its rusty bolt. As the doorway swung open, I saw a glimmer ahead, felt the river breeze, and a moment later stepped out on the main highway leading to the North Ferry Bridge.

XI

It took about ten minutes to find a policeman, who, having directed us to the nearest station, left me and took my uncle home; while I, determined that the diabolical villain I had disabled should not escape, hurried back, with two other men, to the den of horror I had just left.

By way of the foundry yards, staircase, and beach, lit now by the dark lanterns of the officers, we reached the lighted ladder; and, after waiting a while in silence, clambered up through the trap door into the room above.

The lamp suspended from the ceiling had burned low and was smoking badly, throwing the whole side of the place near the cage into shadow. But in the dimmed light I saw the open door of the rats' prison and the white forms of the escaped animals darting about the floor.

"Where's your man?" asked the officer.

He stood looking about the great room. Then, stepping slowly across the floor, suddenly stopped and started back, as some rats scampered out of the shadows ahead.

"What's that!" he exclaimed, in startled tones.

He was pointing to a yellowish litter half covered with wet-looking rags on the floor. I looked at it, and beyond it at the cage. The fallen man had disappeared. The blotched rags half concealed a round smooth object.

"Why, that's a skull!" cried the man. "Good God! Look at the bones! The rats have eaten him up!"

I had hardly heard the terrible words, when the policeman behind me plucked my sleeve.

"Listen!" he whispered. "There's someone coming."

We heard the splash of oars from below and what I took to be the bumping of a boat, and then a low whistle.

I pointed to the closet, and the officer ahead of us slipped in and closed the door, while my companion and I hurried behind one of the lumber piles.

XII

The whistle was repeated. Then the ladder shook, and I saw the ill-shaped head and close-cropped hair of the doctor's accomplice emerge from the opening.

"Hello, doctor!" he cried. Then, after hesitating a moment, he climbed into the room.

"What's the matter? Hello, there!" he called again. "What's all this?"

He must have seen the rats, or noticed that the cage-door was open, for there was a puzzled look on the bleared face as I saw him step to the workbench, pick up the lamp, and, holding it high above his head, walk slowly across the floor. Before reaching the cage he stopped and looked downward, while his eyes assumed a fixed stare of abject terror. The uplifted lamp was shaking visibly. Just then the closet door opened behind him. I saw the tall figure of the policeman step out with extended arm and pointed pistol and heard the shouted word, "Surrender!"

The man turned. A moment later came a quick report and the crash of broken glass, as the lamp fell from the outstretched hand. But the surprised rascal had escaped the bullet. He leaped along the side of the cage and around its corner, while the officer, firing again, ran after him. There was a loud rattle of boards in the dim-lit background, when I rushed out with the other man, to see the fugitive dart over one of the lumber-piles and disappear in the darkness.

His pursuer, who had stopped and turned back, was pointing at the lower end of the rat-cage, where a tongue of fire had flared up from the grass-stuffed packing boxes. He sprang to the work-bench, seized an empty bucket, and, dipping it into the half-barrel, stepped forward and threw its contents towards the floor near the cage, which by that time was ablaze with the oil from the broken lamp.

Instantly a bright blueish flame, redoubling that of the kerosene, rose against the boxes, quickly transforming the tufts of protruding grass above us into gleaming torches that lit up the walls and ceilings of the vast room.

"God only knows what that is," exclaimed the man, stepping back in dismay. "I thought it was water."

"There's water down the ladder there," said his companion. "Hand me the pail, and I'll pass it up."

"It's too late!" cried the other, throwing down the bucket in terror as he turned towards the trap-door.

With startling rapidity, the fire had overwhelmed everything in its reach. Forked flames, catching the high-stacked boxes and straw, with far-hurled volumes of smoke and crackling sparks, were rising in all directions upon the piles of combustible rubbish.

"Hello, back there!" I shouted at the top of my voice, at thought of the escaped villain hiding in the background. "The building's on fire."

"He's safe enough by this time," declared the officer, who began climbing down the ladder. "Come on, I tell you, and come quick, or we'll never get out of this alive!"

We followed him through the opening and downward to the beach, and for a few moments I stood by the ladder, shouting, but looked up in vain for the terrified face of the criminal who had escaped us.

One of the officers with his opened lantern had found the boat left by the runaway.

"Get in here," said he. "Quick! The yards won't be safe by the time we're out there."

We clambered in and, rather by pushing and pulling at the piers than by the oars, got out into the river. By that time the blanketed glass of some of the windows in the doomed building had yielded to outbursts of smoke and flame, whose intermittent flashings upon the water ended the night; for the dawn was breaking and the tide at its lowest ebb when we reached a landing down the river and got ashore.

XIII

I had a long run back to the station with the men, and when they left me to give the alarm, I hurried to my uncle's house, where I found him in bed and asleep.

The old housekeeper took me into the brightly-lit kitchen, and there listened to my hasty account of what had happened, with the horrors omitted. Then, utterly exhausted as I was, I accepted her invitation to rest in one of the spare rooms, got rid of my wet clothes, and soon fell asleep.

When I awoke the morning was nearly gone. Through the open windows I heard a loud noise of shouting and ringing of bells; and, calling downstairs for my dried clothes, got them on and went out. The streets were full of hurrying people, whose frightened random words prepared me for the fiery havoc that I soon saw. The whole water-front of the city was enveloped in flame and smoke. Most of the great warehouses had sunk into smouldering craters. From others, outbursts of flame, seen through water-jets, were leaping across wide intervals, to seize upon their wooden prey. Where defeated firemen, helped by volunteers from the onlooking crowds, were yielding in all directions, I did my share. But it was late in the afternoon before the wind lulled and ruin halted its fatal march.

XIV

Bridgenorth was saved. The fire, destructive as it was, seemed to clear the air of a contagion that, after the conflagration, made no headway; and, gradually yielding to the precautions taken and a wholesale poisoning of rats, soon died out.

Before my uncle recovered, I learned in a talk one evening by his bedside the full story of his imprisonment by his ferocious and vindictive enemy, who had kidnapped him in one of the boat landings, and whose latest frightful project, as a sequel to earlier crimes, threatened the whole city with destruction. The purpose of the weird laboratory we had seen was explained. For months past the deserted foundry had been used as a breeding-place for the agents of monstrous revenge,—rats poisoned till they were turned white by the deadly infection that soaked their straw; cholera-bearing rats, caged in a false pedlar's pack to be scattered broadcast by the arch poisoner.

But for my accident on the North Ferry Bridge, his ferocious vengeance would have triumphed.

"Accidents are strange things sometimes," said my uncle. "What theory of chances will explain the hour that you crossed the bridge,—the passing ship,—your jump upon the draw, and your fall?"

"Think of your life," said I, "hanging on such threads."

"No! No! Not that. What was one life in thousands? It was the whole city that was doomed,—cursed. The Powers of Darkness were at work."

As the evening shadows gathered about us, we talked on of those Powers, and that Curse, which was the Malice of a Master Mind, until, out of our words, as if to frighten us, rose too vividly the sinister image of the man himself. The Rat Pedlar whose Pack was Death, the prowling fiend who had opened the doors of his vengeance upon the World, when events defeated his purpose. I thought of my unconscious agency in his destruction without a shudder.

Rather as a blessing than as a calamity came the fire that

had swept away all trace of his terrible fate and of the deadly vermin that had devoured him. His dangerous secret, only shared by his accomplice, who was never heard of again, perished with him.

THE BLACKBIRDS

I

It was a fine June afternoon, unusually cool that summer for Eastport. Charles Carrington, the dramatist, was in his house-top study, talking to his friend Arthur Norton, who had just come in to join him on one of his eccentric suburban rambles. He was standing by an open window, looking out across the city roofs and river at the magnificent uprolled clouds that deepened the distant blue and cast their majestic shadows over the far-off suburb of Fairfield.

"What is there about Midsummer Eve," said he, "that you don't get on any other day of the year? You feel it in the air, particularly toward evening,—a sort of flutter, as if something might happen."

He walked over to the writing-table, where several paper-weighted stacks of manuscript were rattling in the draft. Wedged between them lay a pile of engravings, one of which Norton had pulled out and was looking at intently.

"What a curious print," said he. "What is it?"

"Don't you recognize it? It's the cemetery where they never bury the dead,—the Tower of Silence, as they call it, at Bombay."

Norton held up the picture and turned it about in the light.

"I see," said he; "the vultures are waiting for one of those ghastly funerals."

"Exactly," replied his host. "I had a notion of having it framed as a curiosity, but fear it is a little too suggestive."

"I should say it was," returned Norton with a mock shudder as he laid down the picture.

Carrington pulled out his watch. He had been expecting their friend Pryor, who, having chosen to remain in town that season after the fashionable world left for the seashore, often dropped in of an afternoon.

"Pryor won't join us today," remarked his guest decisively, and then paused. "Tomorrow is his birthday."

"What! Midsummer Day? He never told me that."

"No wonder, considering his point of view. He has a reason. A very peculiar reason." Norton paused again. "Don't tell him I told you. He has been warned."

"What do you mean?"

"By one of his Spiritualist advisers, to escape some calamity, God knows what, that threatens him on his birthday. He is superstitious enough to believe it, and has left town."

The dramatist looked at his friend a moment with an astonished, half-amused expression.

"What nonsense!" said he. "I thought that sort of thing was out of date. There's a story that it reminds me of. But come on,—it's getting late."

A bulky-looking satchel, packed with cold supper, lay on a chair. Carrington, after closing the windows, walked over to a large cupboard, opened it, and producing a dingy-looking bottle marked *Château Larose*, held it up gayly to the light, then thrust it into the satchel. When he had slung the package over his shoulder, the two men, leaving the aerial observatory of the writer of plays, descended by a series of dusty office-fronted passages and reverberating staircases into the commonplace world below.

As they hurried down Merchant Street to the Ferry, a lurid glare had suddenly caught the eastern house-fronts. Against the deep shadows in the cross streets, it gave the city a threatening, unfamiliar look, as if the lights were out of order, as Norton expressed it.

"Shifting for the climax," said Carrington. "Tomorrow the sun turns. These shadows are the warnings of winter."

"Or a storm," muttered Norton. "We ought to have brought umbrellas."

"No," declared his friend, "look! the west is clear. We shall have a fine evening."

II

Within an hour they had reached Fairfield, where, after lagging behind the crowd at the wharf, they gained the street, to find the pavement blocked by their fellow-passengers. A funeral procession had halted the impatient throng. The dramatist got out on the cobblestones and looked up and down the gloomy cortege extending indefinitely along the river front. Then, quickly pushing across between a pair of black horses' heads and the rear of a curtained carriage, he stopped to wait until his friend, who had hesitated and drawn back, took the next chance and followed him.

"Not a very lucky thing to do," remarked the latter, as the two men stepped upon the pavement on the shady side of Brooke Street. "Pryor would have kept us waiting here an hour."

"Or gone home," said Carrington, laughing, and then, after they had walked on a while in silence. "But this runaway of his is absurd. Did he tell you where he was going?"

"No."

"He ought to lock himself up in a cellar, or hide in a cave like the calender in the *Arabian Nights*—if that's the story I'm thinking of——"

"Don't get it wrong," interrupted Norton. "It was the boy who hid in a cave to escape his birthday. The calender found the little fellow there and killed him, you remember."

"So he did," Carrington admitted. "But the idea of the thing! A man running away from his birthday on Midsummer Eve. It's a plot for a play."

Keeping in the shade of the rustling poplar trees as they hurried onward, the dramatist had begun to describe one of his discoveries, an extraordinary place, called Deadlock Meadow, which he had planned to show his friend, when they reached a corner where a narrow street turned eastward. There, by one of those chances that happen so often as to have become proverbial, they almost ran into the very man they had been talking about.

The fashionable artist, dressed in white flannel, with glittering patent-leather boots, and one of his gorgeous cravats, stood with a sketching satchel slung over his shoulder, leaning against a curbstone tree. He was looking despondently down the side street, and turned suddenly as his astonished friends confronted him.

"Why, Pryor," cried Norton; "we have just been talking about you. You told me you were going out of town."

"I wish I had," said the handsome painter, with some hesitation. "Unfortunately, I changed my mind. I came over here to do a little sketching. But there's nothing to sketch."

He looked about contemptuously at the gingerbread porches, rows of white marble steps, and dreary intervals of a spike-topped board fence that shut off the background.

"What inspiration a celebrated poet like Whitwell finds in this sort of environment I fail to see," he added gloomily.

"You are on the wrong side of things," exclaimed the dramatist, with a flourish of his cane. "We must get behind the scenes. Did you ever see Deadlock Meadow at high tide?"

Pryor had never heard of the place, and Carrington pictured it in glowing terms as a watery freak of Nature,—a lake unmarked on the map, which had no existence except at certain tides.

"But you're just in time to join us," he urged.

For various insufficient reasons, Pryor seemed unwilling to accompany the wonder-hunters, but his final counter-proposal for supper at a neighboring hotel, where he said he had engaged a room for the night, was overruled, and the three men, after a polite controversy based on the contents of the supper satchel, at last started eastward along the newly-built street.

III

As they passed the boundary between the city's encroachment and undevastated Nature, the blocks of fresh brickwork gave way to half-dug cellars, vacant lots, and dismal-looking sheds roofed with corrugated iron. Then came exposed culverts, pools of stagnant water, with here and there vistas of open country. At last the street ended in a board-fence of unusual height, starting at the walls of a foundry. Carrington pointed through one of the open gateways at grimy expanses of high-windowed brickwork and smoke stacks, which had ceased to smoke, he said, when the place closed down, years before, on account of a lawsuit.

He crossed the street into a bleak rubbish-littered yard and stopped before the formidable partition, nearly twenty feet high.

"The trouble began here," he explained. "They call it a *spite fence.*" He pointed along the boards. "The man on the other side kept just inside his line, you see, beginning at the foundry and bringing it around the corner there, so as to block off his neighbor."

"And block us off," said Pryor dejectedly, as he walked back to the rear of the dirty, sun-scorched enclosure, to peer along the obstruction and point to a barbed-wire fence just beyond. "We might as well go back."

Carrington looked triumphantly at the baffled artist. Pushing through some blighted gooseberry-bushes, he leaned down and pulled back a loose board.

"There," said he, "is the stage entrance to the theatre."

His friends looked at him in astonishment, hesitated a moment, and then got through the opening, after which the dramatic explorer, holding back with difficulty the elastic board, squeezed after them.

IV

They had come suddenly out of the hot sunlight into a refreshing coolness. Just beyond the outrageous fence, under high trees, stood a dilapidated farmhouse, several sheds, and an old stone barn.

"There is always some nonsense of this sort to shut off what you want to see," declared Carrington.

Pryor looked around him suspiciously, walked slowly forward across the mossy grass, and halted. He called attention to a board, painted with the words *Keep Off,* nailed against the house corner.

"Never mind that," said Carrington, stepping past him, "No one cares. The place has been deserted for years."

He pointed to two planks forming an outdoor table, wedged in the shade between tree trunks. Then, going across to one of the open sheds, he unslung his lunch satchel, pushed it into what looked like the top of an old iron stove, half-buried in rubbish and rejoined his friends.

"My idea is to come back here for supper," said he. "Deadlock Meadow is over beyond the orchard yonder,—miles of woods,—shut off along the water. But it all depends on the tide."

The two men followed him past the rear of the vacant house and along the walled barnyard overgrown with jimson weed. Back of this a path led on under some apple and cherry trees, and they kept to it until it brought them to the wood. Just then Pryor, who was walking ahead, started back as two turkey-buzzards rose from the grass with a loud flapping of wings and, without flying far, lit again on the open slope above them. He picked up a stone and was about to throw it at the birds.

"Don't do that," interposed Norton. "They are protected by law,—and ought to be. They eat up anything that's dead."

"They look as if they would like to eat me up," muttered Pryor, with evident disgust at the black scavengers staring at them from the bank. "Why don't they fly away?"

Carrington supposed that there was something in the neighborhood that attracted them, explaining that they were never seen on the Eastport side of the river, though common enough where they found them at that time of year. They were believed to come up from the south about midsummer.

"I never heard that," said Pryor, dropping the stone. "But come on. I can't bear the looks of them."

V

The path had led the trespassers into a rocky tract of rubbish-littered, tramp-defaced woodland, which, according to Carrington, extended eastward for several miles. Blocking the city's extension, it owed its prolonged existence, he said, to certain legal disputes, the details of one of which he had begun to recount to his friends, when they reached the edge of a bluff, where the green shadows yielded to glimmerings of light ahead. There, on mounting to the top of a flat rock, the trees opened upon an enchanting view of distant meadows, cliffs, and a village, seen across an expanse of water. The eastern sky had changed to rose color. The water's shimmer was broken by the breeze into deep-blue paths of ripples. Clouds, more gorgeous than ever, robed in white, gold, and lavender, floated overhead.

"Now," said Carrington delightedly, "what do you think of my lake that's not on the map?"

Pryor's face lit up at last, as he began to unstrap his sketching satchel. "How in the world did you ever find this place?" he asked. "Where have I seen it?"

"Nowhere. You must have dreamt it. It has no existence, except at these high tides."

"It's Holland, all but the windmills and a ship or two."

"The ships are in the sky," said the dramatist. "Did you ever see such clouds?"

Just then a series of distant explosions, lasting several seconds, followed each other like thunderclaps in quick succession from across the water. But Carrington explained them as blasts ending the day's work at some neighboring quarries visible in the distance. Pointing to the far-off yellow cliffs, he told them that the excavations faintly seen followed the hills for miles. Several recently-exposed caves lent interest to the place and to a large settlement of imported quarrymen, nondescripts of varied nationality, who were known to live there in very primitive style. The distinguished ethnologist, Professor Blackmore, had established himself in Greenmarsh for the summer, expressly to study their languages and habits.

"Cheap ethnology," declared Norton. "Why doesn't he go abroad and do the thing properly?"

"No need of that. These people come to him, with their birthmarks. You can't obliterate language overnight, you know. I call it a very clever idea." Carrington glanced at his watch. "If it's not too late," he added, "we might have a look. Some of them, they say, have taken possession of the caves, some live in sod-huts without chimneys and make fire with the bow-drill or something of that sort." He proposed going up around the point and crossing the railroad bridge on the trestles.

"No railroad bridge for me," grumbled Pryor, who had begun his sketch. "It makes me dizzy to think of it."

Norton had walked out to the edge of the rock and was looking with delight up and down the watery expanse. "Why don't we have supper here?" he asked.

As a compliment to his taste, the suggestion pleased Carrington; but when Norton offered to go back to the farmhouse and get the satchel, a discussion followed, in which the leader of the party asserted his authority, left his friends, and undertook the errand himself.

VI

Half an hour passed before Carrington returned with the provisions, to find Norton on the rock alone.

"Where's Pryor?" he asked.

His friend explained that he had left the artist, a short time before, to take a walk, during which the latter had disappeared, probably to hunt another point of view.

"The buzzards annoyed him," he added. "I never saw so many. There must be something here that attracts them."

"Easily explained," said Carrington. "It's the chickens and animals caught in the tide."

The men sat down, and the dramatist, in his picturesque style, entertained his companion with an account of the topography of the elusive flood, which owed its freakish existence to certain half-finished dykes and the phases of the moon. He compared it to a mirage that might fade away at any moment. Like other reprieved solitudes, sometimes seen within the zone of city development, the whole scene awaited its doom, in the onrush of so-called improvement, which would suddenly drain the meadows, and overwhelm the woods with streets and houses. An epidemic of smallpox at some neighboring quarries had frightened off trespassers.

"It's an odd place," he continued, as if entertained by the thought. "Anything might happen here. I expect to come back some day and find nothing that I remember,—absolutely nothing."

"Except turkey-buzzards," said Norton, looking skyward at a black train of soaring shadows.

By the time the talk had ended in an amusing sketch of a proposed musical burlesque, with a cast of characters who had lost their way or identity in the approaching catastrophe, Norton had grown restless.

"Pryor ought to remember that it's suppertime," he declared, walking out to the edge of the rock, where several calls at the top of his voice were mocked by echoes.

"Suppose we hunt him up," suggested his friend.

And the men climbed down the rock, to follow the water's edge for a while in the direction of the headland they had noticed. But after wetting their feet in grass-hidden encroachments of the tide, they remounted the slope and pushed onward, by several rock-built ovens and devastated patches of charred underbrush, which Carrington accounted for as "tramp kitchens." At length a disused path, winding upward along the ridge, brought them to a halt, where an opening in the bushes suddenly revealed the brink of a deep excavation. Far below them glittered a pool of water, enclosed by cliffs.

"Look out!" warned Carrington, as his companion stepped near the precipice and looked over. "The bank has just given way there."

Evidently it had, for a tree, with leaves still fresh, hung by its bared roots, head downward into the chasm.

"Pryor oughtn't to miss this," said Norton; "but if he is sketching it, he wouldn't have heard us. Hello, Pryor!" he shouted, at the same time pushing a heavy stone out of the tree-roots over the brink.

Following the crash and a rattle of the stone, came a curious muffled rustling, and then, to their surprise, a flock of buzzards rose from below and flew about in circles over the pool. Norton watched the funereal birds until they had disappeared under the cliff.

"No use of looking for Pryor down there," said he.

VII

They turned back, reached a clearly-visible branch in the path, and followed it by its windings down the hill. In the late afternoon the shadow of the bluff had fallen upon the wood. They had stopped calling, and several times halted to listen to an illusive mimicry of approaching voices.

"It's the high tide," said Carrington, "or the way the wind strikes the trees. But Pryor must have heard us. Why doesn't he answer?"

Walking on, they realized that it was getting too late to sketch. Norton advised going back to wait for their friend, when, as the path led them down a steep bank, they noticed a faint smoky smell, with a peculiar disagreeable taint, which seemed to increase as they approached the base of the cliff. Turning a corner, they came suddenly upon the unmistakable signs of an abandoned quarry. Near a rusty derrick and some blocks of stone they stopped before a black, rotting shed, with partly collapsed roof, built close against the rock. The dismal ruin had lost its lower wall of boards, a pile of which lay along its open front in the high grass. Its dark interior, half concealed by weeds and poison-ivy, revealed faint outlines of rusting machinery and, contending with the glare of an opening in the rear, the flicker of a fire. The men hesitated a while in the approaching twilight, and then, stepping cautiously forward, looked into the place, to the right of which, by an open stair-case, a rope hung downward, ending in an iron hook. Around the smouldering fire the ground seemed freshly swept.

"Some tramp has taken possession here," said Norton. He stepped forward, but stopped suddenly at a slight rattle of boards overhead.

"Who's up there?" he called, going over to the staircase.

The noise ceased; but was followed by a loud, rustling sound. Norton cautiously mounted to the top of the steps, then paused as if looking at something upstairs, and a moment later disappeared through the opening.

He had hardly gone, when, with a creaking of boards, Carrington heard his quick shout,—"Get out of there!"

Following a still louder rustling, and a few moments of silence, his friend re-appeared, and hastily descended the step-ladder.

"The place is full of buzzards!" he exclaimed. "I mean just outside, on a ledge of rock, where the wall is down. The infernal birds are feeding on something,—some sheep or cow, I take it, that has fallen over the cliff. There were two or three of them in the shed, and I drove them out."

As he stepped back, Carrington went to the ladder.

"I wouldn't go up there," said Norton. "It's a disgusting sight."

The dramatist hesitated a moment, then, despite the warning, quickly climbed into the room above. He was gone longer than Norton, and when at last he appeared, he nearly fell in his hasty downward scramble.

"I warned you," said Norton, catching the startled look in his friend's eyes. "But,—what's the matter?"

"That's not a sheep those birds are tearing to pieces up there."

"What is it?"

Carrington looked uneasily at his friend.

"It's a man."

"What!" exclaimed Norton, with an incredulous stare, as he walked to the ladder and listened. "I didn't notice that."

"You can't mistake a human skull," declared his friend. "Did you see a bundle of blankets on the floor?"

Norton remembered that one of the buzzards he had driven out had been sitting on something of that sort, at which Carrington asserted that he had seen the blankets move. "Don't you think we ought to go up and look into it?" he urged.

"Let it alone," said Norton, glancing nervously around him. "I should say the sooner we get out of this place the better."

But Carrington had again started to mount the steps, when both men turned at a sound outside the building, this time unmistakably a murmur of voices, at first low and confused, then louder and clearer, as if rapidly approaching up the hill. Carrington, who had stepped toward the entrance and looked out, sprang back, pointed to the opening in the rear, and, followed by his friend, hurried through the shattered machinery, to halt at the collapsed wall, where a pool of water close against the rock completely cut off their escape. They glanced quickly around the wreckage; then, taking advantage of the brickwork of an old furnace under some wheels and shafting, stooped down behind the projecting boiler-ends.

When, a moment later, they looked through the crevices, a tall man was standing by the fire. He was dressed in black and wore a dark straw hat with curled brim pushed down upon his ears. For a while he stood in profile, and though he made no sound, his lips seemed to be moving, as if he might be whispering to himself. Then, stooping down, he built up the fire with some sticks held in his left hand, pulled a bag from his pocket, opened it, and sprinkled some of its contents on the flames. A dense smoke rose over him under the ceiling, and as this partly hid his emaciated face, he stepped across the light and out of the building.

Hardly a minute had passed when he reappeared against the daylight, with another man dressed like himself. Helped by the latter, he was carrying a large bundle into the shed, a rope-bound package, apparently very heavy, which swung between them on a flexible shoulder pole and swept the grass as they came in. On reaching the middle of the room they stopped, set down their burden, pulled out the pole, and laid it on the ground. The watchers scarcely had time to observe more than the quick agile motions and long glossy hair of the men before the pungent smoke, which was filling the place, hid them from view. When it cleared a little, the bundle was swinging in the air. Suspended on the rope they had noticed, it slowly rose, while one of the men, with arms uplifted, pushed and steadied it, until, as it disappeared through the ceiling hole, he followed it upstairs.

The intruders listened a while to the voices and rattling boards; then, hurrying to the entrance, got through the weeds and down the slope into the woods.

VIII

Across a gutter that must have drained the quarry, the path brought them upon marshy ground where Carrington, who had walked into a pool of clear water without seeing it, turned about upon his friend.

"Listen!" he said; "did you hear that rattling sound?"

"No."

They were well away from the shed, but he spoke in a low voice:

"This thing ought to be investigated. We must go back."

Norton objected. Declaring that the affair could be reported to the police, he pointed out the obvious danger of interference, under the circumstances, with the men just seen, besides the injustice of forgetting Pryor, who must have got back to the rock by that time and would be waiting for them. After an argument, Carrington yielded, and the two men, following the base of the bluff, at length reached their starting point, where, to their surprise, after mounting to the stone summit, they found no sign of the missing man. They examined the unopened supper-satchel, walked about the bare rock-level, and called loudly in all directions.

It was getting dark. The wind had risen and was making a loud noise in the trees.

"He must have gone home," said Carrington, looking up at the sky. "I was wrong about the weather. We are going to have a storm. But we can catch him yet."

At a distant rumble of thunder, they scrambled down the rock and had started westward along the path, when Norton suddenly stopped.

"I didn't agree with you a while ago," said he. "But what do you think about examining that shed?"

"Too late now," replied Carrington, looking about him nervously in the twilight. "Come on; we had better catch Pryor."

"We may never catch him," said Norton. "Can you get those infernal blackbirds out of your head? You saw more of it than I did."

"What!" exclaimed the dramatist. "Do you mean to tell me —that you believe—that Pryor could be in any way——"

"I don't know what to believe. But the more I think of it, the more——"

"Good Heavens! Come on, then!"

They turned back along the ridge by a path they thought they remembered, but soon lost their bearings. Whether because of the failing light or because the bluff had broken into several confusing spurs, the place, found so quickly before, seemed to have changed its position or passed out of existence, while the woods that Carrington alleged to be of trifling width, defied their efforts to get out into daylight or back to the water's edge. Judging by sky-gleams, seen through the tossing boughs as they climbed up and down the slopes, the sun might have been setting in all directions. At length, when their difficulties had doubled with the downfall of night, a gleam of light ahead suddenly brought them to an opening in the trees, beyond which they got over a fence and stepped out, not upon the water side, but a swampy meadow, with a high embankment just ahead.

"The railroad!" cried Carrington in disgust. "We have come east instead of west."

Wading through mud and briars, they gained the slope and mounted it.

Far away on either hand the sharp lines of polished metal

were lit by flashes of sheet-lightning and gleams from the rising moon. To the left, a distant watery reflection, the lake, blending with the horizon, lost itself in the darkness.

Norton proposed going back.

"No. We've wasted an hour," said his friend, pulling out his watch and holding it up in the moonlight. "It's after nine o'clock. Pryor is half-way home by this time. The thing to do is to walk into Fairfield and find him at his hotel."

Again Norton objected; but after a discussion in which he failed to suggest anything practical, he yielded, and they started westward along the rails, but had not gone far when a distant noise and a flash from the trees ahead halted them. They stepped half-way down the bank, waited while a train rushed by, and when it had slowly slackened its speed and stopped apparently on the distant bridge, watched it for nearly five minutes, until the cause of detention, whatever it was, ceased. By that time Carrington suddenly remembered their chance of catching an incoming train at a small freight station just across the lake and, turning eastward, the two friends followed the retreating noise to the bridge and stepped onto the trestles. Ten minutes later, after a dizzy balancing of foot-steps on the open framework, and then by way of a long plank foothold and trackwalker's shed, they got to the station.

The stormclouds had blackened. Intermittent windy gusts, with loud rumblings overhead, proved that they had reached the deserted little waiting-room just in time. As they entered it, by the light of its flickering lamps, the ticket agent, a heavily-built, sullen-looking man in a blue shirt, who had been struggling in the wind with some freight boxes, came in to close the windows.

"What right have you men got to hold up the nine-thirty on the bridge a night like this?" he asked angrily, turning upon the trespassers and scowling at Carrington. "She never stops here."

Carrington declared that they had come over behind the train.

"Then, what did she stop for?" grumbled the man. "There

have been three men killed on this bridge since I came here."
He went into the ticket office, closed the door, pushed the tickets through the window, and was about to say something more, when the noise of the expected local train and a howl of wind drowned his words.

Carrington and Norton got on board barely in time to escape a whirling downpour of heavy drops, followed by a tremendous roar of wind and thunder, while the train crept cautiously across the bridge. For several minutes the car trembled and rocked, until successive flashes of lightning ended in a deafening rattle of hailstones on the roof just as a sharp curve in the track saved the window glass.

IX

The storm was over by the time the friends stepped off the cars at Fairfield in the cool night air, to look in vain about the platform and adjoining pavements for a belated cab. The fact that they had forgotten, or never learned, the name of Pryor's hotel caused a delay, during which, after several inquiries at the ticket office, they hurried about the hail-strewn streets from one possible destination to another.

Tired, discouraged, hungry, still hoping to make up for their spoiled picnic with a festive dinner, they at last found the deserted chair-littered porch and overlit lobby of the suburban tavern sought for, where the clerk, a stout sleepy-looking young man, had been winding up a cuckoo clock. He got down from a chair behind the counter and, after listening to their questions, led them along a dingy corridor into the cloak-room.

"There's his valise," said he, "just as he left it. We haven't seen him since."

"But he got a room," said Pryor.

"No. We offered him number thirteen, but he wouldn't take it. Said he would wait. Some people don't like that number," he added, with a compassionate smile.

Norton pulled out the fresh-looking, well-kept valise, examined it nervously, and looked up at his friend.

"I thought you were wrong," said he solemnly. "What are we to do?"

Carrington hesitated. "He has been caught in the rain," he answered at last; "or he may have gone back to Eastport. We can go on to the ferry, if you say so, or order supper and spend the night here."

They had walked again to the desk, and while they stood there deliberating, the clerk had dipped his pen in the ink for the usual ledger endorsement, when Carrington felt a hand laid on his shoulder, and turned quickly upon two policemen whom he thought he had noticed at the station.

"You're wanted, you men," said one of them, a tall red-haired giant, with a strong Irish accent, as he seized the dramatist's wrist. The latter drew back. But a violent wrench of the arm failed to free him.

"You've made a mistake. We've got something to tell you," he cried indignantly.

"You've got a good deal to tell us," the big man muttered, tightening his grip, while the astonished captive, seeing that resistance was useless, submitted to the quick onthrust of a pair of handcuffs.

The thing was over in a minute; and when Norton was treated in the same way, the officer turned to the clerk:

"They won't need supper here tonight," said he. And while the clerk looked on with an amused smirk, the helpless prisoners, more astonished than angry, followed their captors out into the street.

A half-hour later, in separate cells at the end of a long gaslit gallery, at the station house, they were left to reflect as they chose upon what had happened: a police blunder, a possible newspaper sensation. Bad enough. But it was not that, nor the prison blanket, nor the evil atmosphere of the dirty cell, dimly lit through its door grating, that robbed the supperless Carrington of his rest that night. Wild waking fancies, ghastly suspicions, ended in an oft-recurring nightmare, when, projected against the illusive background of Deadlock Meadow, he would see the figure of a man pursued by nothing visible, yet running in frantic haste,—now as if upon the clouds, now plunging through muddy grass or the waves of a rising tide,— till exhaustion and daylight at last brought the half-hour of rest that prepared him for what followed.

X

The sun was shining bright in one of the upper offices of the station house, where the two dejected friends, who had got through their prison breakfast, were anxiously waiting, when the door opened and an active, well-dressed, dark-bearded man, whom Carrington recognized as an old acquaintance, stepped into the room, halted suddenly, and stared at the captives.

"What, Mr. Carrington!" he exclaimed. "You arrested?"

"Yes. For crossing a railroad bridge. Is there a fine?"

"It's not that. It's what happened to the train near Green-marsh. A man they found lying on the track. You must know that the express stopped for him just before you went over the bridge."

"Good God! It's Pryor."

"Yes, William Pryor, the artist. I know him."

"Is he dead?"

"No, but it's a case of attempted murder. He has been as-saulted and drugged. Professor Blackmore, who found him at the station and took him home, has wired us about him."

A rapid explanation by the two prisoners of what happened to them before their capture soon threw a new light upon the situation, without diminishing its mystery.

"This thing must be looked into," said the chief, after listen-ing with grave attention to Carrington's narrative and asking a number of questions. "There is a ten-thirty for Greenmarsh. We had better take it."

Quickly following a telegram to the professor, and a second breakfast at the hotel, the released friends, in company with the officer and two policemen, were looking out of a car window at the altered scene of their last night's adventure.

The lake of yesterday had disappeared with the ebb-tide,

leaving in its place a wide sunny outlook of waving meadow grass. Fading northward into mist and steeples, it still confronted them at Greenmarsh, and there a walk of ten minutes, in sight of several quarry escarpments, brought them to a shady lawn and a little flat-roofed, vine-clad villa, where the distinguished ethnologist was waiting for them. But there was an anxious look on the kindly aquiline features as, waving his Panama hat, he came down the porch steps and out upon the gravel walk to grasp his friend Carrington's outstretched hand.

"This is a strange business, gentlemen," said he. "Did you get my last message?"

"No."

"He has gone."

"Gone, why? Where?" asked the astonished officer.

"We don't know. He must have dressed when we thought he was asleep. Poor fellow! I know him well; but I don't think he recognized me. He went off without a hat."

"Is he bewitched?" cried Norton. "What on earth can he mean? What did the doctor say?"

"He called it a case of attempted suicide, at first. So I thought, until we woke him up for a few minutes this morning. He must have been out of his head ever since they found him on the track."

"How did he get there?" asked Carrington.

"We missed that. He had been drugged; but, strange to say, not robbed. We made out that he had jumped out of a window in one of the old quarry sheds."

"In the Fairfield Woods?"

"Yes. He had been terribly frightened in some way by turkey-buzzards. But the drug would have accounted for his ravings. We thought he said the birds had been sitting on him."

"What!" exclaimed Carrington. "Could he explain how——"

"That shed will explain everything," interrupted the chief. "Have you seen it?"

"Yes, this morning," said the professor. "A heap of charred wood and ashes,—struck by lightning, no doubt, during the night."

"Deliberately set fire to, I should say," declared the officer excitedly. "Good-bye, evidence!"

"What are we to do?" asked Carrington.

"Find this man," said the chief; "and the sooner the better. We may learn something at the station."

The disappointed officer pulled out a time-table from his pocket and, with his dark intelligent face bent over the leaflet, slowly followed the astonished party into the scholar's study, a cool, book-walled museum of Oriental trophies scented with sandalwood, where the disordered outlines of a large writing-table showed dimly in the artificial twilight. The professor pulled up the Venetian blinds.

"There can't be any doubt about the shed," said he, when Carrington had got through his strange story. "These men you saw must have caught him sketching the place. Why didn't they rob him? And where was he? Why didn't you see him?"

"Why didn't he see us?" added Norton.

"But the rest of it? The buzzards? Are you quite sure of that?"

"That's the point," declared Carrington. "I saw a human skull, not the slightest doubt of it."

The professor turned to the chief, as the latter, who had been listening impatiently, rose to take leave of the party. "The thing gets more and more mysterious," said he. "Have you no theory?"

Stopping at the door before following his two subalterns out of the room, the officer looked back, with a last word: "You have heard of Resurrectionists."

The professor had walked to the open window, and for a while stood watching the men hurry down the path and out the gate.

"Resurrectionists," he repeated at last. "We never thought of that."

"But the place was not a graveyard," objected Carrington. "And why should dealers in dead bodies allow vultures to destroy their stock in trade? The thing is incomprehensible."

"Must we wait here?" Norton asked impatiently.

"Yes," said the professor. "The chief will find him before we finish dinner."

But adding new danger to the situation, the final disappearance of the artist seemed to grow more and more threatening as they discussed it, until the ringing of a bell interrupted them, after which the talk, returning to the ghastly subject of the vultures, continued upstairs. The theme was wisely abandoned during dinner, but introduced soon after, while, as no news came to verify the professor's prophecy, the three men sat anxiously smoking their cigars in the little dining-room. Looking at the affair from half a dozen different points of view, they guessed, they argued, they theorized, without reaching any reasonable conclusion. Several times the professor seemed distracted by some idea that he hesitated to express, until at last Carrington, lacking a night's rest, grew too sleepy to think clearly, much less talk, and at his host's suggestion, followed the latter into a matting-floored parlor, where, in the curtained shade, he lay down on a sofa and fell asleep.

XI

By the time he awoke it was too dark in the parlor to see anything distinctly, and for a while he failed to recognize his surroundings. He heard a distant sound of voices as he groped through the dining-room into the hall; then, following the glimmer of a light downstairs, he at length reached the half-open door of the professor's study, where he found his host talking to Norton.

The windows of the laboratory were open, and the mellow glow of a student's lamp fell upon the book-littered table by which the scholar stood. He was leaning over a large portfolio, and turned at the sound of footsteps,—and Carrington's question:

"Has Pryor been found?"

"What?" came the excited answer. "No! not yet; but I have just made a discovery, and I think I have explained the mystery." Reaching over the table, he pushed an engraving from the portfolio nearer the light. "Did you ever see that?" he asked.

The dramatist stepped forward, to stare with astonishment at the picture. It was a duplicate of the print he had shown to Norton the day before.

Carrington picked it up, inspected its title under the lamp, and remarking the strange coincidence, held it out before Norton, who was standing behind him, but who evidently objected to examining it.

"It accounts for the whole affair," said the professor. "Look here!" He pulled out another picture from what looked like a collection of Oriental prints, showing a circle of robed figures kneeling around a fire, upon which a turbaned priest seemed to be throwing incense. "Fire Worshipers!" he exclaimed. "The pictures are from the first edition of Clark's *India*. I have a copy with all the plates." Holding up the lamp, he pointed to one of the high open bookcases, where, at intervals between the volumes, the sinister fronts of a row of skulls showed dimly in the shadow.

"I should have discovered this long ago," continued the scholar excitedly. "What happens in India may happen here." He paused and looked triumphantly at Carrington. "The chief is wrong. The men who assaulted our friend are Parsees."

Carrington dropped the print: "What, Parsees in Greenmarsh!"

"Yes. In the quarry books they are not accounted for. They never appear in their native dress."

"But,—how would they get here?"

"Easily enough, with all this imported labor, mixed up with Caribbean Negroes, Gipsies, or Hungarians, by Port officers, who don't know one language from another. So much the better for me."

At a sudden gust of the night draught, which blew some of the engravings off the table, he went to one of the open windows and closed it.

"Why should I have studied these people so long without suspecting this? Are we to suppose that deaths have not occurred among them? When that happens, a vulture feast on the carcass of a dead animal would suggest exactly what you met with in the shed."

Carrington had stooped to pick up the vulture print.

"You mean this?" said he.

"Yes. A Parsee funeral."

"So the bundle we saw was——"

"A coffin. The shed was supposed to be infected with small-pox, no one would go there."

"The fire, then, would have been a disinfectant," suggested Carrington.

"No. A part of the ceremony, made by flint and steel. A symbol of what our law of physics fails to explain,—combustion, so called. There!"

The professor laughed scornfully, as he leaned forward to turn down the smoking lamp, around which a droning swarm of summer beetles were scorching their wings. "How easy to classify it, to analyze it as an effect. But the cause,—the Sun,— who comprehends that?"

He paused while Carrington stared at the furrowed face and grey eyes glowing with the youth of an old man's enthusiasm.

"You have heard of reincarnation," he continued; "but you cannot know what I intend to demonstrate, that the Parsee shares the doctrine with the Buddhist."

"You would trace it in the Sanscrit books, I suppose. The *Zend Avesta?*"

"No, half the books are lost. I have discovered it in facts overlooked by science, customs centuries old, which, analyzed one by one, would show what is not generally believed: that the halt,—the back turn in the upward progress,—the universal cure——"

Norton, who had been walking nervously about the room, stopped.

"But what has this to do with Pryor?" he asked almost indignantly. "These men are murderers."

"No," said the professor; "religious fanatics. They may be priests."

"They attacked and drugged him."

"They would rather drug him than kill him. They are afraid of our laws. He might have betrayed them. How would he know that the bodies are given to vultures, not in wanton barbarity, but to avoid the results of common burial,—the passing away of the human envelope into dead atoms? Who would understand their secret?"

"What secret? We would call it a curious conception of hygiene."

"Hygiene! No! Sublime theology,—suppressed by persecution; not lost. What is evil? A compromise. I expect to prove—"

The scholar's voice rose as Norton tried to interrupt him:

"You misunderstood what you saw. Reincarnation begins when the lifeless human carcass is absorbed in the flesh of living birds." He paused. "It ends when justice triumphs over the undeserved sufferings of men and animals in the Transmigration of Souls. Pythagoras explained it two thousand years ago."

An excited harangue followed, in which the profound ethics of the case, getting the better of details, seemed to transform the speaker. Years of research spoke in the commanding gestures and flashing eyes, as he declaimed the transcendental doctrine in a passionate attack upon the theology of the West, which, he declared, had failed to solve the chief moral problem of the universe.

They had stepped out upon the porch where, heightening the suggestion of his words, trees, sky, and earth pulsated with the phosphorescent gleams of whirling swarms of fireflies.

Several times Norton attempted in vain to question the professor, until, as if convinced against his will, or overwhelmed by the theme, he listened in silence while the scholar, forgetful of everything but his subject, talked on.

It was late when they parted, the night had darkened, but the gleams seemed to brighten as, after getting through the gate in the intermittent brilliance, the two friends hurried on toward the station, for a while in silence.

"The man is a genius," exclaimed Carrington at length, half dazzled by the illumination.

"Yes," said Norton. "While you listen to him, he carries

you off your feet; but who will believe him? Besides——" he stopped. . . . "The point is not the Transmigration of Souls. Where is Pryor now? The professor has forgotten all about that?"

"So have we," said Carrington. "But the chief is sure to find him."

"He ought to have found him long ago."

An interval of silence followed before Norton spoke again.

"We have forgotten something else," said he.

"What's that?"

"I mean the beginning of the thing,—the Spiritualists."

"They warned him about his birthday,—we know that,—but what if they did?"

"Can you trust such people? They have been imposing upon him for years past. His birthday is not over yet."

They had reached Greenmarsh.

"We had better spend the night here," Norton suggested.

"No," replied Carrington. "What can we do anywhere but wait?"

While they hesitated, the train rushed into the station, and they got aboard.

XII

Following the late homecoming of the friends, a night had passed. Carrington, in an embroidered dressing gown, was seated near a small breakfast-table surmounted with a tray of empty dishes.

The morning light seemed too bright. The city's hum, wafted through the open windows of his lofty outlook, too gay for phantasms.

But Deadlock Meadow, the professor's harangue, and persisting suspicions,—confusing the final exit of his friend with things impossible, grotesque, frightful,—had got the better of his spirits, when, as the thought of waiting idly for news had become almost intolerable, a noise of footsteps on the landing outside was followed by the entrance of Norton.

His friend appeared heated by the quick ascent of many flights of stairs, as he picked up a palmleaf fan from the table and sat down by one of the windows. Fixing his bright, restless eyes upon the dramatist, he began fanning himself vigorously.

"Prepare to be astonished," said he.

"It's Pryor?" interrupted his host.

"Yes. Thank Heaven! Just back. The chief found him at the seashore." He paused. "There's a lot of claptrap about Spiritualism, as we all know. But still, these people warned him. No doubt about that. He disobeyed them."

"And repented later, tried to break the spell. Was that all?"

"Yes. But it explains this second runaway."

"Is he still out of his senses?"

"No. He looks ill, but will be better in a day or two if he manages to conceal the affair from his mother. The old lady must not be frightened, you know."

"Has he identified the men who assaulted him?" asked Carrington.

"No, and I don't think he will, but that's not the point.— How do you suppose he got into their hands?"

"They caught him sketching the shed, of course."

"Not at all. He fell over the cliff."

With a crash of upset chinaware, the dramatist rose suddenly from his chair. "Impossible!" he exclaimed. "It would have killed him."

"But it didn't kill him. It was where you and I looked down. He went over on a landslide, and the bushes on the rock broke his fall. He was stunned, of course, and woke up in the midst of the vultures, just as he told the doctor. These men had drugged him and covered him up with the blankets that you saw. When he awoke again, he jumped out of the window onto a pile of boards, which accounts for the clatter you heard."

"But they must have caught him in the woods."

"No, he got out ahead of them. It was the drug that overcame him when he fainted on the bridge."

Carrington, who was walking restlessly about the floor, stopped.

"At last it's over," said he. "No more mystery, thanks to the professor. What a wonderful man he is."

"The chief doesn't think so."

The dramatist glared angrily at his friend.

"Why not? He has explained the buzzards."

"The chief holds to his theory of resurrectionists, as I thought he would, and I believe he is right."

"But that's ridiculous. It doesn't account for the vultures."

"The chief says it does. Some of these resurrectionist villains are dealers in skeletons, and use the buzzards to save trouble in cleaning the bones. It has happened several times in the south. A terrible idea, but ingenious enough to he true. The professor never thought of that. I doubt if he would admit it if he did."

"He would have to admit it if it is a fact. Don't forget that he is a great scientist. Facts are everything to him."

"He has gone beyond his facts. He can't prove his Parsee theory."

"Pryor can prove it," declared Carrington. "All he has to do is to go over to Greenmarsh and point out the men."

"So the chief thought," returned Norton, "but he won't do it."

"Did you tell him what the professor said?"

"I tried to, but he wouldn't listen."

"How utterly foolish," said Carrington. "But it's just like him."

He walked over to the table, picked up the engraving they had looked at two nights before, and held it toward his friend. "Shall I show him this?"

"For Heaven's sake, don't!" protested Norton. "He has had a terrible nervous shock."

"What shall I do with it?"

"If it were mine, I would destroy it."

THE WOLF BOOK

I

The once celebrated Slavic manuscript, known as the *Wolf Book*, lost to science soon after its discovery about the middle of the last century, has always been associated with the name of the late Professor C——. Nevertheless, the great scholar was invariably reticent on the subject. Whether from unwillingness to figure as the hero of his own anecdotes, or distaste for publicity, he for a long time declined to admit that he had discovered the treasure, much less discuss with his friends the scarcely credible experiences that had put him in its possession. These are now, at last, made public,—prematurely, perhaps, since his own posthumous notes on the facts of the case remain to be published.

It was in the summer following the Hungarian Insurrection of 18— that the professor, putting to the test a plausible theory, undertook his long-planned search for classic manuscripts, supposedly forgotten or misplaced in the monastic archives of Hungary and Servia. His clever plan led him to descend the Danube in a houseboat, thereby curtailing land travel and book transport by easy access to libraries from his floating headquarters.

But by the time he had neared the celebrated defile by which the great river breaks through the Carpathians, he realized that he had misjudged the situation. Disappointing stories, told him by the monks, of robberies, fires, books given away or sold, gross carelessness, dull indifference, met him everywhere, until, disgusted with his summer's work, he had concluded to end it. Then, at the eleventh hour, Fortune smiled upon him at the Monastery of Jollok.

Overlooking an enchanting valley where, through grainfields and vineyards, the River L—— takes its great bend to the southward and peasants wash its sands for gold, the historic Jollok might well have roused his hopes earlier in the summer. But he saw nothing to cheer his dampened spirits in the bulbed steeples and century-marking shifts of roof and turret when, on the morning of a hot summer's day, after a night spent in the neighboring village, he rode up under the limetrees to the great door and rang the bell.

His letters of introduction soon brought the usual welcome from the hospitable monks, ending in an interview with the abbot, a small, stooping, white-bearded priest, with glittering black eyes, who met him in the fragrant garden. After listening politely to the traveler's brief explanation, and protesting that the library upstairs was not worth seeing, the polite old man led his visitor by way of several vaulted staircases to the end of a whitewashed flagged corridor in one of the upper gables. There he stopped before a large unpainted door, chalk-marked with fading symbols, unlocked it with difficulty, and pushed it open.

"I am ashamed to show you such a place," said he.

The dilapidated room, commanding a vast view over the great bend of the river, was lighted by two very high broken windows, through which the protruding boughs of an ash tree scratched and rattled in the wind. Save for a few cheap-looking modern books, the rotting doorless cupboards were all empty. Withered leaves of past autumns scattered the floor and half buried a lot of dark leather rolls stacked in one corner.

The professor stepped forward.

"Here is something," he remarked as, leaning down, he brushed away some of the leaves. The priest laughed contemptuously.

"Only our old farm ledgers," said he, approaching the rubbish and stirring it with his foot; "for you utterly uninteresting, and for us,—not worth shelf-room."

He pulled out one of the cylinders, undid the thongs, and unrolled it about a foot, pointing out rough blocks of coarse manuscript, with here and there a large floriated initial letter in black. Then he tied it up again and tossed it back upon the leaves.

"Farm ledgers, without the farms," said he sadly. "Our lands are gone, and so are our books. You should have come here a hundred years ago, before they were stolen."

Rather out of politeness than interest in the kind of tale he had listened to so often, the professor asked for particulars.

"It came of a lawsuit," explained the priest, "ending in an outrage. You have no doubt heard of the celebrated Baron Trenck,—Trenck the Pandour."

"Yes."

"A terrible man. History tells us, you know, that the law meant nothing to him. Yet, his lawsuit with us, which began with his grandfather, was decided against us. There was a delay in the matter, and the story goes that Trenck, who in spite of his well known avarice was said to be highly educated, agreed to take a certain book out of the library, in part payment of his claim. If so, the book must have been, as they say, either bound with gems in gold, or very valuable. However that may be, during the proceedings, and before the matter was finally settled, our abbot died, and when Trenck came to claim his volume, it could not be found. The thing occurred a long time ago, and it seems almost incredible that a book like this could have been mislaid, or, if hidden, that anyone would have dared to thwart such a man. But so it happened. The result was what might have been expected. At first Trenck ordered his pandours to burn the monastery, but finally compromised by carrying off the whole library. Everything that we had was packed up in wagons, which he forced the peasants to supply, and off it went."

"Had you no redress?" asked the professor.

"The Empress Maria," continued the priest, "on complaint by our patriarch, ordered Trenck to restore the books. Of course, he pretended to comply, but, of course, evaded the matter in his usual way. There is our redress," he continued, kicking the roll tossed back upon the leaves. "All that ever came back. The rest, he might as well have devoured. No wonder they called him werwolf."

"I have heard him accused of almost everything," remarked

the professor incredulously, "but never of that."

"It was suppressed in print through family influence. Never-theless, it is a fact. He was brought to trial for it at Temesvar, in 1753. What they proved I never heard. As for the superstition, it is one of those horrible survivals of the Middle Ages, which, it seems, cannot be rooted out. No matter. I mention it as show-ing the popular opinion of the man, if he was a man and not a monster."

The professor took a final look at the book-pile, then, com-menting on the form rather than the contents of the ledgers, which as extended rolls, *Kulandri*, and not foliated volumes, had survived into comparatively recent times, asked to buy one as a curiosity.

"Buy them all!" exclaimed the priest. "They are of no use here."

The disappointed visitor pulled the spurned roll out of the leaves and dusted it off with his handkerchief.

"This will do," said he. Whereupon, after paying the mod-erate sum demanded, he followed his venerable guide out of the room and upon a brief tour of inspection through the great building. But before they reached the lower floor he re-gretted his purchase. The clumsy bundle, nearly two feet long, about eight inches thick, and very heavy, seemed a useless en-cumbrance, and he was several times on the point of leaving it behind him; but at last, when the horses were brought up, man-aged to make it portable by tying it to the back of the saddle. Then, after a grateful farewell to the monks and their obliging superior, and without waiting for the midday meal, he rode off with his peasant guide.

Jollok was the last monastery in the professor's itinerary. But the more he reflected upon his visit there, the more disgusted he became with his summer's search for treasures that had ex-isted only in his imagination. Jollok again proved the fact. For if Trenck had taken all the books, in the days of its glory, why had no scholars heard of valuable manuscripts in the inventories made during his celebrated law suit with the Crown? Above all, a book of immense value, bound in gold, coveted by the great marauder, and hidden by the Monks. What had become of it after Trenck's death?

The abbot's story was probably a myth, which the professor might well banish from his mind, and with it his plan of pushing his fruitless search down the river, into Bulgaria. The evening breeze failed to refresh him. In gloomy meditation he watched the pink of ending day fade from the eastern sky, while the meadows gave up their golden green to long, stalking shadows from the swaying acacia trees.

The thoroughbred horses hurried their riders northward, but the sun was setting by the time the professor had reached Semendria, paid off his mounted guide at the hotel, and found his way to the houseboat.

II

His servant, a powerful, sunburned, flaxen-haired young fellow, with eyes as blue as his fresh shirt, had been taking down the deck-awning for the night, when the dejected scholar crossed the floor of a dilapidated boat-house and stepped on board.

"Everything went all right, I hope, sir, while you were gone," remarked the young man, as he took his master's dusty coat.

"About as usual," answered the latter gloomily. "I found nothing."

"Well enough, sir, if it's no worse,—but I've had a very queer dream about you."

The professor tried to smile. "Nothing very cheerful, I suppose," said he.

"I can't say that it was, that is, the last part of it. I dreamed that one night you had caught a very beautiful kind of insect, like a glowworm,—the brightest I ever saw. While you were studying it a woman dressed in red came to look at it. All at once she snatched it from your hands. Then, when you tried to get it back, she turned into a wolf, and began to eat you up. The dream came back a second time."

"I am glad I escaped the woman, or the wolf, whichever it was," remarked the professor. "The glowworm, I always miss.

This good-for-nothing book," laying his hand on the bundle
he had brought with him, "is what they call a farm ledger. It
ends my list of failures. I have had enough of them. Sell the boat
at once. We will take our passage on the next up-going river
steamer."

He tossed the despised bundle upon the cabin roof and was
about to give further directions for packing, when the young
man surprised him with the news that, owing to proposed
blastings in the channel below them, river navigation had been
suspended during his absence and the last steamer had left that
afternoon.

As no railway existed in those days, the information, which
completely cut off his easy return home, confounded and
provoked him. He waited a while to hear the man confirm it;
then picked up his package, crossed the roof, descended into
his cabin and lay down on the berth, determined to dismiss the
disagreeable subject from his mind until after supper. But, tired
and hungry as he was, his vagrant thoughts, contending with
the new difficulty, had half mastered him; when, by way of a
possible diversion, after glancing contemptuously at the bundle
on the chair, he got up and unwrapped it. No last flicker of sunlight lit the shadows in the cabin. No sound broke the stillness
as he laid it on the bed and began slowly unrolling it.

The scroll, owing to the stiffness of the leather, opened with
difficulty. Holding it down on the coverlet, the scholar rolled
and unrolled the ends until he had reached about the fifth or
sixth revolution, when a long waxed bundle, exposing a deep-
cut cavity in the interior, slipped out on the bed and fell on the
floor. He picked it up. It was heavy, compact, and tightly bound
with what seemed to be a sheet of linen covered with beeswax.
Carefully inserting the point of his knife through the envelope,
he slowly removed this; when, to his astonishment, a second
cylindrical manuscript, or *Kulandros*, rolled like the first, appeared. It was tied together with two thongs, wrapped upon
ornamented buttons or discs, apparently made of gold. The
well-preserved leather, light gray in color, was richly embossed
on its outside, and opened easily, until after about two revolu-

tions the professor's eyes caught the unfolding characters of a closely-written text. Opposite this, the outer side of the roll showed a yellow surface of gilded felt or wool, under a magnificent fretwork of gold beads embroidered with blue and sparkling stones that seemed to glow with a self-contained light.

Trembling with excitement, he lifted the thing from the bed, and was about to carry it outside for better inspection when he heard voices and a shuffling of feet, followed by the familiar tramp over head.

"What shall we do, Herr Professor?" whispered Karl a moment later, leaning forward into the cabin; "the customs officers are here,—two of them."

Hastily rolling up his manuscript, the startled traveler thrust it under the mattress, pulled out his purse, and handed several Austrian bank notes to his servant.

"Get rid of them," he ordered. "I have found something here that they must not see."

And when with a wink and significant squirm of thumb and fingers the young man had climbed up the ladder, the scholar sat down on the berth and listened to the sound of voices that followed. By the time the disquieting murmur ceased, it had grown dark,—too dark to see his treasure-trove as he pulled it from under the mattress. He got up and stepped across the cabin. When the boat was built he had taken advantage of its doubled partitions to insert a closet behind a small cupboard, in the interval. He turned a clothes-hook, which released the cupboard, placed the manuscript upon the hidden shelf, and had closed the opening, when the bell rang, and he went to supper.

But he had lost his appetite for Vienna coffee and kümmel-brot. Amazed, thrilled, confounded, by the events of the last few moments he hurried through the meal in silence, scarcely hearing the details of Karl's mercenary transaction. At length, he suddenly realized the danger of a second visit from the officers, and rose from the table.

"I have found your glowworm," said he.

Mounting the ladder, he hurried off to his cabin, to return presently with the new treasure tied up in paper.

"We can't afford to run any risks with this thing," he declared, holding out the bundle in the twilight, while with suppressed emotion he astonished his servant with an account of his astounding discovery. "It must be soldered up in a tin, water-tight case, and we must leave here tonight."

He walked down the gang-plank and jumped ashore. The man followed him, and they went up the bank together, after which, with a few more words of explanation, he hurried away.

The lights of Semendria were brightening, and the din of its night life waking on the river breeze, as the excited professor jostled the crowd among its torch-lit booths and tunnel-like shops till the clang of a hammer and anvil brought him to the place looked for,—a smoky labyrinth, lighted with several hanging oil lamps, where a half-naked tinsmith, working at a furnace, laid down his hammer to listen to the uncommon requirement. A promise of extra pay hurried the job, and within an hour the manuscript was safely enclosed in a water-tight cylinder, soldered under a close-fitting lid. Hanging it, as a satchel, over his shoulder, by a strap run through two attached rings, he thanked the man, paid his bill, and hastened back to the boat.

A light in the kitchen, shining through its open door, showed Karl leaning forward upon the table, asleep upon his stool. The professor roused him and, with his help, pulled in the gang-plank and dragged the houseboat by its cable about twenty feet up stream. Then, on quickly lifting the anchor, a strong push with the boat-hook, and double-pull at the oars and rudder, swung the heavy craft out into the stream.

No moon lit the great river as, swept out into the night, they watched the lights of the noisy city grow dim; and, guided only by star-gleams, the shifting of shadows, and the rustle of ripples upon forest wreckage, drifted on until about midnight. Then with the sweep of branches over the deck, came the rattle of boat-hook and anchor that brought them to rest under the bank of a wooded island.

But for a long time the professor lay awake in his cool and comfortable cabin. The sinister figure of Trenck, cheating himself of his booty, appeared and reappeared in wakening dreams.

Vain theories, at variance with the abbot's tale, to account for the singular hiding-place of the manuscript, doubts as to its magnificent embellishment, so imperfectly seen, regrets that he had sealed up his treasure, impulses to get up and file off its lid, banished rest, until, exhausted nature at last asserted itself and he fell asleep.

III

Through the trees the sunbeams glanced on the cabin roof-deck next morning as the professor sat by the breakfast-table smoking a cigar. Karl, who had finished clearing away the dishes, stopped and looked a moment at his master.

"Do you believe in dreams, sir?" he asked.

The scholar had been gazing up through the fluttering leaves at the sky, across which floated white summer clouds of the familiar shape often compared to the fleeces of sheep. "What kind of dreams?" he returned. "We all have dreams."

"That dream I told you about yesterday at Semendria. I have had it again, sir, and I don't like it at all."

"About my finding a glowworm?"

"Not so much the glowworm as the rest of it,—that red woman who turns into a wolf and tries to eat you up."

The professor laughed as the young man pushed the floating house out of its shadowed harbor. He rose from the table.

"Here is your glowworm," he cried, laying his hand on the tin satchel suspended from his shoulder.

*   *   *   *   *   *   *   *

Several days had passed. The Carpathians were rising to the eastward. The channel had narrowed to half its width as the current swept them toward the dangerous rapids that they purposed passing as usual, without pilot or chart. Seated on the gunwale one afternoon, with his hand upon his tin-sealed still-unopened treasure, the professor was looking anxiously down the river, listening for the warning roar of waters as yet inaudible.

Island after island, village after village, had faded into the background, the grotesque Parrot rock had risen in mid-river and was disappearing, when, at sight of a vast ruin blending with the cliffs to the right, he seized the rudder, and hastily deciding to take advantage of its high skyline, as a viewpoint around the sharp bend just ahead, with the help of a few oar-strokes from Karl, brought the boat into slack water under the rocks.

The castle of Golubacz had a bad name on account of an insect of obscure origin, known to naturalists as the *murder fly,* which in poisonous deadly swarms issued from it about mid summer. But the professor, in answer to Karl's question, de-clared that they were a month ahead of the insect danger, and sprang ashore.

Following the blasted wreckage of a once mighty wall, which skirted the rock for about a hundred yards and then turned up the hill, he found a breach and clambered into a stony waste, beyond which the bleak monument of race hatred and cruelty rose upon the rock.

The drawbridge was gone, but the double-winged doors of wood, which still mounted the gateway ahead, stood open. Passing these, a very steep path over ramparts wrecked by the Turks and by way of several vaulted openings, which might have served as egresses for the murder fly, brought him at last to the top of the Great Keep, where the eagle's view, with its flash of impetuous river, brighter than the clouds, broke upon him. He took up his field-glasses, swept them over the moun-tain panorama, and was about to focus them upon the doubt-ful waterway, when, to his disagreeable surprise, he saw that he was not alone.

In the shadow, near one of the towers, two white-skirted men were leaning against the wall, and beyond them he noticed a very abnormal-looking woman, hideously deformed in pro-file by a bristling mass of facial hair. But as he stared at her, and as she left her companions and approached him, the apparent beard changed to a grotesque mouth-mask of coarse brown grass. Around a dingy red gown glittered a very conspicuous polished belt, made of large metallic discs, mounted on strings of shells, or teeth, that jingled as she walked.

She stopped and pointed to the professor's tin satchel.

"Excuse me, my gentleman. It is for the murder fly." She tapped the pavement with her foot. "Come with me, sir. Gipsy woman will show you the murder fly."

Her muffled words buzzed curiously under the mask while the professor again raised the glasses to his eyes, and then, politely declining her services, walked toward one of the battlements.

The woman followed him.

"It is too soon," she mumbled. "When the murder fly comes out, the sky is black."

She laid her hand on her mask.

"We must not breathe him, my gentleman, when we go down into his house." Again her foot tapped the pavement.

The professor heard her words die into a hiss while, as he crossed to the other side of the rampart, the jingling behind him proved that the woman was still dogging his footsteps. He turned about, and taking a silver gulden from his pocket, handed it to her.

"Let me alone," he said sternly. "You are worse than the murder fly."

Instantly her manner changed. She held the coin in her hand, looked at it a moment, and then, with a contemptuous shrug, tossed it over the precipice.

"This is bad money," she hissed. "You are a cheat!"

Under her pink-hooded handkerchief he could see a dangerous glitter in the greenish eyes as she shook her fist at him. Then, turning, she walked back to her companions and disappeared with them behind the wall.

The incident was decidedly disagreeable. But the professor was too much preoccupied to concern himself long with it, and took time enough to make sure that the suspected rapids were not yet in sight. Descending as he had come, and without stopping to examine the much-discussed exits of the murder fly, he at last got to the base of the ruin.

It was getting late by the time he reached the outer wall, and he had just passed the gateway, when, at a startling rattle of stones, a rock struck the ground at his feet and rolled into the open space ahead. He looked up, but saw no one on the wall-top, when another rock, missing him by a few inches, bounded after the first. Suddenly realizing his danger, he started to run, while one heavy mass after another crashed past him down the hill, until, thinking he was beyond their reach, he stopped. Just as his hand grasped the tin can, to make sure that it was safe, a heavy blow on the back of his head ended everything. He felt himself falling. Sensation and consciousness vanished.

When he came to himself he was lying, wounded and dazed, on the hillside. Karl was leaning over him. But for a time the scholar was unable to recall his surroundings, much less account for his condition to the astonished servant, who searched his pockets, to find that his watch, field-glasses and pistol were safe.

"And your tin box?" asked the young man.

With a wild sweep of his hands over his coat, the professor felt that it was gone. He staggered to his feet, and in the hope that the swinging package might have been broken from him in his fall, searched the surrounding stones and weeds. Karl lit several matches, in vain.

"They have stolen your box," observed the young man as they groped down the hill in the twilight. "But why not your watch and the other things? Three of them, did you say, sir?"

"Two men and a woman."

"A woman?" repeated the servant slowly, looking in astonishment at his master. "Was she dressed in red?"

In spite of his condition, the professor laughed.

"Boy, you had better get that infernal dream out of your head. The thing is bad enough as it is."

IV

Following a restless night on the river shoals, several days at anchor above the rapids near Bavna, brought back the professor's strength, but not his spirits. For a long time the loss of his manuscript was too much for his philosophy. In vain he tried to console himself with the thought that, having so imperfectly seen his treasure, he might have exaggerated its value. But the doubt remained, and with it a vague foreboding of approaching danger, half-felt among the rocks, in his cabin, or seemingly muttered under the roar of waters. As the disaster ended his further need for river travel, he might have left the Danube at Ravna, had not the hope of disposing of his houseboat at one of the larger landing ports induced him, as he thought, for the last time to buckle on his life preserver and steer into the rapids below Islas.

St. Brenkova, Dol Milanovac, Tiscovica, swept by. Then, after a long halt in the historic cliff-shadows at Kazan, where the throttled river pauses for its final plunge, they hurried again into the bright light.

Sunny meadows smiled. Trees waved their welcome. Ripples flashed as down the valley they sped, until early one afternoon their race was unexpectedly challenged in mid-river by some soldiers, in a boat, waving a flag.

"You are breaking the law, my friends," shouted one of them, a heavy, red-faced petty officer, who held the flag and was standing up.

He pointed along the waterline toward the housetops of Orsova. "Don't you know that we are blasting over there? You are smugglers."

"No; traveling for science!" answered Karl.

His boat slid along the gunwale, and the soldier stepped aboard with two of his men. Ordering one of them to take Karl's oar, he seized the rudder. The current was running like a millrace. But he knew how to steer, and holding the bow up-river, soon swung the houseboat skillfully along the side of a large moored barge, where a man caught it with a boat-hook.

The barge was full of workmen, busy in adjusting a piece of machinery, and the soldier-pilot, climbing aboard, stepped up to a tall, handsome man, in the white uniform of an Austrian general, who was directing the work. The latter listened to him a moment, then came to the side of the barge.

"A houseboat, it seems," he remarked, evidently impressed by the stately appearance of the scholar, who stood at the door of his cabin, without a hat. "No cargo?"

The professor declared their purpose.

"But you must have heard that the river is closed, for blasting."

The challenged traveler apologized for his venture, took out a card, and handed it to his questioner whose highly intelligent face brightened at sight of the noted name.

"Nothing is happening just now," he said; "but we must look out for you."

An explanation followed in which the traveler inquired as to the possibilities of boat sale at Orsova, while the chivalric engineer justified his rules as safeguards for commerce and against lawsuits. As they talked on the professor soon found that in the directing mind of the great river project he had met a warm friend of science.

"You must spend the night here," continued the hurried general when, after several eager questions, the conversation was interrupted by an orderly. "And in that case, dine with me. Yes? At my headquarters up the hill yonder." He pointed to a grove of trees above the town, and naming the dinner hour, climbed down into another boat, which had meanwhile joined them, and was carried away among the barges.

v

Several hours passed, spent by the professor in examining the engineering works that had overwhelmed the little village of Orsova in those days, and it was late in the afternoon when he left his floating house and, after a hot walk up the mountain side, reached a many-pillared, dingy wooden building, set upon the slope of a lawn under high trees. No fairer evening ever shone over the town and river. The birds were singing overhead. A mellow glow in the light mist seemed to gild the porch and newly-set dinner-table, where, in the fresh white of his gold-faced uniform, the tall soldier met his guest.

"Is the air too much here?" he asked. "If so, we will move inside."

"By no means," cried the heated professor, looking around him and up the hill at vistas of sky and cloud, framed in green. "You have the ideal background,—the indescribable *plus ultra,* orchestra included. Just listen to the nightingales."

"Yes," said the general, "the lay of the land is very attractive. A broken-down hotel, with an old pleasure-ground, now a sort of birds' paradise. There is a stream beyond there that you don't see. I came upon it by chance, but am here very little, except at night, when, as you notice, I am alone and depend upon guests like yourself."

As they waited, two white-gloved soldiers hurried to and from the table, while the conversation, introduced by the host's hasty sketch of the great engineering work under his supervision and the difficulties of blasting in the rapids below, soon turned to the unfortunate literary expedition of the professor.

"It hardly seems like a common robbery," observed the general, after listening to a description of the thieves at Golubacz. "The Gipsy woman with a mask gives it an odd look. But as long as the origin of the murder fly remains uncertain, we shall have these dangerous impostors posing as guides. Besides which the caves there, supposed to breed the insect, are known to contain gold. Hence the Gipsies, who are all gold hunters, as you know."

These caves, he continued, had never been properly explored, notwithstanding their traces of mining operations by the Romans, thus fully accounting for the ancient celebrity of the neighborhood as a source of precious metal. The fact was further established by certain local customs, such as the singular process of washing gold in sheepskins, described by Agricola, and still practiced by the Gipsies.

As the Tokay passed around the table and the candles flickered in their glass globes, the learned engineer declared that the Greeks in the narrative of Herodotus had first associated the surrounding mountains with the terrible and still-surviving superstition of the werwolf, and gave his reasons for believing, further, that the great historian had confused the country with the ancient Colchis, in Jason's classic search for the Golden Fleece.

"But here," said he, "history fades into prehistoric darkness, —myths, many of which we may discard as baseless fancies, while others, like that of Jason, still show their prototype."

Some of these sheepskin trophies of the gold-washers, he declared, were still encrusted with gold and were more absorbent than others. Some that he had seen were so heavily gilded that they had become fetishes in the eyes of the superstitious peasants, who, fearing to remove the precious dust, buried them with the dead, or even burned them, as votive offerings to the werwolf.

He was about to continue, when the sudden appearance of an orderly interrupted him. He listened for a moment to the man, then, with apologies, rose and followed him into the house.

VI

The professor sat looking at the sparkling glasses and silver before him. Over long intervals of time, linked by mysterious events, his wandering thoughts, inspired by the general's conversation, soon returned to earth. From Jason and the Golden Fleece, Colchis and the sorcerers of Herodotus, to the werwolf of modern times, unconscious comparison had exaggerated his own failure. He helped himself to the delicious Tokay. But, in spite of it, memories, tantalizing, distressing, vivid, of his defeated plans had got the better of him by the time the general returned.

But the latter seemed preoccupied with some very pleasant thought as he stepped quickly up to the table, stopped, and stood a moment looking at his guest. Filling a glass, he lifted it to his lips.

"Allow me to drink to your health, professor," said he. "I have some news for you,—almost too strange to be true."

The professor rose.

"Retribution on earth. Rare, you know, yet not altogether out of the question."

The general paused, and the professor, little suspecting what was to come, looked inquiringly at the masterful face and the kindly grey eyes that sparkled with suppressed emotion.

"Those rascals that robbed you, it seems, have not confined themselves to Golubacz, but have been here, breaking into one of our storehouses. Our sentinels fired on them, of course. One fellow met his end, and upon him they found——" The general paused again and rang a little table-bell. "Something that you may perhaps recognize——" As he pushed back some of the dishes, one of the waiters appeared with a tray, which he placed upon the table.

The professor started in speechless astonishment when his eye caught the unmistakable form of his tin can, wrapped in its leather strap, lying upon a napkin.

"The villains have opened it," said the general; "but examine it. Your treasure is safe."

Overwhelmed, half-frightened, the professor picked it up, to see that the solder had been filed off around the edge of the lid. The brown bundle was in its place. He slowly pulled it out and removed the waxed cover. No sign of disfiguration or injury marked the embroidered leather as, with trembling hands, he unbuttoned its thongs and displayed the gorgeous scroll, only half-seen at its former examination. Disregarding the exposed text, he rapidly unrolled the whole manuscript and, pushing aside the dishes, turned it upside-down upon the table, where, like the wind-swept embers of a fire, it seemed to glimmer in shifting tints of red, yellow, and blue.

The general leaned over it, touched it several times, and turned to one of the candles, to examine his forefinger. "This is a very strange coincidence," he at length said.

"A splendid piece of embroidery," declared the professor.

"Yes, but do you realize that it is worked upon a sheepskin? If

I am not mistaken, one of the fleeces of the gold-washers. The gold has been fixed."

The magnificent fretwork, outlined in minute beads of gold and blue stone or glass, interwoven with sparkling threads, appeared to be wrought upon a background of luminous wool, in panelled designs, showing a series of human figures. The professor was overcome. He pointed to one of the larger of these. "There," said he. "If you have been in the catacombs at Rome, you must recognize the favorite emblem of the early Christians,—the Good Shepherd, carrying the sheep."

The general pulled out a small magnifying-glass and held it close to the embroidery.

"Pardon me," he objected, "the head is not human." He handed the professor the glass. "Look at it again. It is that of an animal, a wolf; or, rather, a man with a wolf's head. We spoke of the Devil, the werwolf, and here he is."

He stepped back, while the professor again leaned forward, and carefully examined the figure.

"I agree with you," he admitted at last. "But what an outrageous freak of monkish decoration."

"Rather, black magic," the general contended. "The monks never made the thing. The sheep is the victim. Look at the children devoured by wolves, in the small medallions. They repeat the diabolical idea. The text should correspond."

The professor turned the book over and for a long time examined it in silence. It consisted of isolated passages in several Balkan dialects, with illuminated designs at intervals, representing the sun, moon, stars, and the planet Mercury. Some of the texts were in rhyme, and some, partly decipherable, stood, he said, rather for exorcisms of an evil spirit than prayers, since the names of God, the Virgin Mary, or saints, nowhere appeared.

"The work of a sorcerer," said the general, "one of the *Wolf Books*, as the peasants call them." He left the table and began walking up and down the terrace.

"I have heard of these books," he continued, "used by exorcists in connection with this infernal superstition; but I never until now saw one. To my mind, it would account for your robbery at Golubacz; at least, according to the peasants, who would tell us that if these Gipsy thieves were wolf-men, they would have 'smelt' the book through your tin box. No wonder Trenck wanted it, if he dabbled in this sort of thing."

"But why should the monks of Jollok preserve such an unholy relic?" asked the professor.

"On account of its magnificent cover. Some learned abbot, no doubt, recognized its value. As for Trenck, with all his faults, he would have appreciated it under any circumstances. The wonder is that he let it slip through his fingers."

"As a werwolf," remarked the professor, laughing, "he seems to have lost the gift of smell."

The general enjoyed the joke, then sat down again.

"These coincidences are very remarkable," said he, after several moments of silence.

VII

He was leaning upon the table, his grey eyes fixed steadily upon the magnificent scroll spread out before him.

"There is something else," he continued slowly and with hesitation, "another coincidence. I have not mentioned it because I thought it rather too ghastly for the dinner-table."

He stopped to offer a cigar to the professor; then, taking one himself, proceeded:

"When the Gipsy who carried this tin package of yours was shot, as I told you, a very strange thing is said to have happened,—too strange, in fact, to be believed."

He paused again to light his cigar.

"Without parallel at this season of the year, our storehouses on the other side of the mountain were attacked, they say, by wolves. There are large sheep enclosures attached, and it chanced that the day before the occurrence a little daughter of one of the shepherds died and was laid out in a vacant stable near the gate of the stockade. The gate was open. There was plenty of noise, clatter among the sheep and howling. But when the sentinels fired in the dark at what they took to be wolves, they killed your man, as I told you, with this tin can hanging about his neck. One or more wolves,—wolves, remember, so they say, escaped.

"But the shocking part of the story," he added, rising from his seat to blow out one of the guttering candles, "rests on the evidence of the sentinels and an old woman, who rearranged the child's shroud before the funeral next day. Consequently, it can't be proved, without exhuming the body. The lamps around the little dead girl in the shed had blown out. When they came to relight them, they declared that one of her legs was missing, cut off (or bitten off) close to the hip. Your thief, therefore, according to them, was a werwolf."

"Yet, the body was that of a man. Do you mean that these people would say that the wolf had regained its human form at the time of death?"

"Precisely."

"I have understood that the change is said to work in exactly the other way."

"It works both ways, according to these fanatics, depending on circumstances, charms, and so forth. The whole thing is hypnotic, if you will; a jumble of contradictions. If it were not so horrible and fatal, it would be ridiculous. But what I could not realize before is the association of the thing with your manuscript. What are we to make of that?"

"Curious, of course," said the professor. "But if we leave out the doubtful mutilation of the little girl, I can't see anything supernatural about it. The man killed is one of the Gipsies I met at Golubacz. The others escaped. Why wolves? Why not dogs? The whole thing happened in the dark. Of course it is a coincidence."

"Too many coincidences," objected the general, who, again walking up and down the terrace, denounced the hellish dementia, as he called it, which for centuries had fixed its fatal blight upon the surrounding region. "Leave out the supernatural," he continued. "These grave robberies, kidnappings, and domestic outrages that defy the law and the efforts of the Church have never yet been explained. Nine times out of ten there is no motive. The victims are children, whether by natural death, as in this case, or murder or infanticide. In other words, cannibalism in its most frightful form."

"Who proves these things?" asked the professor.

"The priests. They tell us of whole villages at times depopulated of children. If they exaggerate, half of what they say would be terrible enough."

As over their cigars they discussed the possibilities and theories of lycanthropy, the higher interpretation of the manuscript was forgotten, and the conversation, in spite of themselves, narrowed itself to the details of the ghastly tale, which the general himself refused to believe.

It had grown late. The Tokay stood untasted on the table, while associations more and more sinister gathered around the gorgeous object that glowed and flashed in the candlelight, until the professor, shrinking from the task of escaping from the country with such a thing in his possession, almost regretted that he had found it.

To circumvent the latter difficulty, the general proposed a special passport, under the seal of the International River Navigation Treaty, and the talk ended.

VIII

"These dinners! These dinners!" exclaimed the hospitable soldier, with a touch of sadness in his sonorous voice, as he greeted the professor the next day. "Friends made at night, and lost in the morning! I'm afraid I am getting a little too old for that."

He explained that the promised passport, lying on his writing table, though available at large river ports and at the Turkish frontier, would not be comprehended by country officials, nor by the truculent Roumanian sentries. Then he conspicuously stamped it with the Imperial Seal.

"Jason's adventures were dangerous," he laughed, as the professor turned away. "Keep clear of the peasants. If you take my advice, you will not land at any of the river villages."

Again the magic sweep of the current seemed to reverse the

laws of motion, while, as if they stood still, it was the world that moved backward. The professor had recovered his spirits. Standing on the cabin-roof, in his life-preserver, with his precious canister slung over his shoulder, he heard without fear the threatening roar of waters. The "Iron Gates" were open, and away they went, dancing, trembling, leaping, whirled from shore to shore, till by oar-plunge and rudder-sweep they had cleared the last reef and whirlpool. Then suddenly, unaccountably, just as they drifted into smooth water, the rudder broke.

As the boat became at once unmanageable, several vexatious delays followed. But they soon found that their makeshift splicings of the highly-efficient, enormous oar, balanced by a rope-twist on the stern-post, failed to insure their safety when, in island channels, they contended with shoals, eddies, or the branches of submerged trees.

The Carpathians were fading away to the westward, their foothills sinking into the great Dacian plain, where the Danube, broadening like a lake, seems to lose its current. Jom-palanka and Rakoviza had come and gone when, at last, the professor, compelled to disregard the general's warning for the sake of a thing obtainable at most of the river towns, worked carefully out of the main stream and, hugging the shore for about a mile, gained the village of Borobassa, just below several large moored barges.

IX

The boat had grounded on a muddy beach, under overhanging acacia trees, where a few cows stood knee-deep in the shallow water. They heard the cackle of unseen chickens, and then the clang of an anvil, but saw no one till they had stepped ashore, when a gaunt heavily-built man in gray uniform and wearing a sword suddenly came out from behind the barges, and seeming surprised at the professor's explanation, led him up the beach, into a wattled enclosure littered with boat wreckage.

"Who told you to come here?" he asked, stopping to look at the stranger, with a troubled gleam in his swollen eyes. "You can get oars at Cusjak, or Provo, or Rakovisa. There's a fire-feast here today. You know what for?"

"No."

The man paused at a faint howling noise from beyond the trees.

"Do you hear that?"

"I am not afraid of dogs," laughed the professor, holding up his heavy walking-stick.

A frown crossed the haggard face of the man as he nodded his head contemptuously. "It's none of my business," he added. Then, pointing to a thatched shed and leaving his puzzled hearer, he hurried off.

"What did that man tell you?" asked an old blacksmith, who was standing near a forge-fire by the open shed-door when the professor approached.

"He said I could get oars across the river."

"So you can; but I can make oars too."

"He warned me against your dogs."

"Dogs? We have no dogs. He knows that."

"Is he a customs officer?" asked the traveler.

"Yes, poor devil,—till they get rid of him. He is crazy."

Learning that the job of finding and dressing the new rudder would take an hour or more, and having made his bargain with the old man, the professor stepped out of the smithy.

By way of a vegetable garden, a gate led into a wide, shady lane, where a group of peasant laundresses, in Bulgarian village fashion, were at work around the public well; and, as he went by, he stopped to notice that several of them were in holiday costume. One, a tall, athletic young woman, in a red-embroidered jacket, had just manipulated the pole of the great well-sweep and, without acknowledging the stranger's greeting, had swung two buckets of water upon her shoulder-yoke, when her headdress, a red cap, set sidewise on her black hair-braids, lost its pin or balance, and whirled off in the wind.

As it fell and rolled near the professor's feet, he leaped forward, picked it up, took off his hat, and reaching it out to the approaching woman, placed her cap upon his head while, apparently more astonished than amused, the other laundresses looked on. He stepped backwards. The woman threw his hat contemptuously on the ground and followed his evasive retreat until at last he stopped and, with a polite bow, returned her cap. She snatched it from his hand and stood awhile looking angrily at him. Then suddenly, to his amazement, the young Amazon sprung upon him and, seizing the tin box hanging upon his shoulder, wrenched it from its strap. The professor ran after her, caught the flying end of the broken strap, and, with a quick jerk, pulled the box out of her hands.

The woman turned and again stared at him. Something inhuman gleamed in the green eyes, while a singular distortion of the mouth so disfigured the handsome face that the professor, repelled if not startled, turned away. His hat had rolled down the hill, and he had just found it and picked it up, when he heard the voice of the blacksmith close by his side. The old man was speaking low.

"Excuse me, my gentleman, you are a stranger, sir. Will you take Hungrian man's advice?"

"What is it?" asked the traveler, surprised at the question.

"We are not in my country. I am from Semlin. But here, in Borobassa," he added, with a whisper, "we let such a woman alone."

"Is she married?"

"God knows! But she is a very bad woman. Excuse me, my gentleman, it is not safe."

The professor had followed the old man into his garden.

"Turkish jealousy!" he muttered. "More and more of it, I suppose, as we go eastward."

His critic seemed anxious to say something else. But without waiting to hear what it was, the professor thanked him, left the garden through another gate, and by way of a narrow lane walked slowly up the hill.

X

Unlike the river-villages thus far seen, the whole extent of Borobassa's huts, gardens, and lanes seemed buried in trees, a young forest, in which the scholar saw no sign of life, until the solitude began to astonish him. Then, at last, came a faint, resonant hum of voices, interrupted by the ringing of a bell. The cause of the noise was explained at the end of a lane, where, through an opening in the leaves, the sunlight caught the sheepskin caps and white shoulders of a dense crowd of men.

They were sitting upon the ground and, as the professor found on drawing near, along a narrow, circular row of planks, set with earthen bowls and dishes. He saw a black-robed Greek priest upon a platform, and opposite him, over the swarthy faces, a sheep, garlanded with flowers, held close to the table by two crouching men. Fastened to the animal's horns, two burning candles, shielded by several extended hands, flickered in the draft. Presently the singing ceased. The priest raised his hands in prayer, and the approaching professor, with the uneasy feeling of an intruder, took off his hat. He had stepped backward into the lane and was walking away when, at the touch of a hand softly laid upon his arm, he turned to look, with amazement, upon the woman he had offended at the well.

"You will not go away," said she gently.

The handsome face had lost all trace of anger as, with a laughing apology for what had happened, she held toward him a bunch of pink flowers. He took them, listened with surprise to her invitation to what she described as a public feast, and then followed her out of the lane into the crowded square. They had walked by the noisy table, where several of the peasants turned to look at them, when she laid her hand upon his tin box. "What do you carry in it?" she asked.

"Flowers. I am a botanist."

Passing a pile of faggots, partly covered with a black cloth, which he had not before noticed, he and his guide entered what he took to be the kitchen, a long thatched shed, open in front, and extending backward into a roofless bakery, in which several fires were burning and where a group of peasants seated around a bowl of broth politely made room for them.

The stranger sat down on a stool and took his turn with a

wooden spoon at a highly-seasoned stew, while the villagers, some of whom wore brightly-colored vests and had the swarthy look of Gipsies, examined his carved walking-stick, and would have entertained him had they meddled less with his tin box, which he had again tied to its strap. They came and went, laughed and drank, until when several earthen wine bottles had been emptied, one by one, they left him, and he found himself alone with a solemn blue-eyed old peasant woman, who had been stirring the soup.

Her light, sun-bleached hair had begun to turn grey, and her brown mantle, open at the throat, showed a triple-strung necklace of red berries, knotted upon little silver coins.

"Have you a saint for today?" he asked, as the woman, who held a rosary in her hand, laid it on the table.

"For our Holy Saint Basil," said she devoutly,—"the friend of children. It is a fire-feast."

"What is that?"

"You are a stranger, sir,"—she paused. "But you must know that we have no children here."

"No children!" repeated the astonished visitor. "Where are your children?"

With a strange expression, the woman looked at him a moment in silence. "What! Have you not heard?" she whispered. Then, glancing suddenly over her shoulder, she stopped.

The other woman had come back, bringing a wine bottle, and, without sitting down, stood looking at them. Her peculiar greenish eyes had a slightly supercilious look as she turned them from the professor to his companion.

"I have brought you some wine," she said, placing the earthen bottle on the table and laying her hand on the old woman's shoulder; "to drink her health. Did she tell you who she is?"

"No," replied the professor.

"She is my grandmother."

The old woman grasped her rosary and looked up. Her face flushed with anger, and she rose from her stool.

"She tells you a lie," said she angrily; "I am no Gipsy."

While the indignant peasant walked away, the offender laughed mischievously and sat down at the table.

"Why did you do that?" inquired the puzzled scholar.

Without answering, the woman drew her stool nearer.

"Did you show her your flowers?"

"No."

She laid her hand on the tin canister. "But you will show them to me, my friend?"

"I have only roots," said he, "not flowers."

Leaning forward, his companion clutched the tin box. Again he saw the threatening glitter in the green eyes. He started. For an instant the masked Gipsy at Golubacz flashed upon his sight and vanished.

"Let us see the roots," said she.

He grasped her hand, pushed it away, and, following the example of the old woman, walked hastily off into the crowd.

XI

In clouds of steam, among the hurrying cooks and waiters, the professor wandered awhile. At length, noticing his late aged companion near the entrance, he stopped. She was sitting on a bench with the customs officer he had met at the beach. The singular man, who was holding a white package on his knees and gesticulating violently as if in a rage, got up, thrust the bundle into his pocket, and walked away. The professor hesitated a moment, then sat down.

"Why did you leave us?" he asked gently, looking into the still angry blue eyes. "You knew it was not my fault."

"No, you are a stranger, sir. It is that Gipsy woman." The old peasant pointed to the uncouth, haggard man who was standing outside near the wood pile. "Did you hear what he said about her?"

"No."

"Did you see what he was showing me in a handkerchief? He carries it about in his pocket."

"No."

She leaned forward, lowering her voice to a whisper: "It is his child's foot."

"Good Heavens! Is he crazy?"

"Yes. Mary and Joseph! It would make you sick." Again she suddenly stopped. He looked up. The remarkable woman they talked about was standing before them.

The professor was still holding her pink bouquet.

"Are we friends?" she asked, pointing to the flowers, with a laugh. "Come, I will show you my garden."

Near the open window he caught the glow of her red cap and underdress. Her gold earrings sparkled in the sun.

The professor would have risen, but the old woman clutched his arm.

"Don't look at her," she whispered.

"Come," urged the Gipsy.

Her green eyes fixed upon him seemed to expand with a dull, whitish glitter and lose their pupils.

"Don't look at her," repeated the old woman.

With sudden anger at the continued arm-clutch, the scholar felt an irresistible impulse to break away. Just then a bell rang outside, and the Gipsy glanced over her shoulder.

"Come! I must go," said she.

But as the professor sat still, she turned away, and waving her hand, walked quickly across the square.

"I am afraid I have treated her badly," he muttered nervously, holding up his pink flowers; "she gave me these."

"Throw them away! They will bring you bad luck."

"What! The Orpine? I thought it was a fortunate plant."

"You will see, my friend. Do you know what she wants?"

"No."

"It is your tin box. Are you afraid of her?"

Without answering, the professor tightened his grasp upon the canister.

"I will tell you something." The old woman leaned toward him and again lowered her voice to a whisper. "She is a wolf-woman."

Once more the bell rang outside.

"Get up here," urged the peasant, laying her hand on the bench.

He mounted the seat. Over the heads of the crowd he saw the priest approach the woodpile and draw away its black cloth cover, revealing the carcass of a greyish animal stretched upon the faggots. His companion pulled his sleeve.

"Do you see him?" she whispered.

"I see a dog, or a wolf."

She crossed herself. "It is a man. You don't believe it? The town is full of them. When they burn him, the others go away."

The crowd of peasants gathered close, and the priest held up a book and began to read aloud in Greek.

Gradually his resonant voice rose high and clear in passionate declamation. The men had removed their sheepskin caps, and stood in silence, while a low crackling noise was presently followed by a cloud of whirling smoke. The wood-pile was on fire. As the smoke drew into the kitchen, a deep unison of many voices, blending with the tones of the priest, swelled into a hymn. Louder and louder, rising and falling in long refrains, it seemed to jingle in vibrations upon the beams in the shed. Fluttering tongues of flame shot into the sky over the heads of the choir. Cooks came out of the bakery and crowded the entrance, while the professor got down and walked outside, to stare at the dramatic scene.

When the fire had died into embers, the chanting ceased, the peasants sat down again, and the stranger stepped into the shed to find his companion. But she had gone. He walked into the bakery, then came back, to look in vain for her in the crowd.

It was getting late. "High time to return to the boat," he thought, as he slowly passed the smoky square; and then, with a last look at the noisy company, and a bow to the priest, left the place.

XII

Following by guess-work the direction of his former path, the professor slowly made his way down the hill. Wild, half-considered memories of the general's dinner and midnight talk at Orsova crowded upon him. But he had drunk too much for serious reflection. When a curious feeling that something was wrong with his surroundings yielded to drowsiness, he was crossing an open knoll by a deserted hut overlooking the river. There he saw a bench sheltered under the thatch, sat down upon it, and leaned against the wall.

Moments passed as he looked outward upon the evening lights that streamed across the tree-tops and inward beyond the borderland of dreams. The place seemed confused with things astonishing, contradictory, casual, human feet floating in the air, a cave lit by glowworms, an ash tree, the Castle of Golubacz,—a face, framed in the ruins, now laughing, now frowning. He felt a gentle strain upon his shoulder that gradually increased into a pull, and awoke to find himself clutching the strap of his tin box.

A woman was seated close by him on the bench. At first blending with the dream, her head quickly sharpened upon the background, until he recognized his Gipsy companion.

"It is late, my gentleman," said she, leaning toward him. "You will not sleep here?"

"No," he replied, rising. "I am going to the river."

"I will show you the river."

As he walked away, she joined him. "Have you forgotten your flowers?" she asked, pointing to the pink bouquet lying on the bench.

"Let them go," said he. "I am told they will bring me bad luck."

Again the angry glitter in the Gipsy's eyes. "Yes," she sneered. "What else did that old fool tell you?"

"She was telling me about St. Basil."

"And miracles. Do you believe in miracles?"

The professor pointed at the darkening sky. "I believe in that: no beginning; no end. What are miracles to that?"

The answer seemed to suppress his companion, who walked beside him in silence, while, heedless of a strong misgiving, he went on. The wine was in his head. With the fall of night, the unending lanes seemed to turn in the wrong direction, rather uphill than down, until he began to suspect that his guide, who had lagged behind, was misleading him.

They had passed a gate in a wattled fence, beyond which the walls of a house glimmered faintly through the trees. He noticed the perfume of flowers.

"It's very dark here," said he. "What's that?"

He stopped suddenly at sight of a large animal seen for an instant in the twilight upon the path ahead of him.

The words brought no answer. He turned around. The woman was gone. He listened; then called, half-startled at the sound of his own voice. The dark openings in the trees gave no sign, while as he felt again the curious sensation, as if his surroundings were slipping away from him, or did not exist, a heavy concussion upon his back sent him staggering forward. With a sharp quick pain in his shoulder came a loud report close behind him. The weight fell away, and he turned upon the officer he had seen on the beach.

The man's face was distorted with rage. He was pointing with a pistol toward the house, and the professor looked back,—but saw nothing.

He was fumbling with his coat. "I have been robbed," he cried.

Out of breath and muttering curses, the officer pushed his weapon into a belt mounted with pistols and pulled out another.

"Are you hurt?" he asked.

"No. But there was a woman here. I had a satchel."

"Do you want it?"

"Yes."

"Come on, then, if you're not afraid."

They hurried through a gate and along a path to a white thatched building with open windows set with flowers, and passed a closed door. Beyond this another door stood ajar. Listening, and hearing no noise, the officer cocked his pistol and pushed it open.

A close, sickening smell met them as they entered a room

faintly lit by the fading window-light and a grease-lamp flickering on a shelf. They saw a garret, a step-ladder, some kettles on a bench, and around the walls, or hanging from the rafters, dark masses of clothing and shoes. Some of the shoes were of child's size. The professor had just noticed a miniature row set on a table near one of the windows, when the officer, who was ahead, suddenly stopped, at a guttural sound from the corner of the room. His eyes were fixed upon a partly-opened door to the left of the staircase, when the sound came again,—more distinctly, a low, long-protracted growl. He lifted his double-barreled pistol, but as the door stood motionless, he walked forward and pushed it with his foot. With a loud creak, it swung inward, and the men started back at the sight of two lustrous points of light glaring at them from the darkness.

The officer fired, paused a moment, and then sprang through the doorway.

There was a muffled rustling from beyond the opening, a flash, and a second report. The professor picked up the lamp and came to the threshold of a smoky, windowless closet like a kitchen. He saw a high pile of faggots, near which the officer had stopped. He was leaning forward, and presently began tossing aside a litter of loose sticks and bundles that scattered the floor, until, over the hearth of a dead fire, the unsteady gleams revealed a pool of blood, then the clawed feet, legs, and hairy body of an animal.

"Hand me the lamp," said the man and, taking it, he stooped and held it close to the bloody head and glittering jaws of a wolf.

"Now you know what that woman is," he exclaimed savagely. "You saw her."

"I don't know what I saw," muttered the professor. "Good God! What's that?"

From outside the house a moaning cry, rising into a shriek, with quavering wails, slowly died away in an answering chorus of distant howlings.

"Come quick!" cried the officer.

He turned towards the door, and the professor stepped away

from the place, when, at a half-concealed glitter on the floor, he sprang backward.

"For God's sake, bring the lamp!" He had stooped to seize the partly-unrolled fleece of his manuscript, and was holding it up in both hands.

"Thank Heaven!" came his breathless words. Turning it about in the approaching light, while the officer muttered something inaudibly, he rolled it up and followed his companion into the outer room. When he had thrust his recovered treasure into his pocket, the two men hurried out into the twilight.

As if possessed by a frenzy, the officer, who seemed to have forgotten his surroundings, went on talking to himself. Once they stopped at a rattle of bushes behind a fence, then hastened on, and a few moments later had reached a lane corner, where the crazed fanatic, refusing to listen to the professor's grateful offers, abruptly left him.

The professor started to run. Down the steep hill he stumbled and sprang in the gathering darkness, until, reaching an opening ahead, the scene seemed to shift suddenly into a place already familiar,—a fading of fences and trees into the great well-sweep with the smith's garden beyond. He stopped at the clutch of a hand on his arm.

"Thank God it's not true," came Karl's frightened voice. "The blacksmith told me they had murdered you."

Faintly seen down the hill, the old Hungarian was beckoning violently from his gate, while from the trees beyond them echoed a wild din of shouts and howlings.

They reached the garden at a run and got into the smithy, followed by the old man, who, pushing them through the rear door of the shed, closed it behind them.

"He said there was a woman following you. Did you see her?" asked the trembling, breathless servant as they stopped on the beach to look back.

The blacksmith had opened the door. He was waving his arms, and again they heard his shout:—"Quick! Get away quick!"

A moment later, reaching the houseboat, they dragged the

anchor out of the mud and, leaving the gang-plank behind, pushed off.

Before they had stopped rowing in the current, the tree outlines had vanished against the yet glowing horizon. For a long time wailing echoes, rising on the night wind from no fixed direction, seemed to follow them in the sky. At last these sounds died away, and as the great river, bending to the southward, bore them on, nothing but the murmur of ripples broke the silence, until a swollen eddy drew them into one of the channels of a group of islands.

The young moon had set when, seizing a bough that swept by in the starlight, they found rest and safety at last, in the secluded tangle of an island forest.

XIII

With the professor's safe arrival at Widdin, two days later, our available sources of information end. His own posthumous notes, if ever published, must account for the later history of the great manuscript.

Apart from its fame, established at Geneva, and afterwards at Stockholm, it has often been said that the ill-luck that clouded its discovery clung to it to the last. The scholar's conscientious scruples as to recompensing the monks at Jollok were thwarted by the death of the abbot and by another insurrection in Hungary, and it is well known that several persons died or were injured while in possession of the treasure. Science was robbed of it when the ship, bringing it from Dantzig to Copenhagen, foundered in a storm.

THE DOLLS' CASTLE

I

It was late one hot summer night, at the Templehouse Club in Eastport. The waiters were still busy in the wine-room, where, at several tables, groups of fashionably-dressed members, considering it too hot to sleep, preferred warm discussion and cooling drinks to the use of their latch keys. Charles Carrington, the dramatist, with a tall, ice-filled glass before him and a palmleaf fan in his hand, was sitting alone near an open window, laughing to himself. He was looking about the room, as he had often done before, at the characteristic movements of his genial if argumentative friend, George Westbrook, which that night seemed unusually ridiculous.

Whoever remembers the wine-room of the Templehouse Club in the eighties, remembers George Westbrook and the unique habit he had, which no one who knew the man ever thought of resenting, of introducing provocative, highly-debatable, and sometimes outrageous subjects of discussion among his convivial friends; and then, when the inevitable argument followed, of leaving the scene of dispute, to stir up debate in other parts of the room.

The fact that he appeared to proceed unconsciously and without mischievous intent,—though his topics had the combustibility of slow matches laid to gunpowder,—made the thing all the more absurd to those who could appreciate it, and that night, as the polemical uproar proved, he had succeeded better than usual.

At one of the nearest tables the discussion had reached a climax, on the introduction of a stranger,—a short, heavy-jawed, clean shaven man, whom Westbrook had brought in from outside. Whereupon, Westbrook, or the "Doctor," as he was nicknamed, got up as usual, left the disputants, and came over to Carrington.

"Sit down, Westbrook," said the latter, "what's the matter over there?"

"A worn-out ghost story, about a haunted house, that your friend B—— persists in telling, although it has been demolished over and over again. He says he knows a lady, who knew a man who was found dead there with a bulldog, and so forth. The house is in London, in Berkeley Square. You have heard of it, of course."

"What, Bulwer's 'House in the Brain?'"

"No. That was a mistake. Bulwer never saw the house. Ouida in one of her stories mixed it up with another house. I happened to meet a man in the library who knows all about it, so I brought him up to settle the matter, and I think he has done it."

"And spoiled a good ghost story," said Carrington. "Quite right, provided he has facts, but these haunted houses can't be disposed of on theory nowadays. We must investigate them, one by one, as they come up. Of course you know about the haunted house on Belbridge Street."

"I never heard of it."

Carrington, in his enthusiastic way, described the place as altogether the most typical, portentous, remarkable thing of the kind he had ever seen. He said he had first heard of it as a shunned investment in real estate when reading law with Sharp, Dorrance, and Blair, since which time it had more than once figured in the newspapers.

"It depends on the point of view," observed Westbrook. "Newspaper stories about haunted houses don't appeal to me, and never did."

"Would you like to see the house?" asked Carrington.

Westbrook looked at his watch.

"Never mind the time," urged his friend; "it's too hot to go to bed."

"All right," Westbrook agreed at length. "We will have a stroll down River Street, at any rate."

And they passed out of the noisy forum, into a dark corridor, where "Silence like a poultice came to heal the blows of sound."

Crossing thence a hall, floored with summer-matting and perfumed with the genial aroma of distilled spirits and lemons, they reached the open front entrance and went out into the night.

II

The heat was sweltering, and they walked slowly, so that it took them a long time to get out of the confines of respectability, into the region of the squalid, the disreputable, and the ob-scure. Save for a few belated Jews in their torchlit clothes dens, it was too late for the night life, even of River Street. And beyond that the houses were dark. Here and there a would-be sleeper in a shabby hall-way stirred or yawned as they went by. But the dirty doorstep groups and curbstone gossips had gone to bed, and by the time the two friends had reached Tenth Street and walked down to the corner of Belbridge, the well-lit pavements on either side of the great house, as far as they could see, were deserted.

"There," said Carrington, stopping at the crossway and pointing through the trees at the sinister building; "what do you think of that?"

They walked along the pavement where the black and mag-nified leaf-shadows fluttered under foot, looked up at the rows of closed shutters, and stopped before the high, marble steps that marked the unusual level of the first floor above the base-ment. Westbrook noticed the vile scribblings on the front door, near a dingy sign-board marked *To Let,* with its inscription broken away at the word *Inquire.* Beyond, through the gate-bars in a very high brick wall, a courtyard with a grassy pavement and out-buildings was lost in darkness.

"Porte-cochère and stables," said Carrington, "with out-kitchens and shrubbery in the background. Can you see them?"

"It is too dark back there for anything but the ghost," said Westbrook; and then he looked up at the half-lit, towering walls, swept by the restless shadows of the trees. "All very grand, of course, but I see nothing so remarkable about it, except that the whole thing is out of place, built at the wrong end of town."

"Times have changed, my boy," declared Carrington. "In the old days, this part of the world was in the midst of things. The Polish Jew had not yet appeared."

"He and the ghost came together, no doubt," remarked Westbrook, sarcastically.

"Never mind the ghost. I don't pretend to say that there is proof of a ghost. But it is the appearance of the place rather than its history that strikes me. From a dramatic point of view, I wanted you to see that garden. It is exactly what I am looking for as the background for a play that I have in hand."

Westbrook laughed. "Set to music, I suppose,—another version of the *Contes d'Hoffman,* wonders included. Where will you put Doctor Miracle?"

"Almost anywhere here," returned Carrington enthusiastically. The two men had stepped back across the pavement and were looking along the basement where the barred windows were without shutters, when the dramatist felt his sleeve plucked and turned to see a small, swarthy man close to his side, holding up a piece of paper as if for inspection. A little girl stood behind him, and as the light caught the miniature face and wondering upturned eyes, he noticed that she carried in her arms a large doll. The man tried to say something, but stopped, while Carrington took the paper and, holding it up to the light, noticed the words "Belbridge Street," written in pencil under a number upon it. Beckoning the man to follow him, and continuing his conversation with Westbrook, Carrington walked to the corner, turned up to the left, and stopped before a small white building across the way.

"There's your house," said he, "ten hundred and thirteen Belbridge Street," as, once more reading the scribbled address, he glanced over his shoulder and handed back the paper to the man. The latter again held it up in the light and again tried to say something; but Carrington was talking and had turned away, when the voice behind him seemed to rise in a sharp crescendo, dying into the words, "away—away." When he looked again over his shoulder, the man was gone.

"What in the world became of that little man?" exclaimed Carrington, turning to Westbrook. "Did you see him go into the house?"

"No; I was looking across the street."

Carrington stepped down to the corner. Westbrook joined him. They walked along Tenth Street, and looked up and down the brightly-lit but deserted pavements.

"The man was a Negro, wasn't he?" Westbrook asked.

"An East Indian, I should say. I noticed that he wore one of those embroidered skull-caps and that the little girl had a doll. But wait a minute."

He ran back, and across the cobble stones into an alley behind the great house, groped his way past several closed doors, along the narrow, bricked passage, reached its end, and turned back. Over the wall to his right a faint light touched the upper stories of the deserted mansion, where he noticed that one of the windows was open. Just then, to his surprise, a soft object with a muffled reverberation struck the pavement near his feet.

"Who's there," he called in startled surprise, staring up at the dark window-opening. Then, hearing nothing, he stepped forward, and, leaning down, struck several matches, to discover that the fallen object was a large child's doll. He turned it over with his foot, picked it up, and held it high enough to make out that the dress was torn and rotting, and the paint battered off the face. Bringing it to the end of the passage, he stooped down and placed it on the ground, against the brick wall.

Westbrook was standing at the corner below when Carrington reached the street.

"Come back here, Westbrook; I want to show you something. Look along the wall there on the left," said he, pointing into the alley, as his friend joined him.

Westbrook turned into the shadows, stumbled about for a while, then came out again.

"There is nothing there," said he. "If you are playing me a trick, I don't see the point."

Carrington stepped into the alley. "By George, Westbrook, I put a doll here,—not two minutes ago. But it's gone. What do you make of it?" he continued as, after coming out into the light, he explained the singular incident.

"I don't make anything of it," returned Westbrook, "except that you are getting things mixed. It is too dark in there to see dolls or anything else. That little girl we saw with the Negro, or whatever he was, had a doll, I admit. She may have dropped it. But my idea is that the man took her into that little house over the way there when you gave him his paper."

Walking impatiently across the street, he knocked loudly on the door with his cane. They listened awhile to the hollow echoes. Then Carrington noticed that the light he thought he had seen over the transom had gone out, and that a board had been nailed across one of the closed shutters.

"Why, the place is deserted," said he. "Look here." He opened a gate in the wall adjoining a high building next door. Then the two men, after hesitating a moment, stepped into a litter of waste-paper and rubbish. Following a narrow, slimy footway, they reached a walled enclosure, lit by the electric lights from an alley beyond. The pavement, under a little ruined porch, was scattered with broken glass and tin cans. The windows had been boarded up. Pushing aside a rotting dog-house, the intruders tried the back door, to find it either locked or nailed shut. From the dismal yard beyond, as they looked up over the kitchen wing at the diminutive windows, ancient brick chimney, and hip-roof, a disturbed, wailing cat ran along the porch-cornice and over the adjacent wall.

"I told you so," said Carrington; "our man never came in here."

"But he brought us here," insisted Westbrook; "and you saw the number of this house on his paper. How do you account for that?"

"I don't pretend to account for it,—unless——"

"Let's get out of this," said Westbrook; "we'll be arrested here, if we don't catch some disease."

"What I meant to say was," continued Carrington, closing

the alley door behind him as the two men reached the street again, "that we may be getting to the bottom of the business without knowing it. Suppose, for instance, that the Lascar we saw had no existence at all. This thing ought to be reported to the Psychic Research Society."

"You don't mean to say that you believe that we saw the ghost!"

"I don't know what I believe," Carrington replied, "except that the key to the situation is not over here but in that house across the street. I tell you, the fellow we are after is in there now. If so, we can run him down. I've got what I call my dead-latch candle in my pocket and a box of matches. What do you say to going in through one of the cellar windows and settling the matter?"

"My boy, you're crazy," said Westbrook, looking at his watch. "Do you know what time it is? When I'm locked up and fined, it will be for something more sensible than that. For Heaven's sake, come home."

"But that doll in the alley," objected Carrington. "We ought to investigate that."

"Never mind the doll. I didn't see it, and I don't believe you did," added Westbrook as his friend yielded; and they walked up the street.

III

It was on a cool autumn afternoon nearly two months after this adventure that Carrington, homeward bound from one of his eccentric suburban rambles, happened to be walking down Eleventh Street. He was alone, as usual, with his notebook full of dramatic suggestions, gathered in dilapidated found-ries, through holes in fences, and beyond broken viaducts. His thoughts were in the clouds. It was late in the day. The life of the city had waned into a drowsy, low-keyed hum. The sun's rays were losing their heat and began to catch a false fire in the glitter of west-fronting windows. When he reached the corner of Belbridge Street, he stopped and looked eastward. Down at the angle of Tenth Street, where the pavement trees had begun to show to the brown touch of the season, he recognized, to his surprise, the familiar figure of his friend Westbrook. Dressed in the height of fashion, in silk hat and frock coat, with beflowered buttonhole, the latter was standing with his back toward the great deserted house, looking at the small buildings opposite.

"Hello, Carrington," said he, as that explorer of the underworld turned down the thoroughfare and joined him; "you are just the man I wanted to see. I have made a discovery. I have demolished your ghost."

In answer to Carrington's question, Westbrook explained that he had been examining a map of the city and had found a singular duplication of names, which he had come down to verify.

He paused and looked knowingly at his friend.

"Where would you say that that East Indian or Negro, or whatever he was, slipped away from us the other night?"

"About where we are standing," said Carrington, pointing to the little white building in front of them. "There is the house, number ten hundred and thirteen."

Westbrook laughed in his most triumphant style: "Not a bit of it. The man never came near that house."

"What do you mean?"

"I mean that we are on the wrong street. This is Belbridge Street. We went up Bridge Street, the next street below. Belbridge; Bridge. Notice the similarity of names. But come this way. I'll prove it to you."

He walked down to the corner and along Tenth Street, with Carrington following, turned at the first street they reached, crossed it, walked up the pavement, and stopped.

"There's your house," he pointed out: "Ten hundred and thirteen Bridge Street."

Carrington started with astonishment as he stared at the place. The little white wooden house, with its transom, hiproof, enormous chimney, and alley gate, was apparently an exact duplicate of its Belbridge Street model. More than that, the similarity seemed to repeat itself among the neighboring houses. Westbrook pointed to a closed warehouse behind several trees opposite. "Another version of your haunted house," said he.

"Do you mean to tell me," asked Carrington excitedly, "that we were in a trance,—groped past Belbridge Street, and came up this street instead?"

"Why not? You were talking about your 'Castle of Otranto' and noticed nothing."

"But I ran up the alley back of the big house."

"So you did, but that was later. We were back on Belbridge Street by that time."

"You may be right," returned Carrington in utter bewilderment, "but if I took the man and the little girl to this house and they went into it and stayed there, the people that live here ought to know something about it."

Nervously throwing away a cigar that he had just lighted, he stepped up to the door and knocked with the ferrule of his cane. Following a noise of voices and footsteps inside, it was opened presently by a thin, stooping, bright-eyed old woman. She stared at them a moment; then, after explaining by gestures that she was deaf, led them into a little darkened parlor, where an old white-bearded man was seated on a sofa.

Carrington, in a polite extemporized account, explained that, at the request of certain ladies, he was looking up the address of a little girl, a pupil at a certain Sunday-school, and had brought the child to the house, with a colored man, some weeks before.

The latter part of the statement had just been translated to the deaf woman by her husband, when she angrily interrupted.

"We have heard that story before, and we don't want to hear it again. This house is not on Belbridge Street, I'll have you gents to know. It belongs to me. And when I have to rent it, I don't want any of your 'little girl' stories hanging to it. Johnnie, show them out."

The old man, who had been sitting in his stockings, slipped on his shoes and led the visitors into the hall and out the door.

"Don't mind what my old woman says," he muttered, as,

after listening to Carrington's apology, he followed the two men down to the corner. "I don't know where you gentlemen picked up that story, but it don't belong here. If you will come with me, 'around the corner just,' I'll show you where it does belong."

He led the two friends back to Belbridge Street, turned to the right, and pointed to the house they had just left.

"Look there," he said. "That house looks like our house, don't it? And it's got the same number. That house won't rent. Over across the street there," he continued, shaking his fist at the forsaken mansion, "is another house that won't rent."

"What's that got to do with it?" asked Westbrook.

"You know as well as I do that they say there's a 'dark-complected' man comes out of that big house and goes into this house with a little girl; and the little girl, they say, carries a doll. There's people that will talk you to death about that doll.—Dolls!—They tell you that that house across the street is full of dolls. There's dancing goes on in there."

"Dancing," repeated Carrington. "Who dances?"

"They say it's the dolls,—if you believe it. I don't, for I never saw it, and I don't want to. Stories are bad things," he added. "But I know gentlemen when I see them, and I don't believe you want to take the bread out of a poor man's mouth,—do you? Then shake hands, and I hope you will let us alone with these stories."

"What a superstitious old fool that man is," muttered Westbrook as the shock of grey hair and beard disappeared around the corner.

"Not at all," returned Carrington. "He is afraid of what they call at law defamation of title. That is what our meddling with his house amounts to."

"He has told us nothing," said Westbrook.

"Except that there *is* a ghost, after all. According to his account, we must have seen it. To my notion, your discovery of house number three brings us nowhere, or rather back to where we started,—back to the big house. There it is!" he exclaimed, pointing eagerly over the way. "Look at it. What would Bulwer or Dickens or Wilkie Collins have thought of it? If I ever investigate the thing seriously, I shall drop side issues and begin there, with this doll story."

"All very well, if you are writing a play," retorted Westbrook, "but if you expect to get to the bottom of the business, you had better stick to facts."

They had crossed the street, and Carrington was stooping down, looking at the basement windows. "They have been painted on the inside," he said. "You can see nothing down there." He arose, and the two men walked slowly up the pavement, then stopped, turned, and looked back at the deserted building.

"See there!" he exclaimed, as the western beams of approaching sunset blazed on the glass of its upper windows; "what a gorgeous effect! Exactly as if the place was illuminated inside. Strange you don't notice it on the other houses."

"The dolls must be dancing upstairs," said Westbrook with a sarcastic laugh.

IV

Another year had passed, during which Carrington, more than ever absorbed in his work, had seen little of his friends. What an incessant traveller he was, into the far-away world of his art; how late he sat up, amidst the creations of his dramatic fancy that flitted like gay-winged moths around the flame of his midnight oil, no one knew but himself. Plays, preferred by chance or forced upon him by theatre managers, scene painters, or impressarios, came and went, until, overwhelmed with engagements, he had well-nigh forgotten Belbridge Street and its ghosts, when a chance meeting with his legal friend, Dorrance, brought the subject suddenly back to his thoughts.

Dorrance, still at the old office, had become a great lawyer. A dweller in cities by preference, who never left town, summer or winter. A man behind the scenes in legal situations, who never addressed juries, but commanded verdicts. Always successful; hence, at length, one of the heads of the firm.

The former colleagues rarely met. But when they did, their reminiscences of mutual friends and old times generally ended in an engagement for the theatre, or a dinner at some neighboring restaurant. On this occasion they recognized each other as the great man came out of his down-town headquarters. Carrington, who always associated Dorrance with his first knowledge of the house on Belbridge Street, introduced the subject.

Dorrance turned back, and the two friends passed through several busy rooms, evoking memories of the past, then proceeded upstairs, into a familiar little back office, brightened through its open windows by the afternoon sun.

"Sit down," said the lawyer, "and have a cigar. You don't want to buy the place, do you?"

"No, it might make a Bohemian club or an outpost for the Psychic Research; but I'm not engineering anything of that sort."

"I'm glad to hear it," said Dorrance. "Of course, I wouldn't like to advise against the firm's interest, but, strictly between ourselves, that house is one of the most useless piles of brickwork in the city. A bad legacy; and a worse investment. It has been on the market without a tenant since you were here,—a dead loss to everybody but the tax collector. One of these days it will have to be pulled down."

A brief history of the unlucky mansion followed. Through deaths and sales, it had continually changed hands. There had been contentions in the Orphans' Court, forfeitures of rent, prosecutions for breach of contract. Its lease as a gold cure sanitarium for inebriates had failed because of a newspaper scandal. More than once suits for defamation of title had upset negotiations.

"Do you know," Dorrance continued, "that, though I have had charge of the place for the last ten years, I have never been inside of it? There is a dime-novel-full of stories about it, of course; but they don't interest me a bit."

"Still, I suppose there is some basis of fact in some of them," remarked Carrington.

"If there is, I haven't found it. A bigger jumble of contradictory nonsense raked up at groceries, apothecary shops, and pawnbroker dens I wouldn't want to listen to. All that I know definitely is that, somewhere in the fifties or earlier, a rich widow with an only child lived in the house; that the child was stolen and never found, and that the lady went insane."

"Sudden grief, I suppose?" said Carrington.

"Not exactly sudden," replied Dorrance. "It seems that the little girl had a doll when last seen. The poor mother advertised, of course, and got anonymous letters describing dolls, discovered or traced, as clues to the child. She paid the blackmail, but got nothing,—nothing at all, year after year, but—dolls. These, it seems, she kept, and brooded over as a sort of memory,— washed and dressed, talked and sang to, until the thing drove her mad. There are other details; but these are enough. I can give you the woman's name, if you wish."

"No," said Carrington, "it's not that. All I want is to get into the house,—not so much as a ghost hunter, but from a dramatic point of view. The fact is, I've heard something of the doll story, and the place strikes me as a marvelous background for a play that I have had in mind for years."

Dorrance walked across the room and unlocked the door of a cupboard.

"There is no janitor at present," said he. "Here are the keys."

He pulled a well-kept bunch out of a pigeon-hole and threw it on the table.

"Those for the front door and garden gate are painted red, you see. When would you like to go?"

"Tomorrow afternoon, if it suits you."

"Come down, then, and get them. I may go over with you.— But one more word," he added, as Carrington rose to leave. "You'd better say nothing to anybody about your visit. The present owner, the archbishop, is an easy-going man; but he has had enough defamation of title, and if the newspapers get hold of the thing, there will be more of it. I would be responsible, of course."

"His Grace will never hear of it through me,—newspapers or no newspapers," said Carrington, as warmly thanking his old friend, who had followed him down-stairs, he bade him good-bye.

v

How often must we account for the origin of human responsibility in nothing more definite than shifts of chance! Why did Carrington, whose nights were particularly occupied at the time, go to the theatre that evening; and why was it that almost the first person he saw there in the unfamiliar crowd was his friend Westbrook? It happened that the latter, like himself, had chosen to hear on its opening night the fantastic little musical comedy much in vogue later, known as *Dolls in Toyland*. He had brought his little boy, Archie, with him, and was seated in the pit, near the stage. As the play went on, Carrington noticed the child clinging to his father, apparently terrified at some of the scenic marvels. But as the performance was expected to be a decided juvenile success, he was surprised, at the end of the second act, to meet his friend in the foyer leading the little fellow out of the theatre.

"Most children would delight in it," explained Westbrook, "but Archie seems to be frightened. He has nerves. As I see no use in upsetting them, I think I had better take him home. We will postpone the hobgoblins until he gets older."

Carrington, who had taken his check at the box office, stepped out onto the pavement.

"By the way," said he; "speaking of hobgoblins, how would you like to follow up our investigation on Belbridge Street?"

"You mean the Haunted House, I suppose," said Westbrook. "I thought we had given it up as a hopeless case."

"Why give it up? I have learned a good deal about it since I saw you, and I have got the keys, or will have them; so, if you choose to meet me there tomorrow at five o'clock, we can look it over together."

"It sounds interesting," admitted Westbrook. "I think I'll join you,—that is, if my wife has no other plans."

"Bring her with you," suggested Carrington.

Westbrook laughed. "Quite out of the question. If there is one woman in the world who takes no interest whatever in that sort of thing, I think it's Clara. She's not at all romantic, and your dramatic rhapsodies about the place wouldn't appeal to her at all."

Carrington watched the father and his little boy disappear down the street. But he had hardly reached his seat, when he realized that, under the circumstances, the introduction of the talkative Mrs. Westbrook into the proposed ghost hunt had been a mistake. He left the theatre, found a messenger boy at the nearest telegraph office, and, determining to forestall the lady's gossip and a possible newspaper sensation, wrote the following note:

DEAR WESTBROOK,

It occurs to me that you had better not mention our Belbridge Street project to anybody, not even your wife. [He underscored the latter words.] The newspapers are, as you know, hungry for things of this sort, and if they get hold of our plans, I happen to know that the owner of the house would seriously object.

Yours,

Charles Carrington.

"That ought to protect me," he muttered to himself, as, sealing up the note, he paid for the boy at the window and, after watching him swagger down the street, went back to the theatre, where he became so absorbed in the melodrama that he forgot to criticise it,—as he had intended.

The next day, he again congratulated himself on his precaution and had dismissed Mrs. Westbrook from his thoughts before the appointed afternoon hour found him approaching the place of meeting, with the keys in his pocket.

VI

Carrington was alone. Having heard nothing from Westbrook,

and having parted from Dorrance, who was called away at the last moment, he had resigned himself to the somewhat cheerless prospect of a solitary exploration, when, to his agreeable surprise, he caught sight of Westbrook in the distance. The latter was standing near the great house, close to a carriage drawn up under the trees, and, on seeing Carrington, hurried toward him.

"I suppose you hardly expected me," said he, as they met; "but here I am; and I have brought Mrs. Westbrook and Archie with me."

Carrington had some difficulty in simulating the delight that the unexpected announcement required, but managed to do so.

"I hope you cautioned her about talking," he observed anxiously.

"Yes, but your note came ten minutes too late. When I mentioned the affair to her, for some reason best known to herself, she decided to join us. There she is, you see."

As they drew near, the smiling lady, dressed in the height of the autumn style and seated in a handsome phaeton, waved a paper-covered book at them.

"Don't be alarmed, Mr. Carrington," said she, while the latter paid his respects. "I am not going to interfere. George says you are hunting ghosts for your next play, and I thought you would let me wait out here with Archie until you get through. Archie will be a good boy, and stay with his mother, won't he, dear?"

The little blue-eyed fellow, whose brown hair had been elaborately curled in the style of the day, was dressed in his best clothes, the miniature kilt, bonnet, and tartan of some of his far-away Scottish ancestors. He had climbed out of the phaeton and caught his father's hand.

"How pretty he looks," said Carrington. "Is that plaid a special pattern?"

"Yes, the Campbell tartan. His grandmother was a Campbell, you know."

"You will have to teach him the sword dance one of these days."

"Wouldn't it be pretty? He'll sing *The Campbells Are Coming* for Mr. Carrington, won't he, Archie? Yes, he must learn that tune. But he hasn't been very well lately," added the lady; "and I brought him with us to get the air."

Her husband had been looking through the grating of the large iron gate in the brick wall to the left.

"Why, here is a bench in the garden," said he. "Don't sit in the phaeton. Have you a key, Carrington?"

Carrington stepped across the pavement and tried one of his red keys in the massive lock. It turned easily, and as one wing of the gate swung open, the two men walked in. Mrs. Westbrook had stepped out of the low carriage, with her book, and carrying a red silk cushion under her arm, had followed them, leading her little boy by the hand.

"This seat looks comfortable," remarked her husband, gallantly dusting off the bench with his handkerchief while his wife, arranging the cushion to her taste, sat down, gazed curiously about her and up at the side of the closed house as it caught the sun. Yellow butterflies were fluttering across the grass-grown pavement and about the shrubbery and walls of the dilapidated stable, overgrown with luxuriant vines.

"I wish we had a garden like this, George," she said. "Think of that wisteria in May, and those box trees and flower-beds,—if they were properly cared for."

"There is something here that you don't get in a modern garden," observed Carrington with delight. "I hope you have an interesting book."

"*The Voyage of the Sunbeam.*"

"There's your sunbeam," said he as he watched her stoop down and kiss her little Highland boy,—"just beginning his voyage,"—he added, patting the child on the cheek. "Not a cloud in the sky. But he doesn't realize that yet."

Westbrook had gone out to the phaeton, and Carrington pulled the gate toward him from the street. "Now madam, we will lock you in," said he, and the lady leaned back comfortably on the bench and thanked him.

Westbrook took another look at the halter and neck-strap of

the handsome chestnut horse, then joined Carrington on the
marble steps. His red key seemed to work badly; but finally they
got the great front door open. Noticing as they entered that a
man was looking at them from across the street, they closed
and locked the door behind them.

VII

They were in a long, narrow hall with a very high ceiling, dimly
lit through the transom and a large unshuttered window overlooking the staircase beyond. Corniced doorways opened
into the pitch-darkness on the right. But, across the passage
opposite, a faint twilight penetrated several large bare rooms,
through louvered shutters. A musty smell, with a faint, sweet-
ish tinge as of decaying paint or varnish, hung about the place.
The doors were all open, and their footsteps reverberated with
loud echoes as Carrington, lighting one of his candles, led on
from room to room, into the distant kitchen, back again, and
then upstairs into the third story and garret. On the second
floor, where the shutters were all louvered and many of the
slats broken, the light was better. They saw stuccoed ceilings
and cornices, elaborate panellings, and carved marble mantel-
pieces.

"Places like this have a wonderful fascination for me," said
Carrington, looking about him with delight and holding high
his candle before one of the walled-in mirrors. "Past glories!
Think of all those who have been and might still be here.

'Lords that are gone, come back! For you our hearts still yearn;
The golden days will come again, when you return.'"

In one room, much larger than the rest, apparently overlooking the garden, where a beautiful glass chandelier with innumerable pendants twinkled in the subdued light, they had
stopped to notice the wall-paper. Panelled in blending pictures,
with floral borders,—one of the marine landscapes, with a
smoky volcano in the background,—showed a group of dancing figures under a canopy of palm-trees.

"What a delightful fancy," exclaimed Carrington; "those splendid trees—the colors—the motion—the atmosphere! Why can't they paint drop-curtains like that nowadays?"

"It looks like Captain Cook at Otahietie," said Westbrook, laughing; "only rather exaggerated. Those impossible savages with the ostrich plumes might pass for our dancing dolls. But we need more light."

He walked across to the large window and, with some effort, pushed up the long-closed sash. The shutter-hooks were easily released, but the bolt was rusted fast, and he had to hammer it out with his cane. At length the two large shutters creaked open. As the southern light filled the room, he heard his wife's voice from below, stepped forward, and leaned out of the window.

Mrs. Westbrook, still seated upon the bench, had laid down her novel and was looking up at him from under her plumed hat.

"I wish you would call Archie," said she. "He will ruin his clothes in that muddy garden."

She pointed to what seemed to be a bundle of colored rags, tied to a stick, propped in a corner of the bench at its other end.

"Look at that," she said.

"What is it?" asked Westbrook. "I can't make it out."

"It is a doll, a hideous battered-up doll that Archie has picked up in the garden. You know what curious fancies he has. He says a little girl gave it to him."

"What little girl? There is no little girl down there, is there?"

"No."

"Is there a gate open?"

"I don't know. But I wish you would call him."

Westbrook called the boy several times, who at last came out of the shrubbery, with his little stockings well blackened at the knees and without his cap.

"Archie must be a good boy," said Westbrook, "and stay with his mother. We can't take him with us again if he behaves like this."

Then, as his wife leaned down to scold and kiss her truant,

he turned from the window. Leaving it open, he crossed the room to find Carrington, who had finished his examination of the wall-paper and was standing, candle in hand, in one of the dark bedrooms across the hall.

"What's the matter over there?" he asked as Westbrook joined him.

"I was calling Archie. He is spoiling his clothes. It seems he has picked up some sort of a queer-looking bundle. Clara says it's a doll."

"That's very strange. Where did he get it?"

"He says a little girl gave it to him."

"A little girl!" exclaimed the dramatist. "What do you mean? There were no children down there."

"Why not? If there is a gate open, they would get in of course."

"Yes,—but a little girl—a little girl—with a doll! How do you account for that? If that's not the ghost, what is it?"

"Just what I thought you would say," laughed Westbrook. "But, in my opinion, it's pure chance." Whereupon, without answering his friend further, he left him in the hall and went to close the window. As he did so, his wife called him again.

She was still sitting on the bench. Archie was apparently playing with the doll, near the corner of the stable.

"I wish you would come down and let me out," said she. "I'd rather sit in the phaeton."

"Why, what's the matter?" asked Westbrook impatiently. "I thought you were very comfortable."

"So I was," she returned. "But there's somebody moving about in that stable. I'm sure of it!"

"Nonsense, Clara! But just wait a minute. We are nearly done, and coming downstairs now."

He closed the shutter and window and joined Carrington.

"Clara is getting restless," said he as he followed his friend downstairs. "If you're satisfied, let's go. It's an interesting old place, certainly; but there's nothing ghostly about it."

"The ghosts seem to be in the garden," said Carrington. "But hold on,—we must see the cellar first."

He had relit his candle and was shielding it with his hand in a draught that came up through an open door under the hall staircase.

Westbrook glanced at the front door, hesitated a moment, then followed Carrington down the dark steps.

At the basement level another door had been partly closed by a piece of carpet nailed across its top, and as Westbrook's hat fell off in passing under it, Carrington handed him the candle, and walked ahead.

He had not been long gone, and Westbrook, after some difficulty with the candle in the draught, had just found his hat, when his friend's voice rang back through the passage:

"For Heaven's sake, Westbrook, come here and look at this!"

Westbrook, candle in hand, hurried down the corridor.

The large open basement, with the shutterless windows, which he soon reached, was almost light enough to see objects distinctly. Carrington was staring at a sort of shelf, made of tables, boxes, and planks set on barrels. It followed the walls on three sides.

There, propped close together against the dingy plaster, an unaccountable array of diminutive figures,—dolls, in various dresses and of many sizes and kinds, startling, repulsive,—seemed to gaze at them from the shadows. The slanting rays of evening, through several breaks in the dimmed glass, here and there brightening the display, showed the havoc of moth and damp upon the tattered costumes, mouldy hair, and glassy-eyed faces rotted into paintless knobs.

"Good Heavens!" exclaimed Carrington, lifting up one of the larger figures, to quickly set it back again as a cloud of moths fluttered out over his arm. "Who on earth would want to put together such a damnable show as this?"

"Some janitor's trick, I suppose," said Westbrook.

"There is no janitor. If there were—— Hello! What's that?"

A door, which had apparently been standing open at the distant corner of the room, closed with a distinct bang.

"Come on," urged Westbrook. "I've seen enough of this. Haven't you?"

"Just a minute," said Carrington. "I must look at that door."

As he spoke a loud piercing outburst of screams near at hand and several times repeated, filled the whole place with reverberating terror.

"Good God, it's Clara!" shouted Westbrook as he sprung back in the direction of the steps.

"This way," said Carrington. "That door opens into the garden."

They ran to the end of the room. Carrington seized the knob and tried it; but, to his astonishment, the door that had slammed was locked. Without waiting to examine it, the two friends rushed back into the dark passage, mounted the stairs, got the front door open, then, without closing it, ran down the street to the garden gate.

VIII

By that time a crowd had collected and was looking through the bars. Carrington pushed the mob aside, then squeezed in with his friend. When he had locked the gate behind him, Westbrook was kneeling over his wife. She was stretched on the grass,—motionless. Her hat had fallen off, and her auburn hair lay loose and disheveled. She was breathing, but speechless. The delicate rose tint had left her fair face, which, by a twitching of the forehead and brow, betrayed some unuttered distress.

"We must find a doctor," said Westbrook in frightened tones as, after trying in vain to rouse her, he stood up and looked about the garden.

"But where is Archie?"

The boy was nowhere in sight. The father called several times at the top of his voice. He waited, but the child gave no sign.

"He may have gone into the stable," he said. "I'll find him. For Heaven's sake, get a doctor!"

Carrington pushed through the gate again with difficulty,

hurried across the street, found an apothecary nearby and, jotting down an address given him, hurried away.

He was gone about ten minutes. When he came back he brought with him an old and rather decrepit physician. Westbrook's haggard face was nearly as pale as that of his still-insensible wife.

"I can't find Archie," he cried in broken accents. "This is terrible. Clara has had some dreadful fright. She has been whispering. But all I can hear is that she says she saw a black man come out of the stable and carry off Archie. But she is out of her mind—of course."

The old doctor knelt down over his patient.

"There has been some terrible shock," said he, after examining her for some time. "We'd better get her away from here at once."

"But my boy!" exclaimed Westbrook with a despairing moan. "We can't leave him here!"

"I'll attend to that," said Carrington. "Archie is hiding in the stable, or may have got into the house. We'll find him. You may be sure of that."

Again they opened the gate; and while the barbarian crowd, repulsive in its greedy curiosity, pushed in, the three men carried the unconscious lady to the phaeton. When Westbrook and the doctor had driven away with her, Carrington came back to the garden. There a policeman, who had joined him, ordered out the crowd and locked the gate, after which the two men began a systematic search of the shrubbery and the ruined greenhouse. The shallow cistern, though without a floor, was dry and clean. There was no well in the garden. Apparently there had never been. In the stable, the carriage rooms, hay lofts, bins, and stalls were open and empty. Finding a key to one of the back doors of the house, Carrington gave his candle to his companion, and while the latter searched the upper floor, reëxamined the cellar and again and again reëchoed the shouts of the man upstairs; but in vain.

It had grown dark, the crowd had gone, when, baffled and discouraged, Carrington left the place with the officer, locked the garden gate, and went out into the street. As they looked up at the sinister building, he remarked to the officer that one of the upper windows was open.

"It must have blown open," said the policeman. "I didn't open it. Let it go tonight. I'll go back to the station and start things going. We will find that boy,—if he can be found."

IX

These words of the officer were all that Carrington had to console himself with that night. They cheered him for a time in his vigil as he waited at the corner, walked round and round the illuminated silent streets, and questioned the policemen as they came and went. But at last his spirits sank. The whole force had turned out. The entire district, including the deserted house across Belbridge Street, was ransacked. At Carrington's suggestion, they roused the indignant tenants in its duplicate on Bridge Street. Several times Westbrook, distracted and longing for news, left his wife and joined the searchers,—only to return to her in despair.

When morning broke, the comforting assertion of the officer had not been justified by results,—nor was it in the days and nights of fruitless search that followed. Weeks went by until at last Mrs. Westbrook, who had slowly recovered from her shock, without any clear recollection of what had happened, on the doctor's imperative order left Eastport for a short ocean voyage with her husband.

Meanwhile, the freedom of the press was demonstrated in another sensation. Dorrance had done his best to stimulate the efforts of the police, and for the sake of the suffering lady had urged her husband not to despair. So Westbrook, awaiting the predicted anonymous letters as his last chance, hoped on. But as time passed without sign of such clue, the great lawyer ceased to express a confidence he no longer felt. To him there was nothing supernatural,—nothing more than a very remarkable coincidence of place and circumstance,—in the dark deed, which he classed in the category of unpunished crimes untraced until the dying criminal defeats justice by confession on his death-bed. A last fatal blow had been struck, he declared at the reputation of the closed house, and the hopes of the owners. Nevertheless, as he told Carrington one day soon after the tragedy, while they sat together in his office, the archbishop, contrary to his advice, had had the place cleaned and repaired.

"I hope he destroyed those dolls in the cellar," said Carrington.

"I am glad you mentioned that. There were no dolls."

"No dolls!" exclaimed Carrington. "I saw them."

"You must have been mistaken, or you may have mixed up the house with No. 1013 Bridge Street."

"Really, Dorrance, this won't do," protested Carrington. "The cellar was full of dolls. Westbrook saw them; so did the policeman."

"I remember your saying so," Dorrance returned, "and I asked the policeman; but he says he never went into the cellar. The archbishop and I have just searched. There was nothing of that sort there; nor anywhere else."

Carrington stared at him, no longer surprised, but at last overcome by the feeling of fear and mystery that had so long possessed him.

"As I have said before," continued Dorrance, "the place ought to be pulled down. It is of no use to any one, and I suppose that, under the circumstances, you would hardly want to dignify it in the play you spoke of."

"I am done with the play," said Carrington. "It wasn't to be a tragedy. And I am done with the house. I never want to see or hear of it again."

THE SUNKEN CITY

I

When, in the early summer of 18—, my opportunity came, as a young mining engineer, to report upon the condemned deposits of antimony, in the Bosnian province of Borsowitz, no egotism on my part, no premature guess as to the possibilities in view, tempted me to doubt the verdict of my predecessor, the late Professor D——, who had declared that the Vars-Palanka mines were exhausted. But a series of startling discoveries, entirely my own, of facts, which had escaped him, made my fortune, when, contrary to all precedent, I found the evidence despaired of, in several volcanic cave-fissures beyond the range of the lime stone.

At this point a lack of equipment for underground work, interrupted my survey. Reluctantly compelled to abandon my camp at Jaros, I had just demolished my comfortable laboratory and had set out upon a discouraging but necessary return journey to Ragusa, when my strange narrative begins with a well-remembered incident that happened early in the afternoon of a hot day in August.

My small caravan of pack mules, led by a dragoman and two servants and headed by myself, on horseback, had left the lower hills for a succession of barren rocky ledges bordering the coast. Several minor descents had brought us to an open bridle-path, commanding an immense view of water, sky, and mountains, where, beyond a fringe of breakers interrupted by cliffs, the white walls of Ragusa, beautiful as "Tyrus in the midst of the sea," gleamed against the distant blue.

The way had grown steeper and rougher as we went on, and because the hot rocks at this point were bare of vegetation and very slippery, and because, as we approached several dangerous fissures, my sure-footed horse had twice proceeded in mountain style by holding all four feet together and sliding down the declines, I had dismounted and was leading him by the bridle. It was then, when the path rose again to cross a ledge, that I noticed two broad stripes of white paint, smeared at right angles upon the over-hanging rock.

As I passed the place, my dragoman, who followed me closely, stopped, touched the spot, and held up his whitened finger.

"Some accident, I suppose," said I, halting to examine the thing. "A white cross. No doubt for a death or murder."

The man shook his head. "No, signor," he answered. "No one would paint a white cross for murder. It is a signal. You know the smugglers."

Leaving his mule, he walked ahead, stood awhile looking down the slope, and came back again. Then, suddenly stooping, he picked up a small dark object at his feet.

The little, brown, leather-bound book that he handed me was polished with recent wear and was in bad condition. Under the loose cover, the title, a masterpiece of Venetian printing, in red and black, with the device of a flaming volcano, proved it to be an odd volume of a Latin edition of the historian Ammianus. Here and there the worn and loosened pages, as I turned them over, showed interlineations and marginal notes in fine manuscript.

"This is not the book of a smuggler," I said, "but of a scholar. Whoever painted the rocks must have lost it, and not long ago, at that."

But our time-consuming search of the neighboring rocky levels showed no further sign, and as our shouts were only mocked by empty echoes, I put the volume in my pocket and we went on.

About half-an-hour of careful descent, quickened by dangerous slides, brought us to the foot of the mountain, where a long and very ancient wall, connecting several towered gateways, overhung the great coastal road. Passing under one of these openings, I reached the hard highway, crossed it, and stopped by its outer parapet to wait for the others.

Several hundred feet below, under the cliffs, a small sailboat lay, half out of water, upon the sand. In it, beneath the loosely furled sail, flapping in the wind, I saw a large box, several packages scattered upon the seats, and then a glittering object half-hidden under a piece of black cloth.

Just as I thought I had identified this as a telescope, a tremendous noise and concussion close behind me almost threw me off my feet. I felt the horse's bridle dragged from my hand. Staggering, I turned round, to see a cloud of dust and, close upon me, a mass of moving stones. I ran for my life till the noise had stopped; then looked up. A part of the overhanging wall had crashed down upon the road, and through the blinding dust and still resounding stones and rubbish I saw the figure of a man struggling on the brink above. He wore a white shirt, and for a moment his small, wiry body, with its kicking legs, hung suspended in mid-air. He seemed to be clinging to a bush. But I had scarcely noticed this, when the outline of a bearded face swung out against the sky above him, and a down-thrust bare arm seized him and pulled him out of sight.

A moment later the man's head and shoulders appeared, leaning over the wall-top. He waved his arms in answer to my instinctive shout of sympathy, and as he did so and drew back again, I noticed that his face was splashed with blood.

Shocked and wondering, I stood for some time watching the place, still half-hidden by a cloud of dust whirled upward by the wind. Then, as I walked cautiously backward, to my surprise, the injured man suddenly came out of the nearest gateway and stepped across the road. A bloody handkerchief, tied through several long strands of yellowish hair, under the shining bald head, concealed his lower face. But I saw one side of a small turned-up nose, a very large nostril, and protruding grey eyes, almost without lashes, which flashed with audacious energy. His little sinewy arms were bare and his sandalled feet and well-formed legs, enclosed in tight-fitting trousers, were splattered with white. Just behind him came a very tall, muscular man, with broad-brimmed felt hat and a grizzled beard. He wore spectacles with very large lenses and carried a pair of field-glasses slung over his shoulder.

"I hope you are not hurt?" I inquired of the small man as he advanced.

He laid his hand upon his bandaged mouth, and his tall companion spoke for him in a deep, sonorous voice. "Nothing serious," said he as, with a laugh, he pointed to a whitened bucket that had bounded across the road. "Only a loss of material. We are painters, you see."

Until interrupted by their accident, he went on to say that he and his companion had been painting signals on the rocks. They had mounted the dangerous wall, in order to mark one of the turrets, when a part of it, probably loosened by some of the recent earth-tremors, had given way.

At this, mentioning our suspicion, I described the freshly-painted cross seen by us on the mountain above.

"Smugglers? No,—nothing so dramatic," he returned with a laugh; "we are only studying the marine mollusca along the coast, dredging, hence obliged to fix the position of the deeper shell-beds by bearings visible from a boat. Unless, however, you have gone into the matter, you would hardly know that the murex shell,—that is the purple dye made by the Romans, the royal purple——"

At this, a high-pitched mumble of comment from his wounded comrade interrupted him. But the pack-mules had passed me, and with a few final words of congratulation on the escape, I hurried down the road and soon overtook my dragoman.

This swarthy little man, Silvio by name, with grotesque, beardless face and sparkling black eyes, who, because of his origin, was known in Ragusa as the "Maltese," had caught my runaway horse, and was holding him by the bridle, when I came up.

To my comments on the sensational incident, which had thus suddenly explained the painting on the rocks, he listened without reply. Then, after I had remounted, and had ridden on for some time by his side in silence, he spoke, in a solemn, positive tone:

"This is a very unlucky place."

Under the circumstances, the remark provoked me. But my contention that the hairbreadth escape just seen had turned on good luck rather than bad, failed to convince him. He declared that the massive wall was said to be earthquake proof.

"Yet," he grumbled on, "when this gentleman steps upon it, down it comes. Below here, on the beach, the Count Seismo was standing, when a rock rolled down and broke his leg; and out beyond is Epidauro."

"What is that?" I asked.

"That, signor, is a whole city under water,—drowned in the sea."

Though, during my short stay at Ragusa, I had listened to fanciful rumors of a submarine town or city, shown to visitors by native boatmen, I had not yet heard the place named, and I questioned him as to the nature of the wonder until he had entertained me for half-an-hour with accounts of houses, towers, and streets under water, a view of which depended on the state of the tide, the time of day, and even the season of the year. He ended with a description of the discoveries of Count Seismo, just mentioned, a very rich and learned man, who had not only seen the sunken city, but had dug up wonderful things, made by the ancients, upon the beaches just below.

At this point the man's gossip was interrupted by the collision of our mules with two overloaded carts, ending in the usual exchange of drivers' oaths; after which we followed the hot and dusty road for nearly an hour in silence.

II

It was late in the afternoon when we reached the southern harbor-front of the city enclosing a quay, built, according to tradition, by Diocletian. Near a row of moored ships the way led through a gateway, above which the "Lion and Book," carved symbols of the fallen power of Venice, glowed in the western sun beams. We crossed the now deserted Fish Market, and passing under grocers' awnings, and up a steep street in the spicy air of roasting coffee, ended our journey at a dilapidated house, where, looking down from her smoke-stained kitchen, our old housekeeper welcomed us home. Mounting a stone staircase, we crossed the street by a gallery, and while the mules filed into the garden beyond, reached the once magnificent room that I had transformed into a laboratory.

The old woman opened the shutters. As the sea-breeze filled the place, I threw off my coat, and sinking into an easy chair, to wait for supper, lit a cigar and soon forgot my surroundings in an absorbing mental review of what had happened.

Compared with the immense value of my newly-found cave-buried deposits, not only of antimony but of bismuth, what cared I for difficulties, delays, the equipment of a new expedition, or the fresh concessions extorted by the avaricious governor of Borsowitz? In the roseate light of reverie, certain opening sentences of the Preliminary Report, in which, with studied modesty, I would set forth the fabulous results, so engrossed me, that I might not have noticed, at its start at least, a series of low, intermittent explosions, as of blasts at a quarry, had not a slight shaking of the floors and walls of the room lasted long enough to rouse me completely. I sprang to my feet and called Silvio.

"Is this an earthquake?" I cried, as he came out of the adjoining bedroom, while my hour glass fell from the table and rolled across the floor without breaking.

Beyond a sarcastic shifting of the mouth, the wrinkled beardless face and deep-set glittering eyes showed no emotion. "Yes," said he, with a shrug of the shoulders, "when the earth shakes here, we say, 'God bless you.' If it never shook, people would be afraid."

Surprised at the indifference of the man, I walked to the window and looked outward, expecting to see some sinister darkening of the heavens. But the sky was clear. No diabolical vapor, as from the Fisherman's bottle, in the *Thousand-and-One-Nights,* marred the fair fall of evening upon the sea that flashed in the sun, or faded under summer clouds into the distant mountain tints.

I waited for a recurrence of the noises; but nothing happened. To the southward, a moving speck on the water caught my eye, which, when focussed with a pair of field-glasses, proved to be a boat. In it, against the brightness, I could see the dark figures of two men, one of whom I made out to be grasping the shoulders of a third person, swimming in the water.

"Can you see," I asked, handing the glasses to the old servant, "what is going on there among the fishermen?"

He looked for a while, turned the instrument shoreward several times, then handed it back. "These are not fishermen, signor," said he, in his confident tone. "They are the gentlemen who painted the rocks."

As we had met only two persons, I objected: "There was a third man in the water."

"What we see in the water, signor, is not a man."

"A dog perhaps?"

"No, signor, a water-glass."

Another long look convinced me that he was right. But when I suggested that our friends were studying the shell-banks, the wizened countenance of the Maltese contracted itself into a wise smile, as he closed one eye.

"Would these gentlemen search for shells where the water is so deep?"

"What are they doing, then?"

"Looking for Epidauro," he said; and with a polite bow, as if he had proved something, left the room, while I, after several efforts with the glasses to follow further the shifts of the boatmen in the glare, finally gave up the attempt.

III

Early the next morning, in the laboratory, just as I had arranged my roasting apparatus and acids and was about to blow up the furnace, Silvio came into the room and placed a small brown object upon the table.

"In the signor's pocket," said he, as I recognized the book we had picked up on the mountain the day before. I had entirely forgotten it; but on a quick re-inspection again realized its value. Learning that its probable owners, the men we had met painting the rocks, had been seen in the Fish Market, I told the man to find their lodgings and return it as soon as possible.

After he had left the room, I spent some time in glancing through the well-worn, often-annotated pages, at the catalogue of prodigies, springs that turned hot and cold, mermaids captured by fishermen, dragons, sea-monsters, and tuneful shells, accepted as facts by the ancient writer. Then, margined by notes, among which appeared the names of Ptolemy, Mica Madio, and Apollonius Rhodius, came a grandiloquent passage describing a statue of the god Æsculapius, wrought in gold, highly valued by the Greeks, bargained for by treaty, and even fought for in several wars. I had skimmed through the account without paying much attention to it and was about closing the book, when a passage on one of the loosened pages caught my eye. I read, re-read, and then translated it as follows:

"THUS THE EPIROTES, CONTRARY TO THE ADVICE OF THE AUGURS, BROUGHT THAT WHICH THEY HAD SO NEARLY LOST TO EPIDAURUS, A CITY, THE VERY FOUNDATIONS OF WHICH ARE UNSAFE, FOR SINCE, ACCORDING TO THE ANCIENTS, THEY HAD RISEN FROM THE SEA, THEY MIGHT AT ANY TIME SINK AGAIN. AND SO INDEED IT HAPPENED, WHEN, WITHOUT ANY WARNING, AN EARTHQUAKE SUDDENLY INVADED THAT COAST, DESTROYED WHOLE CITIES, SWEPT RIVERS FROM THEIR COURSE, AND OVERTURNED MOUNTAINS WITH A TERRIFIC CRASH. THEN THE FOUNDATIONS OF THE EARTH GAVE WAY; AND EPIDAURUS WENT DOWN IN THE SEA, AND BECAUSE ITS TWENTY THOUSAND INHABITANTS HAD NO TIME TO ESCAPE, ALL PERISHED IN THE FLOOD, AT WHICH MANY GRIEVED, LESS FOR THOSE WHO SANK THAN FOR THAT WHICH SANK WITH THEM."

I remember that the first and last qualifying words of the passage impressed me at the time; but without examining or attempting to explain the text further, I called back Silvio from the adjoining bedroom.

"What is the name of the place that you tell me can be seen under the water down yonder?"

"They call it Epidauro, signor."

"Then," said I, "here is something very curious, a city actually named Epidaurus or Epidauro, described in this book, sunken, it seems, in the sea, nearly two thousand years ago. And," I added with a laugh, "this explains your story. The ancients were fond of wonders. So are we. Somebody at Ragusa reads this old book, gets the idea, and passes it on. Visitors see what they want to see, particularly under water. And the boatman gets his fee."

The Maltese showed little sympathy with this version of the matter.

"What the book tells is well enough," he remarked, "but what we see with our own eyes is better still. Let anybody who says the city is not there prove it."

"Are you sure that you ever saw anything yourself?" I asked.

"Yes, signor, a whole row of buildings with doorways and windows. Then the weather was cloudy; but the water was clear. It was winter, and," he continued, "I saw other things too; but not what they call the Virgin."

For a time he seemed unwilling to explain this last statement, but at length admitted that the object so called, which in some lights had a peculiar glitter, was not the Virgin at all, but rather, in his opinion, an idol worshipped by the ancients before the time of the Blessed Mother. Many people, including Count Seismo, had seen it, and it was because the latter did not want any one but himself to meddle with such things, that the fishermen, who were all in his pay, rarely showed the place to visitors nowadays.

The name of Count Seismo had already figured in Silvio's talk, and I listened for nearly a half-hour to further gossip as to the enormous wealth of the eccentric savant; stories of false relics detected by him, collisions with impostors, and other incidents until, ending with an account of a wonderful museum in one of the old palaces, my servant finally left the room.

IV

During several days that followed, whether because of Silvio's delay or my own carelessness, the unreturned volume of Ammianus lying on my writing table continued to remind me of my evaded duty. At last, one afternoon I determined to end my responsibility in the matter, and noting down some instructions from Silvio, left my lodgings with the book in my pocket.

Following my pencilled chart half-an-hour's walk, by way of several steep streets and a little windy square near the city wall, brought me to a gateway and then to a hillside garden, where a large gloomy building, with many windows, overlooked the sea.

Under a cloister, here and there reinforced with iron rods and near an obstructing pile of stones, I found a doorway, pulled repeatedly but in vain upon a bell-rod, and was going away, when, at a sudden sound of footsteps, I turned to see the tall, bearded man, whom I had met upon the mountain. Covered with dust, and without a hat, his grizzled hair rose high above a pair of grotesque, black-rimmed goggles, as through their luminous discs he fixed upon me a questioning stare. To my surprise, he seemed unable to remember me. So much so that I had to awkwardly recall our meeting and express more interest than I felt in his marine studies before he turned back along a flagged terrace and, by way of a window-door, led me into a very large dilapidated room, with mouldy stuccoed walls.

The place was littered with heavy packing-boxes, and at one end of a long table, covered with pasteboard trays, sat the small, wiry, red-faced, snub-nosed man of my previous acquaintance. He recognized me and, as he rose, greeted me with an exaggerated and mirthless smile. His tall friend walked across the room to an open inner-door, closed it, and, returning to the table, pointed to the collection of arranged shells. Some of these, he said, were very rare species of the murex that had not yet been classified.

At this, the small man began shifting the trays, and in the

excited talk that followed, shuffled restlessly around the table. With high-keyed outbursts and sudden stops, he continually interrupted the explanations of his tall friend. But his apish gestures and spluttered words failed to offset an impression of profound learning conveyed in his comments. I knew enough of conchology to appreciate this, admire the display with reasonable intelligence, and ask a few questions. After a time I managed to turn the talk to the subject of our former meeting.

The tall man had taken off his goggles. Before he could readjust them, I saw that he was suffering from an affection of the eyes, one of which twitched nervously. I explained the purpose of my visit, pulled the volume from my pocket, and handed it to him, when, as he took it and glanced at it, a hardly perceptible frown like a quick shadow, crossed his deeply-furrowed face.

He thanked me. They had carried the book to the mountains for reference, he explained, and had missed it not long before my coming.

"You probably looked through it," he continued, fixing his watery eyes upon me. "A remarkable book. Obsolete, of course, full of fables, but yet suggestive. There are notes on mollusca that interest my friend here, which ought to be winnowed, as it were. Did you notice several references to the murex?"

"No," said I. "But how strange that the author should corroborate the local myth of a neighboring city, called Epidaurus or Epidauro, sunk in the sea."

Again the quick-passing frown, as he interrupted me: "Unfortunately there are two other ancient cities called Epidaurus, not by the sea, but several miles inland. Diodorus and Pausanias describe them, and them only. Why talk of a third Epidaurus sinking in the sea? Ammianus has misnamed the place, or mixed up some cock-and-bull story with the real Epidaurus."

"Nevertheless," I continued, still tempted to draw out the speaker, "some city seems to have sunken here, if we are to believe the popular story of walls and towers, seen under water with a water-glass, or, as they say, at certain tides."

"Always at certain tides," he answered with a contemptuous laugh. "We have settled the Epidaurus story. We have dredged and we have used the water-glass. Whether you believe these people or not, I tell you that there is nothing here, except several angular rock-ledges, which the wonder-hunter loves to mistake for houses, towers, and God knows what. Then comes the tradition, no doubt several hundred years old, which delights the visitor and fees the boatman. All very charming, of course."

From this version of the matter,—which, notwithstanding the way in which it was expressed, entirely agreed with my view,—the discussion led back to the subject of the murex shells and finally to the reappearance of the lost purple dye, once the celebrated product of ancient Tyre. Here the gigantic speaker again yielded to his companion, who proved by a show of several scarfs and aprons that neighboring peasants had reproduced the noble color that once glorified the robes of emperors. By the time he had denounced the bad taste of certain popes,—who, he said, had supplanted this magnificent hue with a vulgar red,—I realized that it was getting late. Not too well satisfied with my reception I bade my new friends good-bye.

v

In looking back upon the fateful events which followed this curious encounter, I have often wondered what would have happened if on a certain day not long after this I had remained at home and had not, as the result of a delayed errand, chanced to breakfast that morning at a restaurant.

The place known as the Giardino d'Espana overlooked the city harbor, under a porch built, according to a mural inscription, by the soldiers of Diocletian. An immense plane tree, shading the flagstones, accounted for its name. And as I sat there, by one of the high-shuttered windows, enjoying the sea breeze and my second cup of coffee, for which the kitchen was famous, my quiet was disturbed by the behavior of several card-playing fishermen nearby.

They were gathered under the great tree around a table where a pile of coins had probably several times changed hands. The native wine had done its usual work, as the angry uproar proved, when suddenly one of the men sprang from his chair, grasped a small brown object set before him on the coins, and hurled it across the table. By a quick dodge, one of his companions escaped the missile, which, striking the trunk of the plane tree, glanced toward me, bounded over the flags, and fell at my feet. A fight followed, at which the landlord and two of the waiters rushed out, seized, and held apart the offenders.

Meanwhile, I had picked up the projectile and placed it on the table before me. A short inspection showed it to be an ancient lamp of bronze, with surmounting figures in relief, which more or less obscured the shape of the oil cup. Just as the outlines of a serpent and the fairly visible letters of an inscription caught my eye, my scrutiny was interrupted by the approach of the missile-thrower, a black haired, sunburned, ear-ringed fisherman, wearing a gayly printed and very clean shirt.

"I am sorry to disturb the signor," he said politely, cap in hand, and pointing to his adversary, who was still talking loudly to the landlord; "but that is a bad man, and he plays bad cards. You see, signor, we played for this bottle, which belongs to me. If it had hit him," he added, with a mischievous grin, "he would have remembered it."

I held it up admiringly. "This is a great curiosity," said I. "Where did you get it?"

"On the beach down that way," he answered, pointing beyond the ships. "If the Count Seismo were only here, it would bring me good money, for it is very old, signor, very old."

Although not an expert, I knew enough of antiquities to covet what looked like a treasure; so I shammed indifference, bargained in the usual way, and bought the relic so cheaply that, in order to ease my conscience, I felt obliged to nearly double its price.

By this time the other fishermen had gone, and as my cold coffee had lost its delicious flavor, I paid my bill, carefully wrapped up my prize, and returned home.

There I took my time in examining the relic. But after a few experiments had proved the danger of hastily loosening the layers of green rust, which partly hid the work of the ancient artist, I laid down my file. I had made out the figure of an old man, holding a bowl in one hand while grasping the neck of a serpent in the other.

Whether from my knowledge of mythology the thing would have suggested the god Æsculapius but for the passage recently seen in Ammianus, I hardly know, but when it further appeared that the rust had not quite hidden the outlines of a child, seated upon the back of a centaur, college memories, associating centaurs with the youth of Æsculapius, convinced me that I had not mistaken the figure, until I came to the inscription. That puzzled me. For the letters IOV, preceded by the syllable CULA, could only, I thought, refer to Jupiter,—Jove. More and more interested in the waif, I sat for a long time, baffled with the meaning of CULA, and trying to account for the snake, which as an attribute of Æsculapius rather than Jupiter, seemed to contradict the legend. The longer I looked, the more I regretted my hasty return, to its unsympathetic owners, of the book, which, if carefully read, might have solved my difficulty.

But at length I realized that I was wasting time, since reference to any Latin original would settle the matter. Remembering the neighboring library of the Franciscan monks, I placed the lamp in one of the drawers of my writing-desk and dismissed the puzzle from my thoughts.

VI

At that time an insignificant door opening upon a side street led to the famous library of the Franciscans at Ragusa, which, with its noble collection of early printed volumes, manuscripts, and *incunabula,* thrown open to the public by order of Pius VI, filled one of the upper wings of the monastery, overlooking its Byzantine cloister.

On the day of my visit the great room, where Time's censer had swung a heavy must of vellum and old leather over the work of scribe and printer, was empty. But in a small ante-chamber, whose high ceiling seemed lost in shadows, I found the librarian, a pleasant-looking, pale, broad-faced, dark-browed man, in the dress of a lay priest. He was busy with a lot of engravings that lay in piles upon a large table, several chairs and on the floor around him, and as I introduced myself and explained the purpose of my visit, his blue, deeply-fringed eyes twinkled pleasantly. He told me that there were several Latin originals and one or two translations of Ammianus in the library. But, when I described the passage which had aroused my curiosity, a look of puzzled astonishment sobered his boyish face.

"Book Nine?" said he, repeating the words. "You say you are positive of the number?"

"Perfectly," I replied, briefly describing my discovery and recent return of the book to its owners.

"In that case you may not know that you are in search of the doubtful ninth volume of the edition published by Gonelli at Venice early in the last century,—one of the 'lost books,' condemned as a fraud by scholars. Out of print, of course, and very scarce. Some years ago," he went on, after a pause, "our copy strangely disappeared, and things happened here that make me familiar, too familiar, perhaps, with the subject,—not only because my predecessor lost his place——" He stopped a moment, then added, "You speak of a serpent, Æsculapius and a serpent."

"Yes," said I, again stating my lamp difficulty.

"Some such thing," he went on, "is associated in my mind either with this book or a copy that my old friend Count Seismo has in his museum and has several times shown me. Besides, there is a very remarkable bronze serpent, which he dug up some years ago, at Monte Bergato. Yes, the doctor's symbol, Æsculapius and the Serpent, is one of his pet subjects, in some way connected with his theory of earthquakes."

He paused again; then, on my suggesting that I might perhaps be allowed to examine the volume in question, told me that, owing to the absence and supposed illness of the count, the much-admired museum referred to was closed.

"Count Seismo," he continued, "has become very sensitive of late,—absorbed in his studies, difficult to approach. Strange to say, the subject of this particular book would be very distasteful to him. In fact, certain gossip in the matter has ended in a misunderstanding between him and our abbot."

As he said this I noticed a humorous twitching about the corners of his large, expressive mouth and wide-cut nostrils.

"The result is good-bye to one of our chief patrons. Look there!" He pointed to the engravings spread before us as gifts of the highly cultivated scholar, and among them to several rare etchings of Titian, nearly all of the prints of Parmigiano, and a set of transcripts of Cherubino Alberti, which copies on copper, he explained, remained as the only record of the lost paintings of Caravaggio.

"How well I remember them," said I, recalling my own small collection of the works of Alberti, together with several of my adventures as a print collector, until my unexpected comments on the rarities, known as the "Golden Apples" and "The Spoiling of the Egyptians," so much pleased him that, when we turned again to the subject of the Ammianus, he appeared to have forgotten the difficulty of getting at the book. Declaring that he knew the count's janitor, he seemed so loath to let me give up my classic search that, ten minutes later, we were on our way to the closed museum.

As we hurried through the hot streets, I was entertained with a short biography of the eccentric scholar, whose chance visit to Ragusa many years before had been prolonged, said the priest, from month to month and year to year until it had ended in the residence of a lifetime.

"A man with a theory," he continued, "which has unfortunately made him more enemies than friends. An alleged law discovered by him by which earthquakes may be predicted as following one another at fixed times. Based, of course, on many facts, such as the upheaval here of 1650, earlier catastrophes, passages in ancient authors, and other data, partly astronomical, and mixed up recently in his talk with things, which to me, as a priest, seem forbidden and irrelevant. I don't pretend to understand it."

Walking onward, by the shady sides of streets, where ancient shiverings of the earth and Time's heavy hand had in many places left their mark, my polite guide continued his sketch, often brightened with anecdotes of the startling discoveries and immense wealth of his extraordinary friend.

But neither his eulogies nor the half-remembered gossip of Silvio prepared me for the collection shown us by a neatly-dressed janitress, in a magnificently furnished Palazzo fronting the square of St. Michael.

Through high, open windows the sunbeams glowed on fragments of mosaics worked out in lapis lazuli and yellow marble. The glass amphorae, several well-preserved helmets, lamps and braziers, would have been classed as masterpieces anywhere. I noticed at least three stone querns of hour-glass shape, one of which was ornamented with a figure of Ceres, and had admired several bronze and marble centaurs, when we stepped into a small vaulted room decorated with opalescent shells.

"There," said the librarian, pointing to an object mounted on red velvet, in a glass case, "is the count's serpent from Monte Bergato. How does it compare with your serpent, or, rather, your lamp?"

Attracted by a curious look about the head, I walked nearer the case.

"My little lamp," I replied, after a close inspection through the glass, "is a mere plaything. This seems to be a masterpiece."

"No such masterpieces for me," said he, with a mock shudder. "The thing repels me."

"But," I protested, notice the modelling of the mouth and the expression of the eyes. Would you call it good or bad, or what?"

"I would call it the Devil," he returned, laughing. "But look here." He had halted near a bookcase and had lifted from the wall a small volume hanging by a chain. "Here is the book catalogue."

He sat down and turned over the pages until his finger stopped upon the record. "And here," he added, "is the volume we want." He rose from the table and began inspecting one of the shelves.

"Why, the book is missing!" he exclaimed. "Count Seismo must have taken it away with him."

"Let it go," said I, still staring at the serpent. "I don't suppose," I continued, turning to the janitress, "that anyone but the count ever looks at the books?"

"Not often, sir," she replied; "but there was one gentleman who did,—a very tall gentleman; very tall, sir. He came here a month ago, and was more interested in the books than anything else."

"A book collector, I suppose," said the priest. "How did he get in?"

"He brought a letter from the mayor, and he stayed a long time."

"So he would, if he appreciates rarities. There are two or three manuscript Florians and a Livy here that would make him open his eyes. But it is too bad," he continued, as I followed him into another room, "that the book we want is missing. Still, you have your other volume to fall back on. Why not visit your naturalist friends and clear up your lamp difficulty?"

We had left the museum, crossed the square, and turned out of the hot sun into a narrow lane, when my friend returned to the subject.

"By the way," said he, "has it not occurred to you that this volume that you picked up on the mountain and returned to these strangers may well be the very book we are looking for?"

"Lent them by the count," I suggested.

"Hardly lent," he returned, and then paused with a knowing look and a droll attempt to suppress a smile.

"But you don't think," I exclaimed, "that a scholar of this sort would have—would have——"

"Sh-h-h!" he cautioned; "when we come to books and book collectors, who knows what to think?"

The novel suspicion had not occurred to me; yet, thus suddenly expressed, I admitted the probability as I bade my kind friend good-bye. But the doubtful Ammianus and his Æsculapius story had lost interest for me, and as literary frauds and the dishonesty of unscrupulous collectors had always repelled me, I had given up all thought of further pursuing the book or its owners before I reached home.

VII

That same day the sudden arrival of the ship bringing me my long expected instruments put an end to my days of idleness. In the several weeks that followed, devoted to my new surveys at Borsowitz, nothing happened worth noting here, except the discovery that in my absence two of the metallic fissures had been closed, as if by the rock-shifts of an earthquake,—a threatening fact that had to be accounted for in my final Report.

At last I had got through this, sold my equipment, and was waiting one morning late in August to close my ship's contract, when the familiar ring of my distant door-bell and a hasty word from Silvio were followed by the entrance,—not of the captain, but of my friend the priest. There was an anxious look on the kindly face as he held my hand.

"Here I am," said he, "for a second good-bye,—but with an apology. I have a favor to beg."

"Allow me to ask," he continued, sitting down at the disordered table, "whether you have looked up the volume of Ammianus that you returned to your scientific friends?"

As already explained, I had dropped the distasteful subject some time before. When I told him this and added that the men whom he had suspected of book-theft were still in Ragusa, he fixed his blue eyes curiously upon me.

"Our suspicions have been verified," said he.

"How?" I asked.

"By the count. He has just come back. I saw him yesterday, and heard him denounce what he calls a burglary. He has proved that the man who took the book, who is known here as Prelati, and who was seen by the janitress, is the celebrated Dr. Debaclo, professor of physics at Padua some years ago, the great Coptic scholar, discoverer of the *Sourriani Codex,* a sort of giant, too big to be mistaken. He and the Mr. Underbridge, a rich English naturalist, with whom he came here in a yacht, must be the persons you met on the mountain."

Astonished at the news, if not convinced, I asked whether

the count had been told of my book experience with these men.

"No," replied the priest. "In his present mental condition he might suspect you. He knows enough already."

"But he may be wrong," said I.

"So he may; but if not, the thing is a disgraceful outrage that ought to be righted. What we want is evidence, and what I propose, therefore, is a social visit to Debaclo. Then, if we can arrange to get a glimpse of the book, so that I can identify it, the difficulty is settled. The count can do the rest. The law acts quickly here."

The plan seemed justifiable; but, on the eve of my departure, so inconvenient that, to get rid of it, I urged immediate action. As the priest agreed with me, we set out at once on our doubtful errand.

The sun was shining brightly when we started. But by the time our uphill walk had brought us to the house we sought, it had grown prematurely dark, at the threat of a summer storm. As before, I rang the reverberating door-bell, but without result. Then, stepping through the cloistered entrance into the garden beyond, I looked out over the black-blue sea and back at the great building, where all the shutters on the terrace were closed. Painted on one of the walls, the letters of a Latin inscription, not before noticed, forming the legend of a missing sun dial, caught my eye, and while the priest walked down the terrace, I looked at it until in the half-erased words, "at even, or at midnight," I made out the ominous warning from St. Mark, 13:35, which associates the passing hours of night and dawn with the Doom of the World. As my eyes slowly followed the sentence, "at the cock-crowing, or in the morning," and fixed themselves upon the last word, *Vigilate,* Watch, the cloud had darkened the upper sky; but a broad streak on the horizon, deepening the shadows in the garden, glared luridly upon the upper windows of the house. One of the shutters rattling in the wind, or the rumblings of thunder, seemed to echo a noise of pounding from inside the building, when I heard the priest call from the cloister:

"Have you forgotten that we have no umbrellas?"

I followed him out into the street, and without waiting to make inquiries in the neighborhood or otherwise increase our chances of a wetting, we hurried down the hill, until, on reaching the lower city, the cloud, with its spectral shadows, had vanished.

Walking homeward after leaving my friend, a vague feeling of uneasiness, not reasonably accounted for by anything seen or done, might have prepared me for Silvio's bad news. The man, who had been waiting in the street, stepped forward with a gloomy shake of the head to tell me that the ship had sailed without us. The captain, he said, who had come to demand our instant embarkation, had waited a long time for me. At last he had gone off, and now the ship had gone with him.

To make sure of the evil truth, we went upstairs, and from one of the laboratory windows saw the lights of the vessel, beyond the harbor, moving westward in the windy twilight.

VIII

When, on the morning following this exasperating upset of my plans, I set out to tell my friend, the librarian, why I was still in Ragusa, my biassed reflections upon his book errand had put me out of humor. As a further reminder of my troubles, I happened to catch sight of my unlucky bronze lamp upon one of the tables. I had removed some of the rust, and in the slanting light, the bluish-green figure of the old man holding the snake stood out in clear relief. But I had taken a dislike to the thing. Suddenly remembering the librarian's aversion to serpents, and deciding to get rid of it, as a joke, by giving it to him, I wrapped it up and put it in my pocket.

Again my friend the priest welcomed me in his cool little ante-chamber. But I had scarcely told him of my mishap and listened to his sympathetic self-blame in the matter, when he turned anxiously to the subject of our last meeting. Everything had gone wrong, he said. The janitress had been talking too much, and he had found it impossible to explain our library visit to the count.

"Whether he suspects us or not, I hardly know," he went on, as we sat down at the broad table, where he had been taking notes from several open folio volumes. "But, according to the doctor, he is suffering from some kind of mental breakdown, resulting from his speculations in physics. No doubt true in part; but, to my mind, there is something else,—some dangerous discovery that he keeps secret. Still," he continued slowly, leaning back in his chair and looking up at the ceiling, "I may be wrong. What philosopher has ever accounted for the eternal conflict between the phenomena of good and evil, life and death, health and disease, which our Holy Mother Church explains through faith? When the count's talks continually associate these mysteries with so repulsive a subject as serpent worship, what are we to think, unless we suppose either that his mind is unhinged or—unless,——" his voice sinking to a lower tone, "——we are prepared to admit the doctrine of fetishism, that is to say, that there may be objects,—such, for instance, as this bronze snake of his,—which, whether by long worship or otherwise, cease to be entirely material. Our Church has at times, as you know, humored this thing; but——"

He stopped at a confused sound of footsteps and voices in the outer library, held up his hand, and listened. "How very strange," he whispered; "but, if I am not mistaken, here comes the count himself."

He hardly had time to rise to his feet, when a small, well-built, handsome man of about sixty years, elegantly dressed, and leaning on the arm of a servant, entered the room. He wore a blue velvet skullcap with a gold tassel, and the close-trimmed whitening beard and long drooping moustache darkened by contrast a purple flush upon his aquiline features,—somewhat marred, I thought, by heavy eyebrows, which notched his forehead, over rather prominent green-grey eyes. His heavily-ringed right hand grasped a long gold-headed cane and shook nervously. He bowed politely when my friend introduced me, but, declining an invitation to sit down, looked at us awhile in silence.

"Gentlemen, I am sorry to disturb you," said he, at length,

"but there is one detail of this book affair that I don't quite understand." He paused, turned to the librarian, and then, in a louder and somewhat contemptuous voice, glancing at me, continued; "what interest can this gentleman have in the matter? Why should he wish to visit my library in my absence, to examine a book of this sort? If there is any collusion here, any scheme to shield——"

At this, the librarian tried to interrupt him.

"Wait!" exclaimed the count. "That book was full of my notes—upon my next thesis—very important notes—discoveries known only to myself,——" There was a dangerous glitter in his eyes, and the purple flush on his face had deepened, as he stepped nearer. "The man who took this book,—this Debaclo,—is a plagiarist. You don't know him. I do. He has stolen these notes, and will use them to suit his villainous purpose."

The count's voice had risen to a high key. He raised his cane and brandished it in a threatening manner.

Fortunately, the librarian was equal to the quick defense necessary. In his blandest manner, he hurriedly explained my first association with the affair, my lamp difficulty, and chance knowledge of the book-borrowers. Upon which, I added a hasty account of my own, while the count limped to the window, and looking outward, with his back towards us, now and then interrupted with questions.

But, as our talk continued, something curiously suggested in the voice and manner of the enraged scholar,—rather of abstract enthusiasm absorbed in things sought for or imagined, than of egotism or vanity,—touched me with compassion. I remembered the lamp in my pocket. On a sudden impulse, I pulled it out, unwrapped it, and explaining it as the original cause of my visit to his collection, handed it to him. "If it is a rarity, count, your wonderful museum is the place for it."

Slowly, and with hesitation, he took the relic in his trembling hands and held it close to the window. When, after examining it in the light, he turned again, his troubled frown had given way to a stare of astonishment.

"Very kind of you, indeed," he faltered, in a much-subdued voice; "but before I accept this, may I ask you—if you are aware of—if you have deciphered—the inscription?"

As already narrated, my efforts to reconcile the chief figure, apparently the god Æsculapius, with the word CULA had failed. I told him so, adding that the letters IOV might stand, I thought, for some part of a dedication to Jupiter.

"I think not," he said, touching with his ringed middle finger a much corroded spot on the lid; "there is a syllable missing here, AES. You have failed to supply it; and if we prefix this and add a final P, we have ÆSCULAPIO."

I smiled at my stupidity.

"The relief upon the margin," the count went on, "a child carried in the arms of a centaur, can only mean the early education of the god, as described by Apollodorus and others. The V may stand for *venenum,* poison; venom, or for some word of minor importance. Let it go for the present.

"But," he added, holding up the lamp and turning it about in the light, "here is the serpent, never an attribute of Jupiter, but always of Æsculapius, throttled in the hand of the central figure,—a symbol of the stupendous compromise between Good and Evil, which underlies all creation.

"What is it," he continued, sitting down and placing the lamp on the palm of his left hand, "but another proof of the former worship of the God of Healing, at this place, or at the ancient city of Epidaurus, near here?—of events—things—remarkable things—I mean—the genius—the skill, lavished by the artists of antiquity on this serpent,—this Divine Benefactor, here seen in the form of an old man!"

He paused; then, speaking rather to himself than to us, continued in a whisper of suppressed emotion, "But sometimes in the full radiance of Youth."

He stopped. His eyes, showing a predominance of the whites, glared with an entranced look, as if seeing something through or beyond us. But before I could fully account for his change in manner, the color left his face, his hands fell, and the lamp rolled upon the floor. He had fainted.

His servant sprang forward and leaned affectionately over him. The librarian hurried away and came back with a basin of water. But not until this was sprinkled on the unconscious man's face and a little brandy had been poured into his mouth, did he manage to sit up and at length rise to his feet.

But his efforts to talk failed. His feeble voice murmured incoherently, until at last, yielding to the entreaties of his guardian, who had picked up the lamp and followed by the librarian, he tottered out of the room, leaving me alone, to wonder at what had happened.

A long time passed after I heard the noise of their retreating footsteps upon the outer staircase. Then, at length, the priest returned. The large, expressive eyes of my friend had a careworn look as, with a long, loud breath, he sat down.

"Your lamp," said he, "seems to have upset the count completely. By the time he had recovered his voice in the open air, I saw that, in some way, the delusion of which I have spoken,—his secret, whatever it is,—had been strongly suggested to him. Several times, I thought, he was on the point of confiding in me; but he always stopped, and I learned nothing,—except that the thing weighing upon him is in some way connected with this infernal myth of Epidaurus, if there is such a place."

He shook his head ominously and tapped his forehead.

"As a finale, he places himself on a level with the several vulgar impostors,—old women, who have been prophesying disaster here for years past. Imagine his pretending to predict how and when this jack-o'-lantern city should rise from the sea." The priest had followed me across the floor of the great library to the outer passage.

"The worst of it is," he added, as I took my leave, "that he is so certain of the event,—the earthquake,—that he dates it for next month, says he has given up his apartments, and ordered the removal of his collection to a place of safety. Of course, with his public influence, this kind of talk may end in a stampede of the inhabitants,—perhaps a riot."

IX

The librarian sent me no further word. No rumor of collision between the count and the book-borrowers reached me, and I had begun to forget my concern in the affair, when an incident, which happened one hot night late in September, again associated me with the terrible events that follow.

It was past midnight. Long after the uproar of the city below me had died away, I had been drudging at my Borsowitz correspondence, for the avaricious tyrant had heard of my detention and demanded fresh concessions. As the hot hours wore on, the heavy laboratory fumes seemed to grow intolerable; until at length, perspiring, disgusted, weary, I heard a rattle of the windows, that told of a stir in the outer air. Hoping to find relief, I laid down my pen, lit a candle, and went up the narrow steps leading to a large garret above. There I pulled open a rickety wooden shutter and scrambled out through the opening onto the adjoining top of the city wall.

To my tired eyes, the paved footway, with its ascending moonlit staircases, seemed, like Jacob's Ladder, to mount the clouds. I stood awhile in the refreshing breeze. Then, slowly following the winding wall, I walked toward the upper city, often stopping to look, now up, at the blue cloud-swept background, now down, upon the house-roofs, and below, where the waves sang their eternal song upon the crags.

Reaching presently one of the turrets near the gable of a high building, I looked down over the brink and, for a while, fancied I saw the faint moving forms of several men on the face of the cliff. But soon concluding that the rock-shadows had deceived me, I sat down in the overhang and leaned back against the stones. The west wind and watery clamor soothed me, and I had almost fallen asleep when, at a disquieting sound, unmistakably the tread of marching soldiers upon the city wall, I got quickly out of the place.

Unwilling to be arrested by the night watch, I would have hurried home, when, looking over the inner edge of the wall, I

saw the end of a ladder, just within reach, and extending downward at the angle between the house-gable and the rampart.
There was no time to be lost; so I soon climbed out of sight.

The ladder was long but steady. At its foot, I found myself
upon a pavement fronting a large house, where, stepping into
the convenient shadow, I waited until the approaching footsteps passed overhead. Then I walked forward, looked about
me, and, to my astonishment, thought I recognized the recently
visited house and garden of the naturalists.

It took some time, by the clouded light of the moon, finally
to convince myself of the fact. When I did so, and was about
to climb the ladder, suddenly one of the shuttered doorways
opened. A broad stripe of light shot out just beyond me upon
the flag stones. But as nothing followed it, I stepped back into
the shadow, and waited. Presently I heard voices and saw a glimmer close to my face. Then, moving forward a little, I looked
through a crack in the closed shutter upon the laboratory I expected to see.

Several candles were burning upon the long, shell-littered
table, beside which sat a heavily-built dark man with a short
black beard. His frowning face, thrust forward, rested upon one
arm, propped on the table, and his eyes were fixed vacantly on
the display before him. Near him stood Debaclo, whose massive shoulders half hid the opening of a door beyond, through
which a moving light in an inner room showed the corner of a
high cupboard and an expanse of white wall. Upon the plaster
near the floor a very black ragged-edged shadow presently took
the shape of a large freshly-cut hole.

Rather than make myself known, I would have left my
hiding place and climbed up the ladder; but as the light was continually moving beyond the inner door, I feared that someone
might come out upon the terrace, and waited.

For a while, Debaclo, who was apparently suffering from
the heat, wiping the perspiration from his high forehead, stood
before the man at the table. He was evidently talking ear-
nestly. But I could hear nothing distinctly until he walked to the
window before me and suddenly opened its glass casement. I

drew back, to allow the shutter to swing outward; but, as it did not, I again looked through the opening.

Whether the book affair and the consequences involved justified my taking this advantage of the man I had been looking for, I leave my critics to judge. I thought it did.

The talk had now become audible. The dark man at the table was speaking in a deliberate, critical tone: "You say you have the place fixed by buoys?"

"Yes, and by bearings painted along the coast. We can reach it at any time," replied Debaclo.

"Can you see the thing?"

"Dimly, at certain tides, with the water-glass. It is lying on its side in the mud."

"Never mind the mud. I understand that, and don't object to night work in a diving-bell like this, if the buoys are properly placed. I ought to be at anchor. Still, if you insist, I can lie to outside. But," he continued, looking the formidable men before him full in the face, and pointing to the black opening, seen through the inner door, "this crawling into the city through a hole in the wall is more than I bargained for. Suppose they arrest us. What then? In case of a lawsuit, what will be my compensation?"

Debaclo laid his hand on the man's shoulder with a laugh.

"Compensation!" he repeated. "My friend, if you knew Mr. Underbridge, you would never ask that question. He is the last man in the world to quibble over money matters. Make your own terms."

There was a box of cigars on the table. Debaclo handed one to his friend, then, lighting another at the lamp, he continued:

"As to that hole in the wall, and the city officials,—what if they do hear of it? You know them. So do I."

The listening man, who had risen from the table, sat down again, and Debaclo began pacing up and down the room. He was again without the goggles, which before had hidden the stamp of intellect upon his hawk-like face, and I saw again that his eyes were in bad condition. One of them had a peculiar fixed stare, while the other moved restlessly.

"No," he went on, after smoking awhile in silence, "the trouble is not with the authorities, nor the compensation, but with one man,—this infernal Count Seismo, a half-crazy egotist with a private museum. I have been suspecting that he must know of—of—our reasons for using a diving-bell. Now I am sure of it, for I lately managed to look into a book defaced with some of his scribblings,—a lot of rubbish about earthquakes and serpent worship,—which settles the matter. He knows everything, but has done nothing."

At this, Debaclo paused again, laid down his cigar, and stood looking directly at his companion. At length he went on:

"This man will destroy or obstruct whatever he cannot monopolize. When I attacked his earthquake theory in a pamphlet, not long ago, I made a great mistake. The result is that I have to live here under an assumed name until he finds me out. This shell-hunt of ours cannot mask things much longer. I tell you, your ship must never be seen moored near the shore,—and we must proceed by night. We cut through the wall there," he added, glancing over his shoulder, "because we had to find some way of getting in and out after dark."

At this point the talk was interrupted by the entrance of Underbridge from the other room. The restless little man carried a bottle of wine and several goblets. Placing the latter upon the table, he filled them; then, with a characteristic giggle, he lifted one to his lips.

"Let us drink to Æsculapius," said he.

While the others held up their glasses, at this singular toast, I stepped out of my hiding-place, quickly climbed to the wall-top, and hurried away.

What I had seen astonished and puzzled me. Had I misunderstood these men and their marine studies? If not, how account for their extraordinary conversation? Why the ship's captain?—with a diving-bell to study submerged shell-beds? Could this, as a piece of scientific extravagance, justify them in tunneling the city wall and working like thieves at night? The more I thought of Debaclo's fear and abuse of Count Seismo, the more likely it seemed that some desperate, long-planned rivalry had brought the two men into collision in the maritime city. Yet, after all, what had I to do with their schemes, which continually intruding upon my affairs, had become more and more repellent to me?

As I walked slowly homeward by the down-winding rampart, the moon, obscured by clouds, sank in the west. I climbed back into my lodgings, in the hope that my ramble had not been suspected by the watch,—for the unfastened shutter of my garret stood open and was rattling in the wind.

X

Two more weeks went by before I got through my exasperating negotiations with the governor of Borsowitz. All the more anxious to get away, before the tyrant should again change his mind, I had at last found my ship and taken passage. Then after a very regretful leave of the librarian, I set sail from the old harbor one fateful day early in October.

Who that has ever seen the sunrise at Ragusa, said to be peculiar to its climate, can forget the enchanting moment when dawn, first waking the breeze, gilds the waves and restores to the mountains and city their magic colors?

As I sat that morning on the ship's deck, looking eastward, no finer weather ever guaranteed an auspicious voyage. The wind was fair. The sailors sang as the sails went up. The bright sky cast no shadow on land or sea.

Then, suddenly, at about twelve miles from the coast, the day's false promise failed. With startling abruptness, the wind died out, and we met a calm, which indefinitely ended our hope of progress.

By the time morning had turned to midday, it grew very hot. The delay depressed me, and its dismal climax was reached when three men came in a rowboat, bringing a message from the governor of Borsowitz. The latter, it appeared, was in Ragusa, and wished to see me at once.

Disgusted at the selfishness and intrigue of this man, who held the fate of my expedition in his hands, I hesitated, until the boatmen grew restless, before deciding to risk my passage. At last I stepped into the boat despite the last words of the captain, who pointed to some southerly clouds and warned me that, in case of a fair wind, he must sail without me.

It was early in the afternoon, and with no breath of air, the heat was almost suffocating. I gave the sunburned boatmen each a small silver coin, and they began to row away with quick strokes, while I raised my umbrella and from under it, little thinking, gazed out for the last time at the distant rose-tinted picture of walls and towers.

The clouds pointed out by the captain, and which I watched nervously, seemed to spread and darken as we went on. Blending with them, I saw the silhouette of a ship, with furled sails; and then a moving speck, enlarging into the outlines of a row-boat. For a time this came towards us, but just as I began to hope that it might bring the governor himself, or a message of countermand, it turned away, and, to my deep disappointment, I watched the erect rowing figures fade out on the horizon.

At this, I screened my face under the umbrella, lay down in the bow of the boat and fell into an uneasy half-conscious doze.

At least a half-hour must have passed, when I suddenly awoke with a shock. A tremendous noise,—muffled explosions and a continued clearer rattling, resembling quick successive gun-volleys, completely roused me. When I sat up the sounds stopped, and the boat began to rock violently. Clutching the sides, I rose upon my knees and looked about me. At first, un-terrified, my thought was that the fantastic sight that danced before me was a freak of nightmare or sunstroke, since, beyond all reason, I saw that the mountains of the coast were moving, while the city of Ragusa, lurid against a portentous blackness, seemed to be melting into the sea.

For some instants this caprice of vision was noiseless. Then, with loud crashing reverberations, came a weird, half-musical clang of distant shrieks, shouts, and minor echoes, until, overwhelmed with amazement and terror, I knew that I was awake and a witness of the stupendous drama of earthquake. With electric haste, the sinking outline of the city faded into a mist, while a funnel-shaped cloud, as of dust or smoke, illumined by lightning flashes, swung along the horizon and, whirling rapidly upward, overspread the whole sky, turning day into night. Two of the men, lying flat in the boat, were clinging to its sides. The other, who had lost his oar, knelt down and began to pray.

I felt no wind; but the sea's surface around us appeared to have tilted out of level, as the seething water whitened in crests or moulded itself into long, parallel troughs or currents, in one of which we seemed to be rushing towards the coast. Then came a halt, followed by a series of eccentric checks. We stopped, to dart backward, turn around, or skim forward, stern first, in a new direction.

Presently, as if boiling on a gigantic scale, the surface rose in the form of a whirling dome, against which the boat clung at an extreme angle, and then upset.

I heard the cries of my companions. But a stifling cloud hid them from sight; and when this darkness partly lifted, I saw only the shoulders and staring face of one of them.

Sickened, choking, and believing that all was over, I still held on, until a violent but refreshing gust of wind dashed spray upon my face. Dark objects, enveloped in swirling masses of shadow, seemed to be rushing past me, and the boat, bottom upward, righted as it struck one of these. When we swung away again, I saw that my companion was gone.

After this, the current ran slower in a chasm between rising projections, looming higher and higher into rectangular forms. Suddenly, when I thought I recognized the black holes of house-doors and windows, the rope was dragged from my hands. My body glanced upon the sides of a large, smooth object, and my feet touched bottom.

I tried to grasp the thing I had struck, but shrank from it, while a slippery, rounded extension, which seemed to move under my hands, glided away from me. Swept headlong past overhanging masses seen dimly in the twilight, I at times gained my feet and staggered about, waist deep, in a swiftly-moving current. At length, I heard a loud gurgling noise, as of water sucked into culverts or troughs, and felt the flood around me subside.

It must have been early in the afternoon when this happened, and I have thought, from a later reckoning of the time, that for two or three hours afterwards I was unconscious. I came to my senses slowly; and when, at last, I knew that I was awake, saw that I was lying upon a muddy pavement. A cloud of moving mist hung over me, broken by fitful gleams, as if from a distant conflagration. Looking around me, I became more and more aware of a peculiar resonant grating sound, mingled with the echoes of voices, which, like a faint strain of music, increased, died away, and finally stopped.

I shouted, or tried to shout, but waited in vain to hear an answering cry. After this came a relapse into stupor. Then, suddenly, my body was violently shaken. I heard the noise of words called loudly in my ears, and saw a familiar face close to mine. The threatening features at first eluded me. Then I recognized Count Seismo. He was asking me questions, which I could not understand, in a fierce, menacing tone.

While in confused and feeble words I tried to explain my terrible experience, the frown left his face. I remember taking a drink from a flask held toward me, crawling for some distance, rising to my feet, and leaning upon him, as he led or dragged me onward. We went down a steep and muddy decline, and passed through an arch, into an open space. There, in the shifts of light, groups of columns, arches, and roofs, bright in some places and black in others, seemed to change in size and come and go as if floating in the air. Suddenly I heard the clatter of feet and sound of voices. The fog lifted and I saw that we had come upon a group of men surrounding horses harnessed to a sled, and that the sled held a large, blanketed object that was wedged therein with bags apparently stuffed with straw.

Staggering nearer, I stumbled over something lying in my way in the mud, when the count, who had caught me by the shoulder, pointed to the obstruction. It was a large saw. Near it lay several broken pieces of marble, a sledge, and a crowbar. The count stooped down, looked closely at the marble fragments, turned them over, and then seized the saw, a large framed instrument. The wood was dry and fresh, and the tightly-stretched steel blade glittered in the foggy light. He drew a knife, cut the twisted rope, wrenched the cross-bars from their sockets, and, setting his foot on the blade, bent it over until it snapped.

"Vandals!" he shouted, as he hurled the pieces away into the mist.

He was intensely excited. His arms and hands shook violently. "Get in," he said; "you must not stay here."

I took another drink from the flask, then climbed into the sledge.

"Where are we?" I asked.

"What!" he exclaimed. "Here, in an earthquake. And you do not know that—this is Epidaurus? The city has risen from the sea! Ragusa is destroyed! I have come down from the mainland. The whole sea-coast is out of water!"

He turned and hurried away, while the drivers started the horses. The sledge, sliding easily over the slippery stones, followed him. We passed dark passages between blank walls, doorways, porches, and staircases leading to higher terraces, where columns rose upon columns in the mist. I saw a multitude of loose objects, scattered in pools of water, or half-buried in sand. There were places gloomy and terrible, where a greenish-black scum covered everything. Here and there were bright openings that glowed with color.

Under the blankets that covered it, I felt the object behind me roll heavily, while two of the men, grasping the boards at my side, guided us around and over masses of loose stones and rubbish.

For a long time the count said nothing to me. He seemed to be in a desperate hurry and, despite his lameness, sprang over fallen columns, or dashed through pools of water and mud. When we came to obstructions, where fallen walls or pillars blocked the way, he ran ahead, to direct the men or pull away stones with his own hands.

Finally, seizing the edge of the sledge, and following close beside me, he spoke.

"Look!—at the treasures! Saved by salt water. Treasures! Who knows what! About to be plundered by vandals. The vandals are here."

"But this," he shouted, as he laid his hand upon the thing covered with blankets, beside me in the sledge, "—this belongs to me. The villains have mutilated it; but they shall not have it! It is mine!"

He stopped suddenly, then sprang ahead as we turned a corner and came into a wider street. There, descending a steep slope, we reached a gateway, where a sharp current of air met us, and we caught sight of the sea.

XI

The sledge had stopped at a signal from the count, who went ahead under the opening, halted, and looked beyond. As he again walked forward, I felt strong enough to get out and follow him across a beach, where a high wall faced the water. He had reached a corner and had leaned close against the stones. Then, turning, he beckoned me to his side.

"There!" he whispered. "Look! Do you see it? Do you understand now?"

The air was clear. The unobstructed view beyond showed a long reach of wall, following the beach, which here extended outward in the form of a tongue of pebbles. No human being was in sight.

Not a hundred yards from us, and close to the water's edge, a massive glittering statue, apparently made of brass, in human form, stood erect in the sand. Seen only for about six feet, from the waist upward, the figure, nearly twice the size of life, seemed to be deeply planted in the earth.

"They have left it here," he continued, in a low voice, "—left it here and gone back to finish their work. Do you see what they have done to it!"

I failed to understand him. "I see," said I, "that the statue is holding a snake. It is half-buried in the sand."

"It is not buried," he whispered fiercely; "what stands there is only the upper part. The barbarians have sawed it in half."

We had reached the figure as he spoke. Leaving me, he stepped quickly back to the corner of the wall behind us and beckoned to his men. Then, returning, he stood for a moment looking at the thing, walked around it, in quick, jerking steps, and several times drew back after reaching out his hands toward the folds of the reptile coiled upon one of the arms. At length he turned toward me. His face shone with intense excitement.

"Pausanius is wrong. Do you see?" he exclaimed. "There is no ivory."

Again I failed to grasp his meaning. "Has it been scoured?" I asked. "The brass is so yellow."

My words seemed to enrage him. "Brass!" he shouted with contempt. "This is not brass. This is gold,—solid gold!"

He paused while I stood staring at it. The figure was slightly bent. I saw the erect head of the serpent and a vase grasped in one of the hands.

"The great Æsculapius, the masterpiece of Agathocles of Paros."

His voice had failed. I scarcely heard him as I continued to look at the statue. "Two thousand years ago! Two thousand years!" He repeated the words as if talking to himself. "Since then it has risen and sunk—risen and sunk!"

Suddenly, looking directly at me, he exclaimed; "I discovered it. I traced it here. By the law of earthquakes, I knew it would rise again. I waited. The time has come. The villains have broken the marble base, with its inscription. They have dared to saw it in half—because it was too heavy to carry. Shall they rob me of it at the last moment?"

"Where are they?" I asked, still unable to comprehend his wild words.

He continued as if he had not heard me: "They have gone back to finish their damnable work—to get the other piece.— But the other piece is here. We have brought it with us in that sledge."

While he spoke, the horses dragged their burden around the corner of the wall.

Until now, unlikely as it may seem, no thought of my recent experiences had connected itself with the events of this terrible day. But as the count paused, reviving memories of the past weeks confused themselves in my mind with what I saw and heard.

"Look!" said he in a voice quivering with emotion, and pointing at the figure. "Look! Do you feel the power? The tremendous power of thought—concentrated for centuries—upon the mastery of disease."

A cloak, falling from one shoulder of the statue, partly obscured the body. The head was upturned. The short curling hair rose in ringlets. But the figure, bright and dark in spots, appeared to have been recently rubbed. For a time this conflict of light and shadow exaggerated a peculiar contorted expression of the face. Then, while I went nearer, the wrinkles of the forehead and the compressed outlines about the mouth, in the full light, brightened into a look of masterful triumph,—a beauty radiant, unearthly, indescribable, which took complete possession of me.

The count pointed across the beach with his staff. "There is their boat," he shouted, "I ought to destroy it, and put an end to the whole damnable business; but there is no time."

In the rapidly changing light, new gleams had crept upon the glorious figure. The sun was setting under fiery clouds. The wind came and went in gusts.

The men and horses stopped. The former, at a word from the count, approached the statue, leaned forward, and, clasping the body and the folds of the serpent, tried to lift it. But, though resting only on the level of its sawed-off section, as I now saw, it resisted their efforts. For some unaccountable reason, it appeared to be solidly fixed in the earth. The beach under foot was very slippery, and while the men tugged in vain, it gradually became evident that the freshly-cut base of the statue was held fast in a stratum of fine white clay. The air in the hollow casting, rarefied by the sun, had produced a resistant suction.

The count knelt down and examined the ground. He had

drawn his knife and was excavating the surface of the clay, close to the lower rim of metal, when, suddenly, a loud report, with a deafening noise as of escaping steam, shook the whole surrounding earth. He sprang to his feet, while a yellow column of vapor shot over us from just within the city wall.

I saw the horses rear and plunge. The sledge rose at one end and upset, rolling its contents upon the beach. The rope snapped, and in a moment the frightened animals, breaking away from their drivers, had disappeared around the corner of the wall.

While the men, with loud shouts, pursued by the count, followed the animals, I tried to run after the fugitives; but, in spite of the brandy I had drunk, I was too weak to go far, and soon stopped. Dazed and trembling, I watched their retreating figures grow dim in the drifting vapor.

Behind me, between the standing statue and the gateway just beyond, the sledge lay upon the sand, runners upward, and near it, among the blankets and the scattered bags of straw, the slanting sunbeams flashed upon the thing we had brought with us. I saw for the first time the sawed-off lower half of the statue, and walked toward it until, as the glowing legs and sandalled feet showed clearly, with their projecting dowel-pins, a sudden swirl of hot grey vapor hid everything from sight. I heard shouts; and then, when the cloud lifted, saw a crowd of men rapidly gathering round the prostrate figure. One of them, gigantic, grotesque in the misty light, was brandishing a pistol. It was Debaclo. Without a hat, his soaked clothes clung to his body. Under his mud-splashed forehead and crest of grizzled hair, his diabolical goggles seemed to scatter sparks of fire.

"What, signor; you here!" he roared. "Can it be possible that you would undertake to—— Oh no; not you, but the count. Don't explain the snake theory. I understand that."

Swaying with ogreish laughter, he pranced like a huge satyr around the golden legs, and kicked several bags of straw into the air. Then, at length checking himself, he walked towards the standing statue. Pointing at it with his pistol, he turned to his men.

"There is no more danger," said he. "Lift this up and put it into the boat."

The men stepped forward. Grasping the arms and neck of the thing, they pulled it and rocked it, as the two others had done, but without success.

"What's the matter? Pull!" shouted Debaclo, while Underbridge, who had been staring at me, ran forward and helped them.

Then, thrusting the pistol into his belt and joining his followers, Debaclo seized a fold of the golden cloak and pulled with all his might. The statue swayed, but stood firm.

"The thing is buried in the mud!" he exclaimed. "We must dig it out. Bring me——"

A terrific explosion drowned his further words. I felt the ground rise and rock under my feet, with a grinding noise, which, gradually increasing, charged the air with electrical terror.

The men sprang away. Debaclo drew back. A dense hot smoke again enveloped us.

As his colossal form disappeared in the cloud, I heard, despite the dreadful noise, the confused voices of the men, interrupted by his loud commands. For several seconds all was hidden. Then, in the swirl of the mist, I saw the head and shoulders of another man,—a face furious but triumphant, projecting from the vapor close to the statue. Count Seismo,—his right hand lifted high above his head, clenched his cane, and above the hissing of steam came the ring of his fierce shout:

"Too late!"

For some time I could see nothing more, until, when a cool draught had cleared the air, I saw that he had disappeared.

The group of men had scattered. Some stood knee-deep in a pool of water that now extended between them and the city wall. Another watery band, from the right, reflecting the fiery colors of the sky, had nearly reached my feet. The whole sand-bar was sinking. I saw the moored boat in the distance; and as the men, followed by Debaclo and Underbridge, started to wade toward it, I ran after them.

Splashing through the water, I reached the boat in time to jump in, just as Debaclo drew a knife and cut the rope.

Four of the men picked up oars and tried to row. But they pulled at first with wild, irregular strokes. Debaclo, in the stern, held the short wooden tiller in one hand.

The bow had veered toward the beach, and I expected to see it turn seaward; but Debaclo steered steadily in the direction of the erect shining figure.

For a time, though the men rowed furiously, we could have made no progress; for the beach ahead, which had rapidly narrowed, seemed to be retiring from us. Glittering sheets of water had reached the walls of the city in several places. Now they crept close around the statue. One of the men stopped rowing.

"For the love of our Holy Mother, signor," he cried, standing up, "turn us around!"

Debaclo pointed his pistol at the speaker. "Sit down, you coward!" he shouted.

The man obeyed and began to pull again; but a strong current was driving us backwards, in spite of the rowers.

Now entirely surrounded by water, the figure, illumed in the sunset, was rapidly sinking. For a while, whether because of my slightly changing angle of vision or the gathering shadows, the face of the god seemed to distort itself into a repulsive caricature,—a frightful yellow mask that rose and fell upon the waves. But as the rising tide submerged the head and folds of the serpent, the features recovered their expression of triumphant matchless beauty. As I looked, I felt an irresistible longing, overwhelming all other conscious impressions,—then a dizziness. In the gathering darkness, the heavens and sea seemed to revolve and blend together in magnificent colors, till suddenly the upturned golden head, flashing back the last beams of day, blazed like a ball of fire, and I lost consciousness.

XII

I remember nothing of what followed this, but infer a long period of dreamless sleep. I was awakened by a severe shock, followed by blows. Shivering with cold, I saw by the dim light of a swinging lantern that I had fallen from a berth in the small cabin of a ship and was rolling in the water flooding its floor. The door was open. I could see daylight in a passage outside and hear a noise of distant shouting.

With difficulty I climbed back into the berth and, chilled and trembling, held fast to an angle of the panelling, as the water rushed in and out the open door. Then, after a while, when the pitching slowly ceased, I climbed down and, wading outward along the passage, got up a stairway and into the bright sunlight.

The deck of the yacht upon which I looked out was covered with wreckage, which several sailors were busy in clearing away. We lay in comparatively smooth water, in a small harbor, land-locked with cliffs, and had escaped, I learned, a tremendous storm, by several lucky chances and the skill of one of the Greek sailors. At a critical moment he had cut loose the lashings of a diving-bell that had nearly swamped us.

Several boats were rowing about us. In one of them I saw Debaclo, Underbridge, and the owner of the lost apparatus, who presently came on board, gave me brandy and dry clothes, and soon after landed me in the neighboring town. Two days later they left me, to wait a fortnight in the place, and finally to join my own ship at the Port of L——.

In the few conversations I had with my rescuers I learned little more than they chose to tell me directly of several accidents that had delayed too long Debaclo's clever use of the diving-bell. Whether his unscrupulous study of the count's notes had prepared him for the earthquake, I could not learn, though it appeared that, when held by a contrary wind in full view of the risen city, he had at once fearlessly taken advantage of the situation. In spite of his jealousy, he admitted that events had proved the count's theory. But he gave no hint of the process, whether of original research or of plagiarism, that had led him to his own discovery of the lost statue.

It is well known that during the convulsion, which lasted several days, and before the treasure-hunters had dared invade the dangerous place, the whole new coastal area sank again; but slowly, at intervals, and, luckily, without the disaster of a tidal-wave.

The palace of the count, at Ragusa, though destroyed, had not caught fire. Hence the latter, who had previously removed most of his collection, saved the rest by digging later in the ruins. But the narrow escape of my friend, the librarian, who was wounded in trying to rescue a crippled monk, was a great and pleasing surprise to me. Otherwise, the effects of the terrible earthquake of 18— upon the city and the surrounding country are well known.

Rather than overload my story with technicalities, I have omitted the details of the remarkable theory of *The Procession of Earthquakes,* which, as Count Seismo's original incentive, might better have accounted for his researches. For this, I refer the reader to the full text of his noted thesis, in the published *Proceedings of the Academy of Sciences* of the University of B——.

I have nothing more to say, except that my own difficulties and dangers ended when the preservation of all my specimens, notes, and apparatus, enabled me to prove to the Consolidated Mining Companies of L—— the complete success of my labors at Borsowitz.

THE WELL OF MONTE CORBO

I

My association with the following singular incidents began during one of the gay but momentous summers of the late sixties, when awaiting examination for my Doctor's degree at Bonn, I had taken a short holiday. It was at Frankfort-on-the-Main, where one afternoon, in the smoking room of the then newly built Hotel Solms, I had been glancing through the visitors' list in the last copy of Galignani. But it was getting too dark to read, and I was about to drop the newspaper on the disordered writing table, when my eye caught the noted name of my old friend, Theodoric Barron.

Knowing the eccentric habits which had grown upon him with his fame, and the peculiar fancy for secluded research, which, in spite of his great wealth, and convivial tastes, had made him a recluse, I was not surprised to learn that he had not been heard of at the hotel, and soon realized that it would be a difficult matter to find him. So it proved next day, when after a long search, I ran him down at last in a very picturesque, but decidedly second class inn, in one of the distant suburbs.

He greeted me warmly, but seemed surprised that I had discovered him in what he described as a rare relic of the middle ages, a house, built in the time of Charles the Bold, where in sumptuous style, he had cleaned up one of the upper wings, to establish himself in a rambling suite of high-windowed rooms overlooking the river.

He pointed through an open casement at some distant misty steeples, marking, he said, the birthplace of Offenbach, and in the agreeable talk which followed, told me that the famous composer, on a recent visit, had so admired the mediæval details around us, that he intended to reproduce them in one of his opera-settings.

173

The great vaulted-gallery was still in disorder, and as we talked on of our summer plans, I entertained myself looking about the floor and table at piles of books and maps, half unpacked surveying instruments, and finally at a display of unframed prints roughly tacked upon the whitewashed walls. Among these, but under glass, as if of special importance, Barron called my attention to a quite small pen and ink sketch in a flat black frame.

"Do you recognize it?" he asked, smiling.

A quick glance identified a piece of my own handiwork,—a mountainous landscape with a castle, copied from an old wood cut, given him on leaving college.

"Good Heavens, my boy!" I exclaimed, surprised, and flattered by the associations evoked. "Is it Auld Lang Syne, or is it Art?"

Under the glitter of his heavy-rimmed glasses, I saw a well remembered glow in the restless grey eyes.

"Both," said he. "The picture affects me strangely. That castle, and those white mountains under the cloud, seem to suggest something that I can't account for, or that I may have dreamt of. Besides, mediæval fortification is my subject just now. Of course you remember the castle."

"Every line of it," said I, "particularly as my first sketch was condemned, and I had to copy the picture twice."

I recalled facts which he might have known, that our college instructor had photographed an unnamed print, ordered the art-class to copy the scissored-out background, and then, as a clever means of furthering his instruction, expected us to find the original worked from in the library print-room. On taking my degree at the time, I had failed to do this, hence I had never been able to account for the origin of my drawing.

"My friend, Doctor Lysander, has identified it as a Durer," said Barron. "He has a theory that the castle still exists."

"Where?" I asked with surprise.

"Somewhere in Switzerland. He connects it with his Durer letters, which you may have heard of."

I was familiar with some of Lysander's researches, notably his sumptuous folios on the mediæval discoveries at Burg Sonnenburg, but as I knew nothing of the letters in question, Barron told me that the versatile scholar, a few months before, had found in one of the Ducal libraries, a correspondence of the great painter, which was making an unfortunate sensation at the time. In a copy he had seen of one of the letters, an improbable adventure was described or suggested, which together with the authenticity of the documents, had stirred up a bitter controversy. Several noted critics had attacked the Doctor's judgment, if not his morals.

"You mean that they accuse him of fabricating the manuscripts?"

"Sh! Sh!" said Barron. "I think I hear him coming."

The famous scholar, he hastily told me, who was spending the summer in the Taurus, had been passing the day with him, and, when I called, had just gone out to inspect some newly dug cellars, exposing traces of a Roman road.

A moment later a noise of footsteps in the corridor outside was followed by the entrance of a very erect heavily built man in a close-buttoned yellow, double-breasted coat, with huge globular forehead, beetling face, and dagger like beard, balanced by a monkish back-shelf of tonsured hair. He had come to take leave of his host. On being introduced to me, while I politely avoided staring at his grotesque profile, he picked up a cloak thrown over the back of one of the chairs, and had turned to the door, when Barron stopped him.

"Wait," said our host. "I have been telling my friend here about this castle that you say still exists." He lifted my sketch from its hook, brought it to the table, and stood it up against a pile of books.

The Doctor laid down his heavily-felted, broad-brimmed hat and a pair of silver plated field glasses, to listen to Barron's hurried account of my association with the print, then fixed his frog-like browless eyes upon me.

"You have cut out the background of Durer's Visitation," said he, in a deep resonant voice. "Quite a coincidence considering its bearing on my discovery of a batch of Durer's letters, in which this castle is not named, but so well described, that I have been able to trace it."

"To Switzerland, I understand," said I.

"Yes," returned the Doctor sternly. "But I prefer not to name the place."

"My friend speaks of an adventure connected with it," I remarked.

The Doctor frowned. "All in the letters," said he. "There are certain details that should be proved first, and talked about afterward. Still, I will tell you that Durer, while sketching the castle with a friend, whose name is not mentioned, is attacked by robbers. They escape. He throws a valuable church relic or treasure for safety into a well, the castle well, of course."

"Does he describe the relic?" I asked.

"Unfortunately there is a break in the manuscript just there;

several pages have been torn away, but enough remains to make certain that his castaway, whatever it was, had been rescued from a church burned by the Hussites, and was said to have belonged to Saint John the Baptist. A Church myth, no doubt, but judging from Durer's allusions, it must have been a remarkable thing, a very remarkable thing."

"He recovers it, of course," said I.

"No, according to the letters, he never gets back to the place. Therefore, the chances are a hundred to one that it still exists."

He paused and glared triumphantly at me, while as I noticed an angry twitching of the cavernous nostrils, Barron nudged me with his foot.

"I expect to prove the fact in a way that will end this scandalous controversy, which you have no doubt heard of. Winters and his friends will have to apologize. If not——"

He rose excitedly from his chair, picked up his hat and field glasses, and without listening to Barron, who again tried to stop him, strode to the door.

"Let the dogs bark," he cried, turning upon us with a contemptuous sweep of the powerful arm. "The caravan moves on."

Barron smiled, and then shook his head. "Too bad," said he, after the resounding footsteps had died away outside. "A man you can't advise, much less contradict. This is the third or fourth of his notorious wrangles, all the more deplorable when they end in reversions to his old duelling habits at Jena. Did you notice the face-scars?"

"He doesn't look like a man to be trifled with," said I. "But do you believe all this?"

"Not half of it," laughed Barron. "The Doctor has exaggerated the meaning of his letters, which show that Durer has been impressed with a church legend, nothing more. Your castle in the air has nothing to do with it. Durer was not a realist. To my mind the whole landscape you have sketched is imaginary, as far off the earth as the cloud that floats over it."

But as we talked on of the career and appearance of his gigantic friend, Barron's criticisms yielded to admiration. The

Doctor's discoveries, he declared, rescued texts of the Thousand and One Nights mislaid by Galland, decipherments of Hittite inscriptions, excavations at Carthage and Italica, far outweighed his mistakes.

"Look there," he continued, pointing down the flashing river. "Near that fringe of trees he has just unearthed one of the citadels of the 22d Roman Legion. Cartloads of bricks stamped 'Primigenia Pia Fidelis,' prove his theory of bridge construction in the time of Hadrian. Quite enough to offset his meddling with the Agram Manuscript."

As my knowledge of the Agram Manuscript was very indefinite, a criticism of the Doctor's ill judged intrusion upon the great Museum controversy followed, until by the time I had listened to a witty description of the disputed Etruscan text, inscribed on the shroud of a mummy, the morning had gone, whereupon regretting my next day's departure from Frankfort, I bade my old friend good-bye.

II

During two succeeding months at Bonn, ending in a course of lectures on Roman Jurisprudence at Vienna, occasional rumors of the Durer controversy above mentioned, had reminded me of the Doctor and Barron, but I had supposed that the latter was too much absorbed in his researches, or distracted by the proximity of his rival, to write me the letter he had promised, when my next unexpected meeting with him occurred as follows:

It was on a visit to the Albertina, one balmy afternoon. I had paused at the entrance, half tempted by breeze-blown waltz-strains from the neighboring Volksgarten, to give up my proposed hour in the print room, when turning aside to avoid a departing throng of sightseers, I almost ran into my friend at the foot of one of the gallery staircases.

"Upon my word," he exclaimed, with a characteristic cane-flourish. "This is very curious. Come back here, I have something to show you."

Without explaining himself, he sprang up the marble stairs,

and I followed him wonderingly into the long cross-lit narrow gallery, where an attendant, carrying a heavy portfolio, turned at his abrupt call, and placed the volume on one of the small tables near an open window. Barron stepped forward into the bright light. Pointing to the word Titian in gilt letters stamped upon the book cover, he began a hasty shuffle through its carefully mounted prints, to stop suddenly.

"What do you think of that?" he asked, when one of the heavy cardboard pages fell open and my eye caught the familiar outline of my castle sketch. It had a confused look. Apart from its novel foreground, the familiar hillside trees had shifted their position. The details of the castle had been multiplied. The drawing was coarse. But the mountains though turned wrong way about, and the great white cloud were unmistakable. I glanced at the margin to find that the title, if it ever had one, had been cut away.

"My woodcut turned inside out," I exclaimed. "Durer never could have done this."

"No. They ascribe it to Titian. But no matter. Look! here."

He hurried to a neighboring table, where, on following him, I saw in another open portfolio, my version of the landscape just seen, clearly showing one of Durer's monogram labels lying in the foreground. Picking up the heavy volume, Barron carried it back to the table we had just left, and placed the two open books side by side.

Puzzled, but too familiar with the impressive details to be mistaken, I examined both prints closely, to see that the foregrounds, in the Titian, a strangely composed "Flight into Egypt," in the Durer, a prominent group of figures near the doorway of a high building, differed entirely, but that the portentous background, allowing for variations in treatment, had been undoubtedly reproduced.

"The Doctor must see this," I exclaimed. "It throws a new light on his Durer letters. Durer, as he told us, had an unnamed companion. Why not Titian? This landscape is not in the air, as you thought. If Durer and Titian both sketched it, it must have existed. If so, the Doctor may find the castle."

"I hope he may," said Barron. "But wait, here comes an authority on the subject."

While I stood looking at the volumes, Barron went to the desk, and a few moments later, the keeper, who had just come in, a very polite, slender, spectacled man, in a green-faced tyrolese jacket, was leaning over the prints with his magnifying glass.

"Strange," said he. "Very strange, indeed. I am quite familiar with the Durer, but this other print has escaped me. Some vandal has cut away its title. Nevertheless, one of my predecessors has ascribed it to Titian. Or rather, as Titian never made woodcuts, to some engraver who has reproduced one of Titian's sketches. Marc Antonio Raimondi perhaps. But no! Here we have it." He paused to place his forefinger on the engraver's monogram. "F D," said he, "with a little cross stands for Francesco Denanto, one of Titian's scholars, and interpreters in wood. No matter, if Titian produced the original, the duplication of background proves either that he has copied Durer, or vice versa, more probably that both artists have sketched the same landscape."

"From different points of view," I remarked.

"But at the same time," added Barron, "while the cloud retained its shape."

"Quite possible," said the curator. "I have seen these tremendous clouds hang overhead for hours, particularly in the mountains."

"The mountains suggest Switzerland," said I.

"Impossible," objected the curator. "Nothing is more certain than that Titian never visited Switzerland. If the thing happened at all it happened in Italy."

"Have you any proof of that?" asked Barron, who had been listening intently.

"During Durer's visit to Venice in 1506, we can infer that he met Titian. They were rivals, no doubt. Still, according to Professor Winters, certain documents, just found at the Doges Palace Library, prove a temporary companionship."

Barron, who had turned away from us, as if distracted by some sudden thought, started to say something, and stopped. Then, as the chimes of a distant church struck five, he pulled out his watch. "Unfortunately I must go," said he, whereupon, explaining that he was living in one of the southern suburbs, near Ober Sanct Veit, and had to catch a train, he hurriedly left us.

Without waiting longer in the print room, the curator led me into a small bookcased cabinet built, like the study of Rembrandt's Philosopher, under an overwhelming flight of newel stairs, where, following his interesting sketch of the famous collection in his charge, our talk returned to Barron's singular discovery.

"I am sorry," said I, "that my friend got off without telling you a curious story about this castle. Did you ever hear that Durer while escaping there from some robbers, threw a church relic of some sort for safety into a well?"

A politely repressed laugh met my question.

"Doctor Lysander's treasure story. A church legend foolishly mixed up with his Durer letters and passed on to your friend." The curator paused, and then in a somewhat stern voice continued: "But we have heard too much of these letters. They have been discredited by half a dozen critics, notably by Professor Winters, the well known Durer scholar. I haven't followed the controversy, but someone has paid dearly for a patchwork of genuine fragments and forgeries, with an authentic signature."

"You don't suspect the Doctor, I hope," said I.

"There are whispers, of course. But no! No! I know him too well for that, a genius, exasperating, no doubt. But the soul of honour; his appearance is against him. Have you ever met him? A kind of modern Goliath."

He stopped to pull open the upper-wing of a large sealed plate glass window, and as echoes from the Volksgarten again caught my ear, we forgot our subject to listen a while to the magic strains of Strauss, which, according to the curator, had filled the city with visitors, and the Albertina with more print lovers than ever. "Some of them, oddly enough," he added, "in search of this very picture of Durer's, we are talking about. You may not know that a reproduction has appeared in 'Ruskin's Modern Painters,' in which the English Professor sees fit to cut out the great cloud."

"How does he justify that?" I asked.

"He doesn't justify it, he simply saws off the block."

He walked to a bookcase, pulled out a volume, and by help of a previously inserted marker, opened it upon the illustration in question—"no doubt to suit one of his atmospheric theories," he muttered.

After examining the mutilated masterpiece for some time, while listening to the curator's angry comments, it suddenly occurred to me that Titian had reversed the cloud. Whereupon, as the point seemed important, if both artists had worked together, we went back into the print room to satisfy our doubts on the subject, only to find the portfolio gone, whereupon, as

the attendant was closing the gallery, I took leave of my polite guide.

In the several days which followed this, I saw and heard nothing of Barron. I had forgotten to get his address, and as I could learn nothing of him at the hotels, and an afternoon search among the shady villas of Ober Sanct Veit brought no clue, I had to leave Vienna with no more news of him than that contained in a note found one morning in the hotel letter box.

"You will be interested to learn," it read, "that I have a surprise in store for Doctor Lysander. I have discovered his castle, not to mention his treasure. But of that, more later, when I prove my case. With apologies for leaving Vienna without seeing you,—Yours sincerely,

Th. Barron."

For several days the laconic message, postmarked Venice,

puzzled and provoked me, but at last tired of inventing ground-less theories to explain it, I dismissed the subject from my thoughts.

III

According to my holiday plans, I should have spent the rest of the summer in the Carpathians. But reports of floods blocking travel in Northern Hungary had turned me to Italy. Following the tourist beaten path to Innspruck via Munich and Salzburg, I had crossed the Brenner, and after several aimless halts, at last, lured by guide book eulogies of the Dolomites, had established myself, for a week's stay, in one of the new hotels at the little village of Monte Corbo.

As it was not then generally known that the mountain town had been the birthplace of Titian, the note I found in the guide book to that effect, was a pleasant surprise to me. It suggested, of course, my meeting with Barron, and his print discovery, but neither his letter, or anything that had occurred meanwhile, prepared me for what happened on the evening of my arrival. It was in the kitchen of the alleged birthplace of the great Venetian artist, where, just as I had finished an inspection of the overhanging hood and craned andirons of its altar-like fireplaces, I turned at the touch of his hand upon my shoulder.

He looked pale and tired. His clothes were in bad condition, and his handsome face blotched by two disfiguring patches of black court-plaster.

"You knew I was here, of course," he said despondently, after our greeting.

I waited until he spoke again.

"I mean you must have heard of my doings up at the Ruins? Don't laugh," said he, "I have just cleaned out the castle well."

"No use telling you why," he continued. "I didn't believe the Doctor's treasure story, you know, till I found the Titian sketch. Then I changed my mind."

"You were in Venice?" said I.

"Yes, and was shown the Winters' manuscripts. They gave me my clue."

"Why did you come to Monte Corbo?" I asked.

"Because I happened to know that Titian was born at Monte Corbo. If, as the documents proved, Titian and Durer left Venice on a sketching expedition, they would have visited the birthplace of the great Venetian, of course. The Doctor knew nothing of that."

"Did you bring him with you?"

"No! He had gone to Switzerland to identify the wrong castle. I came here."

"But you don't mean to say that you found the treasure?"

"The treasure has disappeared. Durer may have recovered it, or it may be a myth."

"Then you found nothing?"

"Not exactly nothing. I have discovered your landscape."

We had left the unique little kitchen, and were standing in the windswept street. The fantastic pinnacles of Monte Crystallo had begun to blaze in the glow of sunset. Glancing at his watch, Barron declared that we still had half an hour of sunlight.

"Come on," said he. "You must see the place."

Hurrying through the village, we soon reached the great mountain road, and turned down the hill in full view of the Lombard Plain. As our footsteps echoed on the hard highway, our talk turned to the great Venetian painter, who though a city dweller, had yet charmed the world with landscapes.

"What a view!" exclaimed Barron. "How could he forget it? Italy seen from the clouds!"

"It lured Hannibal, when Rome was in danger," said I. "You remember the story."

"Hannibal saw it farther to the West. But wait. There are two views. We are looking in the wrong direction." Barron pointed over his shoulder at some rocks that shut off the upward distance.

At length we stopped where the road at a sharp downward bend escaped a high bluff.

"Now look," said my guide.

Against the darkening sky, Monte Crystallo, seen at a new angle, had taken a new shape. Under the towering mountain wall, the foothill in the mid distance, with its overhanging crag, till now invisible, stood out in unmistakable silhouette.

"Sit down," Barron said. "You are within a few feet of where Durer sat nearly four hundred years ago."

For a long time I looked, too much amazed at the gorgeously colored realization of my sketch, to wonder at its discovery.

"Those rock-pinnacles come to life," I exclaimed, "overwhelm me. Is there anything else like this in Europe?"

"I doubt it," said Barron. "The Dolomites seem to converge here. Titian must have known the place and shown it to Durer. But Durer's sketch records a novelty which until then he could only have dreamt of. It has given me an idea. Have you ever noticed a striking characteristic in early Flemish art, rocky-pinnacles, mountain-fantasies, grotesque, unbelievable, yet continually produced by painters in a country where no such things existed." He paused. "But that's not the point," he added gloomily. "I came here to find the Doctor's treasure."

While we talked on, it had begun to grow dark. The colours had slowly faded out of the great picture, before I noticed that an important detail of my sketch was missing.

"Where is the castle?" I asked.

"Destroyed long ago," returned my friend. "Half the houses in Monte Corbo are built of its stones. No matter. You can see the foundations, and if you choose, look into that infernal well and imagine the rest. I have made a fool of myself."

"You must have found the well very deep," said I.

"On the contrary, shallow. It had gone dry, and was full of rubbish."

As the mountain shadows deepened about us on our uphill walk, he said he had found blacksmith tools, chains, remains of buckets, and a cartload of potsherds and stamped bricks. Nothing else to repay him for an immense amount of trouble with the village authorities, including a narrow escape from a law suit.

"If I stay here, I shall be arrested," he muttered, after declaring his determination to leave the unlucky place next day.

IV

The windy but bright morning following Barron's early departure, found me in the castle-ruins, for a long time looking only outward and upward, so absorbed by the familiar cloud-swept panorama, that I had forgotten the purpose of my climb, until at last a sound of voices brought me to a heap of rubbish marking the site of his fruitless excavation. Two peasants, his employees, with a cart and a gigantic pair of white oxen were engaged in removing the debris. I glanced admiringly at the noble animals, then at a windlass standing near, and at last down the well, while I carelessly listened to their account of the exhausting work. Finally, to satisfy my curiosity, I traced the still visible outcrops of castle foundation that Barron had spoken of. The massive walls, obscured by grass and bushes, had led me by several dangerous precipices, to a neighboring clump of trees, and I thought I had pretty well made out the ground-plan of the demolished fortress, when it suddenly grew dark, and I felt a few drops of rain. I looked up half expecting to see Durer's great cloud in process of transformation. But nothing so spectacular broke the misty blur, and I was about to leave the place, when I forgot the weather at sight of something which caused me to kneel down for a closer look at the hard foothold. What I saw was the abnormal growth of a young oak, which, without sign of adjacent earth, had forced its way upward through a crack in the bare ledge. The tree had split the stone by growing through an artificial circular hole, just beyond which a second round, clean-cut orifice, about four inches in diameter, perforated the level rock.

After pushing my cane down the latter opening until its ferrule penetrated soft earth, I got up, and discovered to my surprise on scraping aside some leaves and brushwood, that the split rock was not part of the solid ledge, but formed a fragment of a thin loose circular slab, about eight feet in diameter.

I looked at the place in the failing light, until I finally grasped its meaning. Then finding a small stone, and again kneeling down, I dropped it through the crack and listened. An expected splash and deep hollow reverberation settled the matter. I sprang up in the fast-falling rain, got out of the bushes, and hurried back to the peasants.

"Did Mr. Barron see the castle well?" I asked excitedly.

"This is the well, Signor," said one of the men, a small, very muscular peasant in a red shirt, with clear cut classic features and close curled hair, who, heedless of the rain, had been looking up at the clouds. "Here is what we brought up," said he, "the gentleman went over it with that sieve."

I glanced again down the opening, at the rubbish pile, and then at the man, until my uncontrollable laugh at the absurdity of the situation, brought a sudden glare of rage into his piercing close-set black eyes.

"You have been working at the wrong place," I cried. "This is the castle cistern."

I walked to the windlass with its short roped bucket.

"Have you no more rope?" I asked.

The scowling man pointed to a large loose coil in the bushes, and then, with his comrade, incredulously followed me back to the split rock. A few moments later, after dropping several stones down the crack, both men were staring with amazement and final conviction at my discovery.

"What did you do all this digging for?" was my next question, as the sun began to shine again.

The tall peasant had taken off his steaming coat and thrown it down upon the rock. "The gentleman said it was a statue made of gold. But he was mistaken about that," said he. "We found no kind of statue, Sir."

"The statue is down this well," I cried. "Will you help me to get it out?"

Before I had explained my already formulated plan to the assenting men, the large peasant had left us for the oxen, and as we only had to deal with half of the stone lid, the two animals when brought up and chained thereto, through the hole

I had noticed, soon dragged it out of the way. Half an hour later, the windlass was in place, the bucket freshly roped, and the small man had descended nearly one hundred feet into the long unbroken darkness. After many shouts to his listening comrade, and cautious haltings by the latter, who continually locked the crank, I could see him light a candle, and as it illumined the clean cut cylindrical walls, and caught the subterranean glitter below him, could hear the rattle of his dredge and thumping of objects thrown into the bucket. I was lying flat for my down-look, and was guessing at the depth of the flashing rock-enclosed pool, when suddenly the plucky little man, to my surprise, got over the side of the bucket, and dropped into the water. For a while he splashed, shuffled and ducked about shoulder deep, while several times, interrupting the reverberations, I heard a tinkling sound, as if he might be jingling a chain.

At last he stopped and looked up.

"Niente Signor," he shouted, and then, as I faintly made out in the glimmer, clambered back into the bucket.

A later call to his companion at the windlass, soon brought him to the surface. He stepped out upon the rock, where after a loud side slapping of his numbed hands, I complimented him warmly on his exploit.

He pointed to the bucket, from which, still soaked and glittering from their bath of centuries, I pulled out, one by one, several battered bricks, two or three fragments of stone and pottery, and the rusted head of a large iron claw hammer.

"This is all, Signor," said he.

"But you found a chain," said I. "I heard you jingle it."

"No, Signor, that was the grapnel. There was no chain."

Not greatly surprised at the result, yet still disappointed, I watched the white oxen pull back the stone, paid the men the price they asked, and left the place.

v

A week had passed, during which several verifications of my landscape, and another look at the castle ruins, had exhausted my interest in Monte Corbo, when on the morning fixed for my departure, an incident happened which suddenly gave a new meaning to my visit.

I had just got through breakfast at the hotel, and had gone upstairs to finish packing, when a knock at my bedroom door, and a word from a ceremonious Austrian waiter, was followed by the appearance of a heavily-built, neatly-dressed peasant, whom I recognized as my tall helper at the castle well.

The man seemed embarrassed. Holding his hat in one hand, and a small paper-wrapped bundle in the other, he looked awkwardly around the room and out the window. At length, sitting down on the chair I offered him, after several long breaths, he spoke.

"The Signor was not satisfied with our work the other day?"

"Why not?" said I. "I paid you for it."

"But we found nothing, Signor."

Prepared for some ingenious scheme of extortion, I looked suspiciously at the rugged sunburned face. "Tell me what you want," I asked sharply.

The man laid his hat on the floor, walked solemnly to the table, and placed his package on its cloth.

"It is what we found in the well, Sir."

Pulling a clasp-knife out of his pocket, he cut the string, and after unwrapping the paper, slowly unwound a gaily printed chintz handkerchief, revealing a globular metallic object resembling at first sight the head of a reptile. Above a long mouth-like slit ending in circular enlargements, flashed two deep red stones close set under uptwisted tail-like projections.

I stared at the semicircular handle formed by these loops, and then again at the gleaming stones which I took to represent eyes, until as the grotesque extravagance of the modelling gradually disclosed the head and body of a frog or a fish, its astounding meaning flashed upon me.

I sprang from my chair, stepped nearer and leaned over the table.

"You say you found this in the well?" I exclaimed.

"Yes, Signor."

He picked it up and shook it, but at a high keyed jingle, quickly set it down again. The musical echoes seemed to offend or frighten him.

Reaching forward, I grasped it, and shook it myself.

"A frog's head!" I cried, "a bell!" Again and again I jingled it, detecting, as I thought, three keys in the sounds.

"You think it sounds very pretty, Signor. To you it is not terrible."

"Terrible," I repeated. "Why terrible?"

"I hear it night and day, night and day, Signor. I can't stand it, Sir."

"What do you mean? Do you dream about it?"

"It is no dream, Signor, will you take it? It is yours."

With my eyes fixed upon its elusive modelling, I rubbed my hand over the dark metal. "Bronze," said I. "The eyes are rubies."

"Yes, Signor, I am a poor man, but——"

"But must be paid for it," I interrupted.

"No, Signor. No pay for me. I can't keep it, that is what I mean. I got it from a thief. He stole it from you."

I listened with amazement. The thing, he declared, had been found in the icy water at the bottom of the well, replaced by his companion, and easily recovered after my departure.

"He promised me to give it to you, Signor," said he, "but he is a liar and a cheat."

"What?" I cried astonished. "I never would have thought that. How did you get it?"

"It was from his wife, Sir."

It appeared that the man he denounced had just been imprisoned for wife beating, and that the injured woman had revenged herself by revealing the hiding place of the treasure.

"If he murders me," added my visitor, with a contemptuous shrug of the powerful shoulders, "it will be when I am asleep."

I looked at the tall peasant, until a glow of admiration that would have depleted my letter of credit, took complete possession of me.

"I didn't understand," I exclaimed. "What can I give you for this?"

"Nothing, Sir."

"But you must have your reward."

"No, Signor, it would bring me bad luck."

"Why?"

"It is my birthday."

I stared at him with increased amazement.

"The twenty-fourth of June. St. John's Day. If I insult St. John on his day, will the bells ever stop? Never, Signor. My name is Giovanni Battista."

He crossed himself, turned and walked hurriedly away, just as the waiter came to tell me that the omnibus was waiting. With the latter's help, I finished my packing, thrust the bell into my valise and reached a delayed company of departing guests, who angrily watched me tip the domestic doorway group, before joining them in the omnibus.

Leaning back on the seat, I forgot my surroundings, and in the long drive that followed, tried to adjust my plans to what had happened.

But for a time, with eyes closed upon the scenic grandeur, doubts as to my responsibility in the matter, the rights of science, my duty to Barron, urged me to turn back. Should I hand over the relic to the village authorities, from whom I had had no permit to find it? Or under the strange circumstances, should I take the law into my own hands? At last on reaching the station, a decision to postpone immediate action relieved my mind, and I stepped into an empty first class car, labelled Vicenza, where, according to our last talk, my friend had planned to spend the autumn.

VI

Barron's visit to Vicenza had been timed for a Triennial Session of the Lombard Archaeological Union there that autumn. But as he had said nothing to me of his extravagant plans, I was not prepared to find him engaged in entertaining a large party of his scientific colleagues in one of the great historic Villas.

A band was playing in the Park, and I stopped at the gate to glance at the Palladian Dome, pillared façade and then at the crowded grounds, in which I caught sight of the gesticulating figure of Doctor Lysander. This induced a detour, and several inquiries, as a result of which, I at last found and interviewed my friend. Leaving him to his duties, I had gone upstairs unobserved. It was late in the afternoon, and I was still in my traveling clothes in one of the great bedrooms overlooking the Park when the music below and uproar of departing guests ceased.

The bell, the chief purpose of my visit, was in the pocket of an Austrian traveling mantle, which I had carefully unpacked. Just as I had rewrapped the relic and thrown the cloak upon a sofa piled with displaced carpet and brocade, my host joined me. He was followed by a servant with a tray, a bottle and some glasses. The windows were open, and as the cross lights of sunset caught the leaves outside, and began to invade the shadows of the room, he held up before a mirror one of the grass-bound flasks that enhance the looks if not the taste of Italian wine.

"Orvieto," said he. "Too good to be kept long."

Several times we exchanged healths in the sparkling beverage with its faint aroma of Hesperidean apples, while in his characteristic style he called my attention to still surviving touches of Palladio in the pilasters of the great room, and then to unique examples of Maize Ears, as trophies of Columbus, modelled along one of the cornices. But though full dressed for the occasion, and bedecked with medals, he looked more worn and tired than at Monte Corbo. His voice had lost its ring, when at last, after a pause, he remarked gloomily that his *fête champêtre* had been a failure. Doctor Lysander, who had just returned from Switzerland, in a prolonged dispute with several of his critics, had spoiled the afternoon.

"They can't come to terms," he continued. "We have had a bears' garden here," and while I did my best to suppress a fit of laughter, at a distant noise of angry voices, walked to one of the open windows, and looked out into the darkening park.

"I thought so," said he, with a sigh. "There he is now. What's he doing to Winters? I must go down at once."

"Bring him back with you," said I, holding up significantly the tempting flask not yet empty.

As Barron left me, the servant reappeared with a fresh supply of the vintage, placed it on the table, and with a long taper, began lighting the wax candles in the Venetian chandelier. By the time the twinklings of innumerable pendants had conquered the twilight, my host reappeared with his enraged guest, colossal, grotesque, yet magnificent in his evening dress. He was perspiring. The belligerent blotchings of his face-scars had deepened. He had torn his sleeve, and his dishevelled cravat had wriggled itself into an ear pendant.

Rolling his browless eyes about the room, he at last grasped my hand, and sat down near the dressing table.

"It's time to put a stop to Winters," said he.

"Why should he refuse to look at the facts?" I asked sympathetically. "Doesn't he admit the Titian print?"

"He says it's a piece of engraver's patchwork," returned the frowning giant. "But it's his infernal suggestions about the manuscript. Hints in place of words he doesn't dare use."

"Do you see this?" he cried fiercely, flourishing in our faces a gold headed rattan cane, broken off in the middle.

"Good Heavens!" exclaimed Barron. "It's Winters's walking stick. What have you done to him?"

"Not half enough. He got behind a tree."

I listened in shocked amazement, while Barron's polite efforts to change the subject failed, until at last, in spite of the Orvieto, the unfortunate affair which had embittered the afternoon, got the better of him.

"You misunderstand Winters," he muttered angrily.

"What do you mean?" thundered the Doctor.

"I mean that this treasure story spoils your case. If you drop it, he may give in."

"You don't know the puffed up book-worm. I do. And he knows me."

The excited scholar had got up overturning his chair, and turned scornfully upon his friend.

"The well you examined, was you say, full of rubbish?"

"I went over tons of it with a sieve."

"But it was dry. There may have been two wells."

"Impossible," said Barron. "I searched every square foot of the ruins."

"Nevertheless, I shall go back to Monte Corbo, and examine the place myself."

Barron sighed. "You will be arrested before you begin," he returned in a dismal protest.

He filled another glass with Orvieto, and handed it to the Doctor, while I looked intently at our host, and burst out laughing.

"What's the matter?" asked Barron angrily.

Without answering, I walked to the sofa, pulled the paper bound package out of my cloak pocket, and placed it on the dressing table at his side. There was a small mirror just behind it.

"How do you account for this?" I asked, untying the string, and pulling away the paper, while the red stones reflected in the glass, caught the glow overhead. I picked it up, and shook it until the walls, ceiling and air of the sumptuous room seemed to dance to the echoes.

"Good God, my friend, what's this?" shouted the Doctor.

"A trick," cried Barron, who as I put down the thing, stared awhile at me, and then leaned forward with a half frightened look, and clutched the weird relic. "Where did you get it?"

"Where Durer had thrown it. In the castle well."

"Do you mean to say that I missed this in the well?"

"You never saw the well. You cleaned out the cistern."

"I told you so," roared the Doctor. "Call back Winters."

"No use of that," said Barron nervously. "He'll be here with a policeman soon enough."

Lysander had tossed the shattered cane across the room, seized the relic and was holding it up under the chandelier.

"Buddhist!" he cried. "The head of a fish, one of the Mu Yu Temple bells of China."

Barron objected. "The Mu Yu bells were made of wood."

"Not always," retorted the Doctor.

"And struck with a drumstick."

"The drumstick is gone. The relic has been tampered with. In place of the drumstick the bronze has been heated and the ring balls inserted through the mouth slit."

"Do you mean to tell us that this thing could have been brought from China in the time of Durer?"

"Long before that. It may be pre-Christian. Look at the modelling of the mouth and brows. A marvel of Chinese fancy. No wonder Durer appreciated it. The eyes are rubies of immense value."

I tried to interrupt them. "You have overlooked something," I managed to say. "Don't forget the church legend."

"What has that to do with it?" asked Barron contemptuously. "A myth."

"No matter. It associates the thing with St. John the Baptist."

"What if it does?"

"It explains Durer's sketch," I cried. "It recalls the Bible story, and the Bible story accounts for the landscape. Look at the mountains. Mary has come over the 'Hill Country' to meet Elizabeth. Read the text, 'Over the Hill Country.' Durer sees the 'Hill Country' in the Alps."

A loud hurrah from the Doctor met my words.

"But the fish," exclaimed Barron.

"The fish is a present, exactly appropriate to the occasion. A bell. A jingling fantastic toy to amuse the expected child."

"Shake hands, my friend," roared the Doctor, waving the relic in the air. "You have it."

"I yield," said Barron, as still staring at the thing, and again shaking it, he listened to the echoes.

"What do you intend to do with it?"

My glass was full. I raised it to my lips.

"I brought it here to give to you."

I could see a quick dimming of his eyes in the protest that followed. But I asserted my moral right as an agent, who by chance had transformed his failure into a triumph.

"Here's your man," said he, looking up at the towering Colossus behind us.

"Never," said the latter, sternly. "I refuse to take it."

"But it proves your Durer letters."

"No matter. I refuse."

A lively argument followed, until at last, as a simple means of settlement, I produced a Napoleon.

"Heads or tails? Do you agree?" I asked the Doctor.

The gargoyle face twitched, while the chivalric scholar behind it hesitated, but at last, urged by Barron, yielded.

"Heads."

The gold coin spun in the air, fell on the table and rolled on the floor. Heads. We tried again, and again heads.

"Doctor, the cup is yours. Let us drink to the Durer letters."

★ ★ ★ ★ ★ ★ ★ ★

The final facts of the case are soon disposed of. When later in the year I met Barron at his old quarters at Frankfort, I was not surprised to learn that owing to the Doctor's inflexible views as to private possession of objects of great historical value, he had placed the relic where he said it belonged, with the Durer letters in the Grand Ducal Library at M——.

"Of course he has had the satisfaction of demolishing his critics," I remarked.

"No," said Barron. "His publication of the manuscript has been indefinitely postponed. Whether because of the devoted Catholicism of the owner, church objection to publicity, in view of the late controversy, or historic doubts as to the antiquity of the relic, the details of the discovery have been hushed up."

"But your own notes on the subject," said I. "Your identification of the two landscapes sketched at the same time by the two great masters ought not to be forgotten. If described in your graphic style, it would add to the interest of your forthcoming book."

"It might entertain a few art students," laughed Barron, "but I am in honor bound to publish nothing without permission. Book notoriety is out of the question this time. Besides, you are the real hero in the story."

THE END

Lightning Source UK Ltd.
Milton Keynes UK
UKOW04f0737250717
305996UK00001B/199/P